THE BARGAIN

THE BARGAIN

Julia Templeton

heat | new york

THE BERKLEY PUBLISHING GROUP
Published by the Penguin Group
Penguin Group (USA) Inc.
375 Hudson Street, New York, New York 10014, USA
Penguin Group (Canada), 90 Eglinton Avenue East, Suite 700, Toronto, Ontario M4P 2Y3, Canada
(a division of Pearson Penguin Canada Inc.)
Penguin Books Ltd., 80 Strand, London WC2R 0RL, England
Penguin Group Ireland, 25 St. Stephen's Green, Dublin 2, Ireland (a division of Penguin Books Ltd.)
Penguin Group (Australia), 250 Camberwell Road, Camberwell, Victoria 3124, Australia
(a division of Pearson Australia Group Pty. Ltd.)
Penguin Books India Pvt. Ltd., 11 Community Centre, Panchsheel Park, New Delhi—110 017, India
Penguin Group (NZ), Cnr. Airborne and Rosedale Roads, Albany, Auckland 1310, New Zealand
(a division of Pearson New Zealand Ltd.)
Penguin Books (South Africa) (Pty.) Ltd., 24 Sturdee Avenue, Rosebank, Johannesburg 2196,
South Africa

Penguin Books Ltd., Registered Offices: 80 Strand, London WC2R 0RL, England

This is an original publication of The Berkley Publishing Group.

Copyright © 2006 by Julia Templeton.
Cover art by Franco Accornero.
Cover design by George Long.

First edition: November 2006

Library of Congress Cataloging-in-Publication Data

Templeton, Julia.
  The bargain / Julia Templeton. — 1st ed.
     p. cm.
  ISBN 0-425-21405-2
  I. Title.
PS3620.E467B37   2006
813'.6 — dc22   2006022129

PRINTED IN THE UNITED STATES OF AMERICA

10 9 8 7 6 5 4 3 2 1

To my treasured friends and critique partners: Beth Ciotta, Jordan Summers, Kimberly Ungar, and Mary Stella. Thank you for your input and suggestions, and also for your constant support.

Special thanks to my agent, Kim Lionetti, and to my editor, Cindy Hwang.

ONE

Northumbria, 1069

h e was coming and there was no one who could stop him.

Aleysia stared out over the battlement, watching the skyline turn black as night. The bastard King William would burn the entire North to the ground, making it uninhabitable rather than admit defeat. Even now her countrymen, starved and homeless, scattered to the border in hopes that King Malcolm of Scotland would give them refuge.

She shook with fury. King William was a coward!

Now the king's trusted vassal, Renaud de Wulf, the merciless Norman baron, skirted the forests of Durham, destroying everything in his path.

And soon he would be at Braemere.

A shiver raced along her spine as a cold premonition forced its way into her mind. The ruthless baron would take Braemere, and with it, any hope of her brother reclaiming his titles and lands. They had come so close, taking back their home from that murderer, Norman Baron de Pirou, the man who had arrived at Braemere a little over two years ago announcing that he had been rewarded with the Fief from King William.

The man who had killed her parents in cold blood.

Pushing the horrible memories aside, Aleysia took a steadying breath and looked out at the rolling hills of her homeland for a final time.

"Aleysia, it is time to leave," Adelstan called from below in the inner bailey. He motioned for her to join him as the portcullis opened and their army filed out the gate.

"Good-bye," she said, blinking back tears as she pulled her cloak tighter against the cold and started toward the stairs.

Just then a horrific sound filled the air, stopping her in her tracks.

"The horn of de Wulf!" Her brother's cry had the hair at the back of her neck standing on end.

The horn blasted again—a death knell that sent everyone scrambling.

Renaud de Wulf looked up at the fortress of Braemere and smiled. No wonder the men sent before him had failed at their task of taking her back from the rebelling Saxons.

She was formidable.

Sitting high on a cliff, the wooden structure with an impressive stone tower had only one entrance by land. Luckily the bridge had been opened, and half of the Saxon army had been caught by surprise. Even now his men pushed through the gate into the outer bailey.

Screams and the sound of men in the throes of battle reverberated throughout the lush, green valley full of tall trees and a fast-flowing river.

Though exhausted, his army rose to the challenge, and soon silence fell over the glen. Already they had burned every village from York to Durham, but this castle was what he had worked so hard for, and it would be spared. Though he already had lands in Sussex, Braemere was larger and far more beautiful than the holding south of London. He could easily imagine living out the rest of his days here.

"My lord, we have captured the Saxon Adelstan."

Renaud glanced at his vassal, Galeran, a man ten years his junior, who not so long ago had been his squire, but had quickly risen through the ranks. "Cawdor's heir?"

Galeran grinned wolfishly. "Indeed, my lord."

Voices raised in excitement penetrated the momentary peacefulness and Renaud turned to find two of his men holding firm a young man who struggled against his captors.

Shock slithered through him. *This* was the man who had taken Braemere back by force? The man who had viciously killed Baron de Pirou? The Saxon could not be eight and ten. In fact, he did not even reach to Renaud's shoulder. And he was almost . . . pretty with his long, pale blond hair and effeminate features, his only masculine trait a square chin.

De Pirou, a bear of a man who had earned his spurs before Renaud had been born, must have been distracted by Adelstan's charm.

3

After all, it was well-known among the ranks that de Pirou had a penchant for pretty boys.

"Adelstan, you are guilty of treason against your king. You will be taken to the tower until your fate is decided."

The boy spit at Renaud's feet. "Release me, you Norman swine."

Stunned by the boy's insolence, Renaud closed the steps that separated them until the young man had to bend his head back to look at him. He had to give the boy credit—he showed no fear.

"What say you, Adelstan? Are there other traitors inside, or have they all fled and left you to your own defenses?"

Adelstan's throat convulsed, his jaw set. "There is no one left."

The news was disappointing, but he did not take the Saxon's word for it. "And what—"

An arrow whizzed by Renaud's head and settled into a nearby tree.

Renaud scanned the battlements . . . and spied a dark cloaked figure, holding a long bow—aimed straight at him.

"My lord, let me have the privilege," Galeran said, his eyes glittering with excitement as he notched an arrow and extended his bow.

"Nay!" Adelstan shouted. "Do not!"

Galeran ignored the Saxon and looked to Renaud. "My lord?"

Renaud shook his head. "Since I am the intended target, I shall take the pleasure of killing him with my own hands."

"Do not!" Adelstan's voice cracked.

"Who is the archer, Adelstan?"

The boy's face paled. "My twin."

"Ah, I see." Renaud smiled inwardly. King William would be delighted to have not only Cawdor's heir, but also his spare. He unsheathed his sword and motioned to his men. Seconds later a whizzing sound penetrated the surrounding air, and a sharp stab pierced his shoulder, nearly knocking him to the ground.

"Jesu—" He heard the young Saxon curse under his breath.

With a grimace, Renaud reached back, broke off the end of the arrow, and tossed it aside. Ignoring the pain, he nodded at three of his most trusted men-at-arms. "Take Adelstan to the tower, lock him in and stand guard. I will be there shortly with the twin . . . if I don't kill him first."

Renaud mounted his steed and rode past his men and the bodies that littered the bailey. An old man with long white hair and huge blue eyes stared at Renaud like he was the devil incarnate. The man crossed himself before running off in the opposite direction.

Renaud dismounted and raced toward the battlements, his men fast on his heels. The wound throbbed with each step he took, the blood seeping into the tunic beneath his chain mail. He would snap the boy's neck like a twig!

He took the final step out onto the parapet and held a hand up to stop the men behind him.

The boy did not even turn at his approach, and Renaud felt a flicker of admiration for such foolishness. His weapon, the bow and arrows, sat a good distance away, a sign the boy had surrendered.

The cloak obscured his features, but Renaud noted the slender form, slighter and frailer than his twin. He stood regally, looking out over the land of his ancestors—an impressive view, taking in the surrounding countryside for what would be his last time.

Fingers tightening around the sword handle, Renaud approached the young man, who abruptly turned.

The breath left Renaud in a rush.

No Saxon man was this. Nay, this was a woman. A striking woman with startling light green eyes, a small nose, full lips, and stark cheekbones that gave her a fragile, almost ethereal quality. Just then, the wind caught the hood of the cloak and it whipped back, allowing pale blonde hair to swirl and whip in the wind.

His twin? Her features were identical to Adelstan's, save hers were more delicate. Renaud's lips twitched. To Adelstan's credit, he had not said whether the twin was male or female.

His gaze shifted over the blue tunic belted at her slender waist, lower, to the braies that covered her sex, and then lower still, over long, slender legs. Her chausses were gartered just above the knee. Heat coursed through his veins, simmering into his loins, causing a deep, throbbing ache in his cock. He had never seen a woman in men's clothing and the sight . . . intrigued him.

"Baron de Wulf," the woman said, her voice soft, pleasant. "I pray you let my brother go."

His gaze returned to hers. "Your brother is guilty of treason and is hereby King William's prisoner. He has been taken to the tower."

Her throat convulsed and her gaze shifted past his shoulder to the looming tower. "I pray for mercy, my lord."

So subservient—this woman who moments ago had tried to kill him. The wound ached, reminding him of the danger beneath the beauty. Yet as he watched her, he sensed the threat had passed. Indeed, hope brimmed in her beautiful eyes, pleading with him. "And again I tell you, your brother is guilty of treason. As are you."

She closed her eyes for a moment, the dark lashes casting shadows against high cheekbones. Her hands trembled before she clasped them together.

His gaze shifted to the pulse beating wildly in her neck. She was not as calm as she appeared. Slowly, his gaze again wandered lower, over the soft swell of her breasts. He wondered if her nipples would be a soft pink or delicate rose. Desire rippled through him, hot and fast, reminding him how long he had been without a woman.

How tempted he was to toss her over his shoulder, take her to the lord's chamber, and fuck her until she was panting beneath him. Oh yes, he wanted her as hot for him as he was for her.

As though she read his thoughts, she lifted her chin defiantly. "My brother fought for what is rightfully his."

"King William has been in power for nearly three years, my lady. He is your king, and de Pirou was given these lands by his liege lord. When you drew swords against de Pirou, you drew against your king."

Her jaw clenched and her eyes sparked hatred. "De Pirou killed our parents, stole our lands, and imprisoned our people. When we took Braemere back, half the villagers were starving. Tell me, my lord, what would you do if you were suddenly stripped of everything you possessed, your parents murdered, your people dying? Tell me. Would you step aside and not fight?"

How passionate she was, and though her words struck a barb with him, he pushed the sympathy aside. He had one duty and that was to his king. And he had done his part. Now he was to be rewarded. It mattered not to whom this land once belonged. It belonged to King William now and he would die defending it. "King William is your liege lord, and it is high time you accept it."

"I hate your bastard king!"

Behind him, his men muttered obscenities.

He put up a hand to stop their cursing.

7

Her hatred was there for all to see. Eyes bright, jaw clenched, color high. In truth, her anger only intensified his desire to have her. She was magnificent in her rage.

"My brother was promised an elevated position with Baron de Pirou. Instead, the Norman tried to rape him, and it was then we fled."

"And what did Baron de Pirou do with you?"

She watched him intently, her beautiful eyes narrowing, telling him she understood the complexity of the question. "De Pirou had no interest in me."

"And what of de Pirou's men?"

Her blush deepened. "I have dressed as a man since I was three and ten."

"Why?"

"It is easier to move in men's clothing," she said defensively. "I ride with my brother, as well as hunt with him. It is just simpler."

Her brother was no fool. He had made her wear men's clothing from the time she had blossomed into womanhood. Using hats, cloaks, and, no doubt, bindings, when necessary, to make sure she would go unnoticed. He must have kept her by his side at all times.

"You were leaving the castle when we arrived. Pray tell, where were you headed?"

She hesitated. "Your arrival was not unexpected, my lord. One needs only look to the blackened sky to know you were coming this way."

There was no mistaking the fierce hatred in her eyes, or in her tone. "That is not the question I asked."

"We were headed north, to the border."

"To Scotland?"

She lifted a tawny brow. "Indeed, my lord. We have lived there these past years."

"Who awaits you in Scotland?"

Swallowing hard, she watched him for a moment, wary.

"Mayhap you did not hear me. *Who* awaits you in Scotland?"

"My betrothed," she blurted, shifting on her feet.

It was not the answer he'd hoped for. In fact, he was unprepared for the jealousy raging throughout him at the thought of some uncivilized Scot bedding this beautiful English woman. "Why is your betrothed not here helping you defend Braemere?"

"He was away when Adelstan and I left."

"You ran from him?"

She shook her head. "Nay, I did not *run* from him. I did my duty to my countrymen and to my brother. There simply was not time to alert him."

"And what will your intended do when he realizes you are gone?"

"He will come for me."

She was so certain; he could hear the confidence in her voice.

"And who is this man who will soon be charging Braemere's gates?"

She lifted her chin a fraction. "Laird MacMillan."

Of course she would be betrothed to a laird and not some lowborn Scot. He forced a smile. "I suppose we must ready ourselves to welcome Laird MacMillan then."

Her eyes narrowed. "Duncan has done you no harm."

Duncan was it? How informal.

"Please let my brother and I go, my lord. I give you my word that we will never return." Her tone implored him, as did her expression.

9

He could feel her desperation. She put her hands together and rested them against her lips . . . as though in prayer.

There was nothing holy about his thoughts.

"Find mercy in your soul, my lord. Let us go."

Let her go, so she could return to the laird? There was not a chance in hell. "I cannot, my lady."

She released a ragged breath and closed her eyes, almost in defeat.

"There are many deaths to be accounted for, de Pirou's murder among them. Your king demands satisfaction."

She opened her eyes and the pain he saw there made his heart lurch. "My lord, please. I beg of thee."

For an instant he wanted to give her what she yearned for, but he had come too far, and his liege lord demanded satisfaction. "Again, I cannot."

Before he could blink, she drew a dagger from her cloak and held the point to her breast. "You will not take me alive."

"Do not!" he bellowed, surprised at the horror rippling through him at the prospect of this gorgeous woman killing herself rather than face her fate.

"I want to see Adelstan." The words were wrenched from her, and tears welled in her eyes. He knew what the words cost her—this woman who clearly was not given to crying or theatrics. A woman who begged for her brother's life.

"What is your name?" he asked, his tone calmer than he felt.

"Aleysia," she said, her voice barely above a whisper.

He stepped forward and she pressed the knife in, drawing a whimper from her perfect lips.

"Aleysia, please do not hurt yourself."

A second later she dropped the dagger and reached out to him, her fingers curling around his. Aside from the shock of her actions, relief washed over him.

She fell to her knees before him. "My lord. Please . . ."

The depth of her plea and the feel of her soft fingers against his rough ones raised his desire to fever pitch. Even the hair on his arms stood on end. He had to remind himself that she touched him not out of desire, but out of desperation. He sheathed his sword and placed a hand on her head, the texture of the blonde locks like silk against his fingers. "Your brother lives. For now let that be enough."

Her beautiful green eyes searched his face as her fingers tightened around his. "Do you give me your word?"

He was astounded by her audacity, yet he admired her all the same. How selfless she was. Begging for her brother's life in front of her enemy.

Renaud's gaze shifted from hers, to the tiny, tipped-up nose, the full lips, lower to her neck . . . and the swell of her breasts. Roughly, he grabbed her by the arm and lifted her to her feet. She fell into him, her soft body against his front. His cock responded, pressing against his braies, rock hard, throbbing.

She swallowed hard. "My lord, I will do anything you desire in order to save my brother."

His gaze locked with hers. "Anything I desire?" he repeated, trying to ignore the exhilaration that rushed through his body at the prospect of taking this woman to his bed.

"Aye." To his surprise her gaze shifted from his, drawing slowly over his chest, down his belly, before settling in the vicinity of his cock. "Anything, my lord."

TWO

Aleysia had never felt so alone in her life. The great hall buzzed with activity, but she knew not a soul. Sitting near the hearth, she watched the Normans file into the room, while harried servants scrambled to fill goblets and tankards with ale and sweet wine.

Gone were the familiar faces of her Saxon brethren, and in their place dirty, smelly, foul-mouthed Normans. Many still bore the stains of her people's blood upon their clothing. The pain and destruction they had caused seemed not to bother them, for they ate and drank as though they had not feasted for a week.

She despised every last one of them, but most of all one man. A man she had made a bargain with. A bargain that would begin this night. Her insides twisted at the thought of sharing a bed with the Norman.

Renaud de Wulf, lord of the keep. Sitting on the high dais, looking down on his vassals and servants with a satisfied smile. He certainly played the part of conqueror to perfection.

How different he looked without his helmet, the nose-plate having hidden his features from view earlier. Now those features were on display.

In truth, Renaud de Wulf was striking, with his long dark hair and contrasting silver eyes. His square jaw, straight nose, jutting cheekbones, and obscenely long eyelashes only added to his appeal. The one flaw she could see was a disturbing scar that ran along his right cheekbone.

In the past fortnight when rumors abounded, she had heard that this monster had been given the scar by his betrothed. The woman, a Norman princess who desperately loved the baron, discovered he had a leman. So great was her fury, she had attacked de Wulf in a jealous rage. If she had scarred him hoping it would detract from his looks, the woman had failed. Miserably so, for the mark only enhanced the baron's untamed sensuality. A rugged, dark beauty—which made him even more dangerous. No doubt he had already littered England with many a bastard.

She prayed she did not add to that number this night.

"My lady, would you like some wine?" a servant asked, jarring Aleysia out of her unpleasant thoughts.

"Nay," she replied, with a forced smile. She must keep her wits about her. Mayhap tonight the Normans would become so drunk that she could escape his chamber and release her brother from his prison. Then she would not have to forfeit her maidenhead to the beastly de Wulf.

The minutes ticked away into hours, and she waited and watched as the ale and wine flowed freely. The noise in the hall grew louder by the second, signaling the soldiers were well in their cups.

A man broke into song, and was soon joined by his comrades. The song was in French, so Aleysia did not understand, nor did she care to. She hated everything about these men and the wretched country that had brought them to England's shore.

Aleysia's gaze flitted over the giant tapestries on the opposite wall. They were enormous and had taken a long time to sew. One was a brutal hunting scene in bold colors, and the other of finely dressed women strolling about a garden, in soft, muted colors.

The latter reminded her of a tapestry she and her mother had embroidered for years, and they had finished it just a year before her mother's death. It had been a depiction of their family. Her mother, her father, Adelstan, and herself, standing in the fields beyond the manor. The tapestry had hung in the manor house, the first thing one saw upon entering. Every visitor had commented upon it, saying how lovely it was. Everyone, save for de Pirou, who had ordered it ripped from the wall and burned shortly after he had murdered her parents.

The horrible baron had laughed uproariously while Aleysia cried, and Adelstan had done his best to comfort her. How she had wished the man dead at that moment.

At least de Pirou was in hell now—right where he belonged.

A woman shrieked, bringing Aleysia's thoughts back to the present. She looked in the direction of the cry to find a woman fighting off the advance of two men. Aleysia went to stand, her fingers curling around the knife in her pocket . . . when she saw the woman smile, and then laugh before she kissed one of the knights. A moment later the three slipped out the door, no doubt off to find a private corner.

Aleysia had considered slipping out that very door a time or two, but where would she go? The Saxons who had been here this morning were all either dead or imprisoned in the dungeon. If what de Wulf said was true, then Adelstan had been taken to the tower, where prisoners of significance were kept, though rarely treated any better than those in the dark, dank dungeons. No doubt each entrance and exit would be heavily guarded.

Nay, she had made a deal with the devil, and she must pay her due. Which meant sticking it out until she could come up with a way out of this mess.

Feeling someone watching her, Aleysia glanced over at the Norman to find his silver gaze settled on her. Her pulse quickened. His was a stare that could make grown men quiver in their seats. No smile, no frown. No expression at all. Just a cold, distant look in his eyes that was more than a little unsettling. Though it was difficult, she forced herself to hold his gaze.

His jaw ticked, as though he clenched his teeth too tight. Aleysia's lower lip began to tremble, but she bit the inside of her cheek to steady it. She must not show fear. He must know she would not back down.

A servant passed by him, and he grabbed hold of her wrist. The woman with copper-colored hair and dark eyes, who Aleysia had not seen before this day, fell into his lap, one arm draped around his neck.

De Wulf's large hand slid to the girl's waist, and she seemed not to mind. Indeed, she seemed excited to have his attention as she rested her head back against the Norman's neck, her nipples pebbling beneath the bodice of her faded kirtle. The woman's hand slid down de Wulf's chest, toward his stomach.

Aleysia knew she should look away, especially since the Norman was taking perverse satisfaction in watching her watch him. He wanted her to squirm. As though reading her thoughts, the slightest hint of a smile played at his lips while his fingers brushed lazily across the woman's stomach.

Heat rushed up Aleysia's neck, toward her cheeks. She lifted a brow, and the side of the Norman's mouth curved slightly. His large, long-fingered hand moved up the woman's belly slowly, to a breast. Aleysia swallowed hard. He cupped the small mound, his fingers rolling over the nipple in a way that had the servant arching her back. The Norman's fingers plucked at the extended buds, pulling, pinching, and to Aleysia's horror, her own nipples tightened beneath her tunic.

Everything within Aleysia rebelled. How could a woman shame herself so, right in the middle of a hall full of roughly one hundred people? She had no shame at all, her hand slipping into the band of de Wulf's braies, cupping his prominent sex.

Aleysia's cheeks burned and though she wanted to flee, pride kept her rooted to the spot.

The woman turned on de Wulf's lap and kissed him, her fingers reaching for the cord of his braies. She tugged for a moment, but seemed to get nowhere. But she would not be deterred. She slipped her hand inside his braies, and for a heart-stopping second Aleysia saw the head of his large cock, swelling up past his navel.

The Norman flashed the servant a wolfish smile, breaking the kiss for just an instant as he whispered something to her.

No doubt some poetic nonsense.

Shifting in her seat, Aleysia watched the kiss increase to a frenzied mating of tongues. The woman's hands wove through de Wulf's hair, and she rubbed against him, much as a cat would brush against a person for affection.

And for an instant Aleysia wondered what it felt like—to kiss like that, to desire like that. She had never kissed a boy in all her years, though she had wondered what it would feel like to kiss Duncan once they married.

She remembered how her parents kissed—gentle pecks on the cheeks or lips. Full of affection, but never a long, searing kiss like the Norman and the servant wench were sharing. God's breath, the woman's tongue was damn near down the man's throat.

And it didn't look like they would be stopping anytime soon. Indeed, the way she stroked de Wulf made Aleysia wonder if he would take the wench right there in front of everyone.

A man's laughter caught her attention, and Aleysia turned to the right to find a knight, well into his thirtieth year, watching her. No doubt he had sensed her shock at the servant and de Wulf's public fondling. He brought the tankard to his lips and drank heavily, the brew flowing over the cup, slopping onto his tunic.

Did the man have no manners? Apparently not, for he proceeded to slurp the stew from his bowl, much in the same fashion he drank his ale. The majority of which had ended up on his tunic and lap.

Disgusted, Aleysia looked away, toward the nearest door where a guard conversed with a servant wench. If she were careful, she could slip out the servant door toward the kitchens, and at least find peace for this night, away from the damned Norman who looked ready to take the wench right here and now, no matter who watched.

Mayhap Aleysia could sleep in the stables, high in the loft, away from everyone, especially de Wulf.

She took another glance at the Norman to find him fully occupied with the servant, who now straddled him, her skirts hiked up about her hips. Worse still, de Wulf's hands were planted on her plump, bare bottom. For all Aleysia knew, the servant could be impaled on de Wulf's large staff.

Confused and disturbed by the way her body tingled just watching them, Aleysia left. Making eye contact with no one, she made it to the door without notice. Once down the stairs, she raced toward the stables as fast as her feet would carry her.

Her heart hammered hard in her breast as she ducked down behind a stall. Two Normans spoke to each other nearby. "How long do you think we will stay?"

"His lordship says indefinitely. Said as much just days ago," the other said.

"'Tis a beautiful place. I do not blame him for coveting her."

"Aye, and speaking of beautiful—did you see the Saxon wench? What a beauty that one is. Shame she prefers wearing men's clothing to gowns."

Aleysia bit her bottom lip.

The other man laughed. "De Wulf does not care either way."

"Indeed, he just wants to see what is beneath those clothes."

"A sweet body to be sure."

Aleysia pressed her lips together and counted to ten.

Let the Norman take his whore to bed tonight. She would sleep with the horses and be glad for it. It would also give her the blessed time she would need to come up with a plan.

"We had best be getting to the hall before all the food is gone," one of the men said. A second later the stable door opened and closed, and soon she was alone, save for the horses, their soft nickering comforting. She recognized her brother's beloved stallion, a gift from their father when Adelstan had turned four and ten. How pleased her brother had been with his trusty stallion. Aleysia reached over the stall and ran her fingers over Galahad's nose. Her throat tightened as the reality of her situation sank in.

If she did not find a way to release her brother and flee to Scotland, then he would die, and she would have lost everyone she ever loved. "We are alone, Galahad. 'Tis just you and I for now, but soon, very soon, I will release Adelstan, and we will flee this wretched pit of merciless bastards."

A bird flew out from its nest above, nearly scaring Aleysia out of her skin. "I had best hide away before someone comes looking for me." She kissed the horse's wet nose and then scurried up the ladder.

Just in time, too.

She had no more than settled in the soft hay when the stable door opened and closed with a loud *thud*.

She held her breath.

On the far wall, she could see a man's form in shadow. He appeared huge, tall, with immense shoulders. Then again, she reminded herself, even the smallest of men could appear giantlike when cast in shadow.

Mayhap those broad shoulders belonged to someone other than—

"Aleysia of Braemere."

Her heart hammered hard against her breast.

Damn! It was de Wulf, and he knew she was here. For the love of God, did the man have eyes in the back of his head? How could he know she had come here when he had been so occupied with the servant wench? Unless, of course, he had finished.

As though reading her thoughts, he said, "I followed you, little one, so you may as well show yourself now. Or mayhap you would like me to climb up the ladder and join you in the bed of hay."

She had never moved so fast in her life.

As she descended, he moved to help her, but she stopped. "Do not touch me," she said, venom dripping from her voice.

He stepped back, a smirk on his lips. "Very well."

Making the final step onto solid ground, she turned. "Why do you follow me?"

"Why did you leave the hall?"

"I wanted solitude."

He watched her intently, his gaze sliding over her in a way that made her stomach flip. "Why?"

How she yearned to slap that smirk clean off his face. "Your men are drunk, as are you. I was not enjoying the spectacle."

He reached out and plucked a piece of straw from her hair. "Were you not? The way you watched so intently made me think otherwise."

She frowned. He had to be joking. "I was merely appalled by the public display. That was the only reason I stared as I did. I could scarcely believe my eyes."

He laughed then, his white teeth flashing in a boyish smile. To her chagrin, he was even more handsome when he grinned like that. "You could scarcely believe your eyes? Now that is a compliment."

Compliment? Was the man mad? "What do you mean?" The words had scarcely left her mouth when she understood exactly what he meant. The size of his cock. God's breath, the man was incorrigible.

"Come Aleysia of Braemere," he said, extending his hand. "I have need of a surgeon and you shall assist."

"A surgeon? You seemed well enough a moment ago."

He lifted a brow. "Do I detect a note of jealousy?"

Feeling her cheeks burn once again, Aleysia lowered her gaze to just beyond his shoulder. "I most certainly am not jealous. However, I believe she would jump at the chance to attend you, my lord."

"I am sure she would, but it is you I want," he said, his voice silky soft.

She had not expected that bold statement. Nor had she expected the leap of her pulse from such a declaration.

When she did not take his hand, he reached for hers, wrapping his fingers around hers. How large his hand was, and calloused, much like her father's had been. The hand of a warrior. Nothing soft about it, and the touch sent a current through her. An odd sensation. She pulled her hand from his, but he snatched it back, frowning down at her. "You will not leave my sight, do you understand?"

"Am I a prisoner then?"

"You offered a bargain, Aleysia—and I accepted. You will abide by that bargain. For now you belong to me."

"And if I refuse?"

"I will kill your brother."

She stopped in her tracks. There had been no apology in his tone whatsoever. In fact, he made it sound as if he would enjoy killing Adelstan. She ripped her hand from his grasp. "What a horrible man you are to say such a thing!"

The moonlight had cast them in shadow, but she could still see his eyes, and she saw the surprise there. "You think me horrible? I let you live. I let your brother live. And you yourself are the one who offered your body for your brother's life. How does that make me horrible?"

Two guards who stood in the shadows laughed, and she wondered if they overheard the conversation.

Ashamed that others possibly knew of her brazen bargain, heat flooded her cheeks. "Aye, you are horrible because you kill innocent people!"

"These are times of war. I do what I must to regain peace for my king. And what of you, Aleysia of Braemere? You fought and killed Norman knights alongside your brother. How are you different than I?"

"How am I different?" she repeated, unable to believe her ears. "You are merciless. You will do whatever you must to get your way—killing, burning villages, starving innocent people. That's the difference between you and I."

He flinched as though she'd struck him. "Am I worse than de Pirou?"

De Pirou had been a terrible man, far worse than any she'd known. A man of no morals. The devil incarnate. A most unpleasant creature—but de Wulf was no better, if his reputation proved true. "Does your silence mean that you have been too harsh in your assessment?"

"I have not changed my mind, nor will I ever. What kind of a man burns the entire north to the ground? You and your men have made the northern country a barren wasteland, my lord."

He ran a hand through his hair and sighed heavily. "I grow weary of such talk, and I am bleeding from the wound that you have caused. You are skilled with bow and arrow, Aleysia," he said, a smile playing at his lips.

Ignoring the compliment, she glanced at his shoulder. "Does the wound pain you?"

"Aye, it pains me greatly."

She smiled, glad she had caused him pain.

He took a step toward her, his eyes narrowing as he searched her face. "You smile, Aleysia. How beautiful you are when you put down your guard. 'Tis like you glow from within."

Her smile melted under his stare, and she looked away, flustered by her reaction to this man. What was it about him that made her thoughts fly right out of her head?

"Are you not accustomed to men commenting on your beauty?" He sounded surprised.

In truth, she was not accustomed to such praise. But she had never had a suitor before, save for Duncan, and he had never complimented her . . . ever. "Nay, I am not."

"Then I am glad to be the first." There it was again, that silky soft voice that made the hair on her arms stand on end.

"Come, let us not dally, little one. I am in need of a bath and some rest."

"Aye, you are," she replied, following him into the armory where men sat or lay on benches and cots, some wounded, others caring for the injured. Seeing de Wulf approach, silence filled the building. An old man with long gray hair and full beard approached Renaud. "There you are, my lord. I've been expecting you. Come." He motioned for Renaud to sit on a bench. "Let me have a look at your wound."

"Aleysia, sit here," de Wulf said, patting the bench opposite him. Aleysia took the seat and was instantly sorry when de Wulf spread his legs. To her dismay, she was caught there, her knees fit snugly between his powerful thighs. She could not move without touching either thigh, so she kept her knees firmly together.

He did not smell as bad as one would think from the days of pillaging. Rather he smelled of musk, and something else she could not decipher. A masculine scent that was not at all unpleasant.

"Remove the tunic," the old man ordered. And de Wulf complied, lifting the shirt over his head and handing it to Aleysia.

She placed it on her lap, trying hard not to look at de Wulf's body, a difficult thing when he sat so close.

"I see a Saxon arrow has found its mark," the old man said, probing at the wound.

"Aye, Henry, and you are looking at the Saxon responsible for said injury," Renaud said, nodding at Aleysia.

Henry frowned. "In truth?"

Aleysia nodded. "In truth."

The old man laughed, a cackling sound that made Aleysia smile.

"Well, we shall have to cauterize the wound. Take a deep breath, my lord, and then release it slowly."

Renaud did as the old man said, his chest rising with the effort. A second later Henry yanked. The Norman flinched, his face turning red, but he did not curse as the old man produced the arrow and blood gushed from the cut. "My goodness, 'tis quite a gash."

"Now this shall hurt a little," the old man said, a moment before he poured liquor onto the wound.

Renaud closed his eyes and took a deep breath, before letting it out slowly. The old man stepped over to a hearth and grabbed a red-hot iron.

To her surprise, de Wulf reached out and took hold of her hand. For a moment she almost pushed it away, but then the old man brought the iron down on Renaud's shoulder.

The Norman's jaw tightened, his stomach clenched, defining the rigid planes of muscle there.

Aleysia winced as the smell of burnt flesh surrounded them. Sweat poured off Renaud's forehead, and she was hard-pressed not to wipe it off with his tunic, but she refrained. Ironically, she felt a pang of remorse for having been the one to cause his pain. She ran her thumb along his and watched his color slowly return.

"My lord, how do you fare?" the surgeon asked with obvious concern.

Renaud opened his eyes and smiled, and to Aleysia's chagrin, her heart gave a fierce tug. "I shall live to see another day, Henry."

"That is welcome news," someone said from the doorway. Aleysia looked up to find one of Renaud's men who had been on the ramparts, coming toward him.

De Wulf smiled up at the younger man. "I am well, Galeran. Have no fear. I shall be in fine form on the morrow. I had thought to keep you all from drills, but I think that would only make the men grow restless."

"I agree, my lord," Galeran replied, his gaze skipping to Aleysia. He did not look very happy to see her.

"Have you grown tired of tonight's amusements already?"

"Nay, I was concerned when I did not see you in the hall, and decided I had best check on you," Galeran replied.

"I am fine, but since you are here, you can do me a favor."

"Anything, my lord." Galeran glanced at where Aleysia still held Renaud's hand. Surprisingly, the Norman did not release it.

"Take Aleysia to the lord's chambers. See that a bath is prepared, and I shall be along shortly."

Aleysia released his hand and gave him his tunic, relieved to be escaping the room . . . and de Wulf.

"I shall see you soon, Aleysia," Renaud said, not moving to let her out of the entrapment of his solid thighs. Rather than climb over him, she slid by him, the front of her thighs brushing against his knees.

More than happy to get away from him and the stifling armory, she followed the young soldier out of the building, feeling de Wulf's gaze on her the entire way.

Renaud watched Aleysia follow Galeran out of the armory, as did every other man being tended to. What a find she had been.

Who knew such a treasure had been tucked away in the north country? A woman dressed in men's clothing, who could best any man with bow and arrow. God knew what other skills she possessed.

He looked forward to finding out.

He smiled, remembering her expression earlier in the hall when she had watched him fondle the wench. It had been cruel to do so.

Little did Aleysia know he had no desire to be with the woman who had serviced his troops for the past eight weeks, since they had burned her small village. In truth, the wench had seemed overjoyed to leave behind an overbearing father to travel with them, spreading her legs for any who would give her coin and attention.

But Renaud had never had the woman, nor did he want her tonight. He merely wanted to see Aleysia's reaction. He had thought the Saxon would blush and look away, or mayhap even cry, regretful of her rash decision to offer her body for her brother's safety. But she did none of those things, and instead stared boldly as though to say, *Do what you will, Norman!*

Even more, he thought he'd recognized curiosity in those haunting green eyes.

But then she had unexpectedly left the hall, and he had followed, much to the wench's displeasure.

Aleysia had trembled when she sat by him just now, trying everything in her power not to have her body touch his. He had trapped her between his thighs just to see how she would react, to see if she would flee as she had done earlier. But she had not fled. In fact, she had tried in her own way to soothe him—her thumb brushing along the edge of his.

Aye, if ever there was a woman ripe for the plucking . . .

"She is beautiful, my lord," Henry commented. The old man had traveled with him these past two years, patching up Renaud and his men, and in turn Renaud gave him protection. He had simply appeared one night at their camp, drunk and bleeding, asking to stay in exchange for his services. A healer, he had called himself, and no one had asked further questions. And he had served Renaud and his men faithfully since that day. "Eyes like I have never seen. Almost haunting, wouldn't you say, my lord?"

Renaud smiled. "Indeed, she is beautiful."

Henry spread a salve onto the cauterized wound and wiped his hands clean with a rag. "Is there anything else, my lord?"

Renaud looked around the armory at the wounded. He would not go to his chamber before he spoke with each man. They had all fought valiantly today, and they would be rewarded, even if it be with just a kind word.

He stood, his body aching, his knees popping, reminding him that he was not getting any younger. Though he wanted nothing more than to retreat to his chamber, take a hot bath, and make love to the beautiful Saxon, he instead rested a hand on his vassal's shoulder. The young man had lost part of his ear, and he trembled greatly. "You did a fine job today, Malgor."

The knight clamped his chattering teeth together. "Thank you, my lord."

"Get well so you can join us in drills in a fortnight or so."

"I will rejoin the ranks long before a fortnight, my lord," Malgor replied with resolve.

"Very well, then. We shall see you on the field when Henry agrees you are well enough."

Next was a knight who had fought with Renaud for the better part of a decade. A nasty-looking gash on his side oozed blood. Renaud clasped the man's hand. "Henry had best put the rod to you next, Gautier."

The Bargain

The man flashed a toothless smile, compliments of a blow to the mouth a month before.

It would be an hour before Renaud made his way out into the outer bailey and toward the tower, where his chamber and a beautiful Saxon woman awaited him.

ThRee

Heaven help her. What had she gotten herself into?

Aleysia's heart hammered in her chest, watching as a handful of servants entered the large chamber. They carried buckets of hot water, and one by one, they poured the steaming water into the large wooden tub.

She knew de Wulf had indicated she could take a bath, but she had no such inclination, especially since she had bathed in the river just last night. Granted, the water had been cold enough to steal the breath from her lungs, but she had suffered through and even washed her hair.

Nay, the bath would be for de Wulf. After all, he would be filthy from his days of pillaging. Given the circumstances, he had no time to stop and bathe—the animal that he was. Too busy killing men, women, and children . . . and sleeping with whores, much like the one he had left in the great hall.

Mayhap he was with the woman now? He had been in quite a hurry to get rid of Aleysia.

Her stomach coiled in a tight knot remembering the baron's gray gaze. Aleysia noted the dark gleam in his eyes when he looked at her, his stare unrelenting. It had seemed the man could see straight through her clothing.

An old woman whom she remembered well from the days her family had ruled the land, glanced at her while she emptied the bucket of water into the tub. She cast Aleysia a sympathetic smile.

They all knew her fate. Even now, she could not forget the knowing grins of the Norman knights as de Wulf had walked with her toward the great hall.

They all knew what she had offered in way of a bargain.

And a bargain it was. Nothing more, nothing less.

Her body for her brother's safety.

Unable to stand still, she walked toward the window and looked out, her fingers curling around the heavy iron bars, yearning for a freedom that now seemed so far from reach.

Her breath formed fog. Night was fast descending upon Braemere. In the distance she could see the manor house where she had been born and raised. The beautiful stone mansion would now be overrun with Norman knights, as was the castle. And in the uppermost chamber of the tower, her brother sat, shackled, awaiting certain death. Poor Adelstan.

Men's laughter brought her out of her musings and the horrible thoughts of her twin's fate. She must find a way to get to Adelstan and together they would escape. They would flee to Scotland and she would marry Laird MacMillan. Duncan had been patient with her delaying their wedding these past months, accepting her excuse that she still mourned for her parents. But even the Scot was growing weary of excuses. When he'd left for Edinburgh, he told her that upon his return, they would go to the chapel and be done with it, once and for all.

It was not like she was opposed to the match. Duncan was a handsome man, nearly twenty years her senior. She felt safe with him, save for his temper, which frightened her at times. Though she did not desire him the same way he desired her, she knew in her heart that she could be happy. She would be a loyal wife to the Scottish laird who had lost his first wife in childbirth.

One *could* love without desire.

And once again she recalled the desire in the Norman's gray eyes. Even now her skin prickled, remembering that hot stare, and the way his gaze lingered on her body.

Running her hands up and down her arms, she knew she must bear the pain of this night . . . for her brother's sake.

Heavy footsteps sounded in the hallway.

Aleysia's heart pounded loudly in her ears as the door opened and the Norman appeared. He seemed even more massive than he had earlier, standing a full head taller than most men, and broader of shoulder. So large was he, he seemed to fill the entire room with his presence. Silver-gray eyes stared at her intently, sliding over her in a way that made her tremble.

She kept her gaze averted to just beyond his right shoulder. Her uneasiness grew with each second of silence, while she forced back the panic that threatened to paralyze her. "May I see my brother?"

"Adelstan is fine," he said, reaching behind his neck and pulling off his tunic, tossing it aside.

She had not been able to fully see his body before, since she had been so close. But now she could see all of his powerful frame. He had white scars that marred the golden skin of his flesh. Battle wounds. He would have another scar on his back, thanks to her.

He rolled his shoulders, as though he hoped to release the ache, the motion sending his muscles rippling. Her gaze fastened on the defined bulges of his abdomen and the line of hair right below his navel that escaped beneath the braies he was busy untying.

Her heart skipped a beat. She had seen a man's naked body before. It could not be helped when she lived in such close confines with Adelstan and his men.

But she had seen no man quite like the Norman. He was perfectly formed—every solid inch of him. Once again she recalled when the wench in the great hall had touched his huge cock. The flesh between her thighs tingled at the memory.

Despite the fact he was her enemy, her fingers itched to touch his golden skin, feel the hard planes of muscle and tendons beneath. Strong and powerful, he made her feel impossibly feminine, even in her men's attire.

Aleysia steadied herself for what was to come. She *would* give this man her body, but nothing else. She would do what was necessary to save Adelstan.

Renaud could smell her fear.

Standing with chin lifted high, shoulders ramrod straight, Aleysia's gaze seemed to be on everything in the room but him. His lips twitched. She might pretend to be unaffected by his presence, yet he

33

had seen the fascination in her light green eyes when he'd taken off his tunic. The way they had followed a downward path over his chest and abdomen, stopping at the edge of his braies. Her throat convulsed as she swallowed hard.

She was curious.

In truth, her innocent stare made him want her all the more. To rip off her clothes, toss her on the bed, and fuck her until she was too tired to stand. Make her forget Laird MacMillan and her pledge to marry him.

Furious that the Scot had once again entered his thoughts, he deliberately pushed his braies down his legs. Slowly. It had the desired effect. Aleysia's cheeks burned and her eyes widened before she turned away, facing the window.

"You did not bathe."

"I saw no need," she replied, a touch too quickly. Silent minutes passed and still she did not move. He glanced at her, to find her on the tips of her toes, gazing out the window.

"I thought it might relax you."

"I have no need to relax."

He fought a smile. By God, she was a proud one. What a magnificent lover she would be.

Walking to the tub, he stepped in and sat down, relishing the feel of the warm water against his stiff muscles. Who did she look for? Her betrothed perhaps? It stood to reason the Scot would come running for his intended. Was Laird MacMillan even now plotting a way to snatch Aleysia out of his grasp—or was he even aware Aleysia was at Braemere? If she were Renaud's intended, nothing could stop him.

He frowned and sat back against the tub's edge, imagining Aleysia without her clothing or the damned cloak that she held so tightly to her, almost like a shield. Already his sac was heavy, and grew more so at the thought of her in all her naked glory.

Two servants entered the room, one a portly woman of sixty, and behind her a young woman about his age. The older woman poured her bucket of water in the tub, averting her eyes. He could not say the same for the younger. She stared boldly. When it was her turn to pour in her bucket of water, she smiled, her gaze skipping from his, down his chest and abdomen, to settle on his cock. She licked her lips and leaned farther as she poured, offering him a nice view of her ample bosom.

A sound of disgust came from Aleysia's direction, and Renaud smiled inwardly. So, the fair maiden had seen the wanton looking at him. Dare he hope she was jealous?

"My lord," the coy servant said, her greedy gaze finding his once more. "Would you like me to wash yer back for ya?"

The older woman gasped and pulled the girl along toward the door. "Forgive her, my lord. She is shameless."

Renaud grinned at the women. "I have someone to wash my back— else I would be delighted for you to do so. Mayhap another time?"

"*Any* time, my lord," the buxom servant replied.

Renaud glanced over at Aleysia. Arms crossed over her chest, she shook her head as she stared out the window. The door closed behind the servants and she jumped, but still she did not look at him. "Come closer," he demanded.

Finally she looked toward him. With a loud, exaggerated sigh, she took three steps forward, the movements slow, as though her legs were made of stone.

"Remove your cloak."

With trembling hands she untied the cord that held the cloak together. She pushed it from her shoulders, where it landed in a puddle at her feet.

The dark braies clung to her long, slender legs, defining their perfection. His blood quickened in his veins, flooding his groin with heat. "Remove your clothing."

"My lord!" she said in a rush. "I—"

"I want to see you."

She swallowed hard and looked to the door, as though she expected to be rescued.

There was no man or beast that would keep him from taking this woman.

Not even Laird MacMillan.

"I am waiting, Aleysia."

Jaw clenched tight, she turned around, giving him a full view of her backside. He stifled a groan. If she thought to thwart his desire by showing him her back, she had been mistaken. In truth, her heart-shaped buttocks enticed him nearly as much as her front. The tight breeches hugged the soft curves of her ass and hips.

Unconsciously, he reached for his cock, his fingers sliding around the rigid length.

Sweat that had little to do with the warm water, beaded on his brow. As he stared, his fingers tightened, squeezing, sliding up his hard shaft and back down again.

She removed her tunic, letting it slide from her fingers to the rug. For the space of a heartbeat he saw her naked back, the slender lines, the indentations just above the curve of her firm buttocks. And then her long hair swung, hiding her from him. He could see her tremble as she slid the braies down her legs and made quick work of the garters, chausses, and boots. He released a groan and shifted his hips.

She was beautiful, and she was his.

The edge of the tub was high enough that she would not know he stroked himself. At this point, he didn't care if she did. He needed release, because he would not spend himself the moment he touched her. Nay, he would savor the taking—caress her until she writhed beneath him. "Turn around and let me see you, Aleysia."

With a muttered curse, she turned, her green eyes flashing with hatred as she met his gaze.

His heart missed a beat. She was breathtaking.

Full, firm breasts with rose-pink nipples gave way to a small waist and softly curved hips. Her stomach was flat, the curls of her womanhood slightly darker than the hair on her head. His stroke increased as he stared at the soft, tight curls there, imagining the treasure hidden within. A virgin, an untouched prize. How hot and tight she would be. He grit his teeth as his blood quickened, his climax coming on, fast, strong. Aleysia reached up and ran her hands down her arms as though to warm herself. The motion made her already full breasts look even more so. He envisioned his cock there, between the soft skin of those ample mounds, thrusting.

Trembling, he closed his eyes and jerked harder, once, twice—and came with a low-throated moan.

Long seconds later his heart slowed a little, and only then did he open his eyes to find Aleysia still standing there, watching him with a confused expression. Did she guess what had made him groan? Would she even know of such things?

Whatever the case, soon the mystery would be over. Virgin she might be, but certainly she knew her power over men. In fact, if she was betrothed to a Scottish laird whom she addressed so intimately, who said she was still virgin?

Suddenly, he had to know the truth for himself.

"Prepare yourself for me now," he said, nodding toward the bed.

Aleysia's heart pounded as she awaited the Norman, regretting the moment she had offered her body to him.

He washed himself with the soap, scrubbing every inch of his hard flesh. Long minutes passed, but still he did not come to her. She had been suspicious as to what had caused such a moan earlier, his head fallen back on the tub's edge, his eyes closed, the thick cords of his neck strained as though in pain. Perhaps the wound she had inflicted upon him?

Nay, he had suffered far worse.

He would not be touching himself, would he? That thought did nothing to help her shattered nerves.

What in God's name took him so long now?

She wanted to get this over with. Hold up her end of the bargain and be done with it. Then she would go on with her plans. She could bear anything if she knew her brother would be safe.

Which meant she must be strong. She must please the Norman, if she and Adelstan stood a chance at escaping. Hopefully, Duncan was on his way with an army. When he arrived, she would leave and *never* come back. Not as long as de Wulf held Braemere.

All thoughts evaporated as she heard the Norman stand from the tub. Fear rippled through her as she glanced at him. Water sluiced down his powerful body, and over that part of him that would soon be within her. Her stomach tightened. It was as she feared. His manhood was thick, long—and far too large to fit inside her. How could she bear it?

Pushing aside her apprehension, she shivered under the covers and awaited him, praying for the strength that would get her through the night. *Remember Adelstan*, she chanted over and over in her mind. *You will escape and this will be nothing but a horrible memory.*

A minute later the mattress dipped beneath the Norman's weight. Aleysia lay as stiff as a board, waiting. He lay on his side, not bothering to cover his nakedness. Instead, he propped himself on his elbow, grabbed the blanket from her grasp—and ripped it down and off her.

Cold air met her body and she trembled fiercely. It took every ounce of will and fortitude she possessed not to flee.

The scent of sandalwood mingled with his masculine scent—a fragrance Aleysia knew she would never forget. His large, long-fingered hand reached out, brushing along her jaw, over her neck, then lower, over the swell of her breasts. She stiffened and held her breath.

Slowly, his fingers rolled over her nipples, circling them, causing a strange ache there, one that settled low in her groin. He leaned over her, his breath hot against her breast, before his mouth covered her there. Her stomach tightened at the new sensation.

He sucked lightly, his teeth grazing her nipple, gently pulling. Her insides burned, and to her horror, she heard a moan escape her throat. Against her leg she could feel his cock, hard like stone. Heat flooded her insides, to the very core of her, making her wet.

Feeling his silver gaze on her, Aleysia closed her eyes, fighting against the strange sensations and guilt that made her want to push him away. She shifted, her body seeming too hot, too sensitive. His wet hair brushed her stomach, his tongue laving her navel before placing a kiss there. Her inner muscles contracted and she lifted her hips. Her eyes darted open, looking down just as he eased her thighs apart.

"Open for me, Aleysia," he said, using his thighs to part her further. She was completely open to him, her thighs spread wide, and he stared unabashedly, his long lashes casting shadows on his high cheekbones. He would be able to see her arousal, the moisture there. Heat flushed her entire body as his gaze wandered back to hers. "You are so beautiful."

Then he did the unthinkable. He lowered his mouth and kissed her there, at her most intimate place.

And it felt . . . wonderful.

Her breath left her in a rush as his long, velvety tongue stroked her moist, heated cleft. Meanwhile, his hands returned to her breasts, cupping them, his fingers teasing her sensitive nipples into pointed peaks.

He seemed to know her body better than she did, touching her in a way that made her heart hammer and her bones feel like they were melting. Her fingers curled into the bedding at her sides, fisting it as a delicious ache built deep within her, there in the place where he pleasured her, making her burn for the unknown. His tongue slipped inside her sheath, and she cried out her pleasure as she was lifted on a silky cloud of sensation.

More. How she yearned to say the word aloud, to encourage him, to keep him doing . . . that. The blood roared in her ears as he sucked hard on the place where it seemed all her nerve endings were bundled. The more he flicked that spot with the tip of his tongue, the higher she soared.

Unable to help herself, she reached out for him, her fingers sinking into the silky-soft wetness of his hair, anchoring him there, urging him without words to continue as she rode out the wonderful new sensations. He inserted a finger inside her channel, and her inner muscles clenched.

"So tight," he said with a pleased smile before sucking her button again. He used the perfect pressure. Not too hard, not too soft, and all the while his finger moved in and out of her.

Her entire being throbbed and she was rocked by something so amazing, her body seemed to be not of itself.

Minutes later, still trembling, she opened her eyes to find the Norman braced above her, his gray eyes dark with unspent passion. His rock-hard manhood rested against the very core of her, the place his mouth had just been—the place that ached for him in a way she hadn't known was possible.

She lifted her hips a fraction, needing to be filled by more than just his finger. The sides of his mouth curved just a little, and then he thrust. She cried out at the momentary pain. The tiny stab that told her she was no longer a maiden. Guilt rushed her, and she pushed at his chest. "Nay, do not."

He didn't move at all, but just lay there on top of her, his cock filling her to the womb. Trembling, he rested his forehead against hers before kissing her softly, speaking to her in his native language, which she couldn't understand. For the first time in her life, she wished she knew the hated language.

Her channel gripped him, adjusting to the intrusion. The pain eased with each second that passed, but that did nothing to ease the shame. Unshed tears burned the backs of her eyes.

"Shhh," he whispered, kissing her gently. "The pain will pass. Soon you will experience paradise."

His jaw was clenched tight, and his eyes closed, making her wonder if he too suffered from a similar ache. It was the same ache she'd experienced just moments before when he'd pleasured her with his mouth, yet more intense.

She shifted again. He released a primitive growl and began to move. Slowly, sliding out, then in again.

Her head fell back a little, her lips opening.

His mouth descended on hers again, his tongue slipping past her lips, stroking hers in the same way he stroked her body. The same rhythm. She tasted her essence on his lips and as he thrust again, she wondered if she would burn in hell for enjoying it so much.

After all, he was her enemy.

The thought slipped away as her stomach coiled and the pulsing began anew. Soon she was clawing toward a pinnacle, higher and higher. With each thrust she gripped tighter to his shoulders, her fingers grazing his strong back, clinging to him.

He winced, and she realized she'd caught his wound with her nail. The wound she had caused. Her hands moved down his powerful back, the narrow waist, to the hips that moved in a slow rhythm, as his tempo gradually became faster, making her body climb higher and higher.

She cried out against his lips as the sensations overtook her, pulsing until the throbbing in her body released, and took her to heights she never imagined.

FOUR

Aleysia was horrified.

Last night she had acted like a whore. Worse still, she had enjoyed the Norman's touch.

She had not realized the pleasure a woman could experience while making love—the sheer ecstasy of the act itself, feeling much like an arrow being shot into the sky, then falling back to earth.

Too bad the rapture ended the moment de Wulf had rolled off her with a satisfied groan.

She should have merely endured his touch, lay still without moving, rather than sigh and moan like a contented mistress. God's breath, she should have at least pretended *not* to enjoy it so much.

Despite the fact she had made good on her bargain to the Norman, from the moment she had opened her eyes, guilt rushed over her in waves.

What of Duncan? How appalled he would be to learn his betrothed had given her maidenhead to another, particularly the very Norman who held Adelstan captive. True, she had offered the bargain in order to save her brother, but she had taken pleasure in the coupling.

Immense pleasure.

Mortified at the idea of facing Renaud this morning, she had considered staying abed, but she would not hide. Nay, she would walk into the great hall with chin held high and act as though nothing had happened. Mayhap de Wulf would think her performance in his bed just that. She worried her lower lip with her teeth. Or would he know the difference?

At least de Wulf had seen she had a bath readied, and she took advantage of it, hoping to wash away every last bit of their lovemaking from her sore body.

There was a forest-green gown, undergarments, hose, and girdle laying over a chair near the fire. Her braies and tunic were nowhere in sight. Obviously, de Wulf did not approve of her men's attire . . . though he had not seemed to mind it yesterday.

She took her time dressing, the fine linen chemise and kirtle feeling odd against her skin. She could not recall the last time she had worn a gown. Having brushed her hair, she started out for the great hall, nearly losing her nerve a half-dozen times.

The bailey was quiet, only a few soldiers about, all of whom nodded as she passed by. As the large double doors of the great hall loomed before her, Aleysia steadied her nerves by taking a deep, calming breath.

Without another moment's hesitation she entered the enormous room full of knights, villeins, and serfs alike, all busy talking as pages scurried about, making sure cups and bowls were filled. Thank goodness. Mayhap she could slip in unseen, eat, and then ask Renaud's permission to see her brother. Scanning her surroundings, she spied a place to sit, on a bench next to an old woman. As she walked across the hall, she made the mistake of glancing toward the high dais where Renaud, Galeran, and several other men-at-arms sat, eating, or had been until he caught her gaze.

Renaud motioned for her to join him.

She pretended like she had not seen him, and kept walking toward the bench. He stood and motioned once more, this time with more emphasis. His lifted brow told her he would not take no for an answer. Forcing a smile she did not feel, she nodded in acquiescence and made her way toward the dais. If there had been some in the hall who had not heard of the bargain made between herself and de Wulf, then that would change the moment she took a place at Renaud's side.

Heat rushed up her neck to stain her cheeks.

Renaud's long, dark hair fell past his broad shoulders in silky, thick waves. Last night she had not been able to see the highlights in the rich brown locks, but now in the light of day they shone brilliantly.

Dressed plainly in a blue tunic and black braies, he seemed uncaring of how he appeared to others. Such a contrast to de Pirou, who had dressed with great care, wearing tunics of only the richest materials, embroidered with colored stitching. Even de Pirou's mantle, held together by an enormous sapphire broach, had been heavily embroidered and embellished with a gold border. Most lords of the realm dressed to impress, but Renaud seemed to have no need for such finery.

Ignoring the whispers that continued all about her, she tried without success not to blush as memories of last night flashed through her mind. This man had seen her naked . . . had done things to her she could have never imagined. Her heart pounded against her breastbone when she finally stopped before him.

"How are you this fine morn?" he asked, a softness in his eyes that had not been there the day before. In truth, his silver gaze was so intense she could not keep it.

"I am well," she replied, biting her trembling bottom lip as she slipped onto the bench at his side.

He sat down, his thigh brushing against hers, reminding her of the night just spent in his arms—of the contrast in their bodies . . . of the pleasure he had given her. She abruptly shifted so they no longer touched, and he laughed lightly, obviously amused by her skittishness.

"Did you sleep well, my lady?" His gray stare burned into her, and she had no choice but to look at him. Her heart gave a mad jolt at the heat she saw there, and to her dismay, her nipples tightened into tiny buds.

"Aye, I did."

His lips curved, flashing a boyish grin. "Good. I am pleased to say I did as well. Already I am eager to return to our chamber."

"You mean *your* chamber, my lord."

How handsome he was—even with the scar, which made her wonder what had happened to his betrothed. Did he love the woman, and were they still set to marry? No doubt she was stunningly beautiful, much as his mistresses would be.

She pushed the strangely disturbing thought aside. It mattered not who his lovers were. De Wulf was merely a means to an end. They had a bargain, and she would live up to her end until she and Adelstan escaped.

Then she would never look back.

Renaud reached for his goblet at the same time she reached for hers and their fingers brushed. She nearly toppled her goblet when she jerked her hand away, but his reflexes were fast and he caught it in time.

"I will not bite you, Aleysia," he said, in a husky whisper she felt all the way up her spine.

"I am not so sure, my lord."

He moved over again, to where they touched arm to arm, leg to leg. "You smell wonderful." He inhaled deeply. "You must have used the oils."

How hot she felt all of a sudden. "Indeed, I did."

"They should help ease any ache."

She knew what *ache* he spoke of. And now she suffered from yet another ache that had returned with force. The one between her legs. Her cheeks burned and she tried to pull away, but he sat on her gown, trapping her.

She took a sip of wine, wishing he would stop staring at her. He mirrored her movements, drinking from his goblet, watching her over the rim. How she wished he would choke on the wine.

His gaze slipped lower to her breasts. Her stomach twisted as she watched him, an idea forming in her mind. She must leave Braemere as soon as possible. From time to time her mother had asked the healer to make her a special potion to help her sleep. And it worked, for her mother would sleep like the dead.

Aye, mayhap she could add a potion to Renaud's wine.

Renaud's heart hammered like a lad's as he watched Aleysia sip her wine.

Last night he had found paradise in the most unlikely place. A Saxon woman betrothed to a Scot, who had given her body to de Wulf himself in exchange for her brother's well-being.

Though Aleysia had offered herself to Renaud under distress, he did not believe for a minute that she did not enjoy their mating. In truth, she had moaned and met each thrust as though she were a well-practiced whore. Yet she had been a virgin, the evidence of which had been on his cock and on the sheets this morning. Knowing he'd been the first pleased him more than he cared to admit. Even more, he yearned to take her to his bed again.

His father's words of warning had raced through his thoughts since dawn. *Never give your heart to a woman—for she will return it to you with a dagger clean through it.* And his father knew of which he spoke, for his wife, Renaud's own mother, had left her family for another. His father had never forgiven her, not even when she returned years later, heartbroken by the very man she had abandoned her family for.

Renaud still could not forget the anguish on his mother's face when his father rejected her, throwing her out in the rain and telling her she would never see any of them again. She had not tried to contact any of them throughout the years, and he had learned she had died about ten years earlier, a sad, broken woman who had been living in an abbey with a small cloister of nuns. Sadly, even after hearing of her death, his father still had been unable to forgive her, and had insisted her name never be uttered around him.

Pushing aside the painful memories, Renaud smiled down at Aleysia. How flustered she was. Her cheeks flushed a lovely shade of pink. It was obvious she hated sitting beside him, and was embarrassed, for no one would be second-guessing their relationship. "What will you do today?" he asked, amazed at her breathtaking beauty. He would have to thank the old servant woman who had found the kirtle for Aleysia. The green of the gown brought out the color of her eyes. How fine she looked in feminine attire. If she were his woman, he would buy her the richest fabrics in the most vibrant colors in which to clothe her slender frame. How he would love to spoil her so. The thought surprised him, even stunned him, for he had never taken to a woman so quickly.

"I would like to go for a ride, and then perhaps see Adelstan."

The fantasy evaporated under her intense stare, and he frowned. Of course she would want to see her brother. She watched him intently, her eyes filled with hope, a tawny brow lifting as she awaited his answer. It was not unreasonable for her to ask to see her twin. After all, she had been true to her word so far. "Aye, but I shall accompany you."

She opened her mouth as though to argue, but closed it just as quickly. "Thank you, my lord."

Aleysia wrinkled her nose as she entered the tower. The large room smelled dank and musty, to the point she fought to catch her breath. The only air came from a small window with large iron bars, which was up too high to see out of. Something scurried out of the corner and Aleysia gasped, placing a hand over her pounding heart.

"Aleysia," Adelstan said, rising from the small cot that had been shoved against a wall.

Aleysia rushed toward her brother, her stomach knotting at the sight of shackles on his wrists and ankles. The skin had already been rubbed raw. "How are you faring?" she asked, hugging him tightly.

"As well as can be expected given the circumstances."

"You are so cold. Do they not give you a blanket?"

"Aye, a scratchy one, but it gives me some warmth. What of you?" Putting her at arm's length, his gaze wandered down her length and up again. He knew she had not worn a gown for years, even though Duncan had requested she do so a time or two.

She forced herself to meet his gaze. "I am well."

His green eyes questioned what he could not ask.

"Do you get enough to eat?" she asked, hoping to avoid any questions pertaining to Renaud, or why she now wore a gown.

"Aleysia, tell me that you have not done something foolish."

Shame washed over her in waves. If only he knew the truth. "I do what I must."

He looked toward the open door, where Renaud and the guards stood conversing. "You gave yourself to him?" The words were little more than a whisper, but she could hear and see his despair.

"I will do whatever I must to save you."

He cursed under his breath. "I will kill him one day. I swear it."

Aleysia ignored the disturbing image his words caused. Though she disliked the Norman, she did not wish him dead.

"Forgive me for putting you through this. You should have stayed in Scotland. Duncan would have looked after you."

"I came of my own accord, and well you know it. I would have never let you go without me."

He smiled a tiny smile.

She squeezed his hands. "What can I do to help you?"

"There is nothing that can be done. All our men have fled into Scotland and Wales, taking refuge where they can. God willing, they will be safe from William's tyranny. If the opportunity should arise, I want you to run, sister. Do not look back."

"I will not leave you."

His hold on her tightened. "You must. Forget me. My fate has been decided." She hated the look of defeat in his eyes, and it scared her. Adelstan had given up.

"There is something I have thought of." She lowered her voice. "Do you remember the potion the healer made for Mother's headaches? The one that made her sleep soundly."

Adelstan nodded. "Indeed, Father said she slept like the dead."

"Mayhap I can convince Renaud to let me visit the healer to have her come tend your wounds," she said, nodding toward his raw wrists. "I can ask her to prepare the draught for us, and I will return to get it. When the time is right, I will give the guards a dose and de Wulf as well."

"Think you it would work?"

Hearing the excitement in his voice, she nodded. "If I can gain his trust in the meantime, then we will have a very good chance."

"But what must you do to gain his trust?"

"Nothing that I have not done already."

He closed his eyes for a moment, but when he opened them again he looked past her, to the doorway. "What if he discovers the draught? You could ruin your only chance at escape, and they could even hang you. I have seen it done before, Aleysia. We are surrounded by the enemy and you must never forget that. Not for a moment."

"I do not want to live in a world without you, Adelstan. I have lost too much already." She kissed his cheek. "We *will* do this. We will. Soon we will be back in Scotland, growing old together."

His eyes glimmered with renewed hope.

"Aleysia, it is time to take our leave," Renaud said, stepping into the room.

She jumped at the sound of the Norman's voice. Surely, he had not heard the two of them discussing their plans? She prayed not.

"A moment only," she replied.

Taking her brother's face between her palms, she kissed each cheek. "Stay strong. I shall visit soon."

Adelstan's nostrils flared in his effort to contain his emotions. "God keep you."

Without another word, she turned and walked toward Renaud, taking the hand he held out to her.

FIVE

He was so quiet.

Too quiet.

Aleysia looked up from her embroidery to find Renaud watching her. He had been sitting in a high-backed chair before the fire, staring into the flames for the past hour, yet just now she had felt his silver gaze boring into her.

Had he overheard her discussion with Adelstan? He had allowed her to go to the healer and ask for her to tend Adelstan's wounds—but he had also sent three guards along to make sure she made it without incident. If he had heard the plan, he would not have allowed her to go to begin with.

The healer, an old woman who had so faithfully served her parents, agreed to tend Adelstan's wrists and ankles. The guards had slipped inside the hut just after she'd asked the old woman about the draught. Thank goodness the healer had readily agreed to help her.

Now all she had to do was wait, and hopefully gain Renaud's trust.

A heavy sigh broke into her thoughts. Renaud ran a hand through his already tousled hair. How restless he seemed. She prayed he did not guess at her treachery.

Her stomach clenched, knowing she flirted with danger, and her brother's life. Unable to stand his intent gaze any longer, she set her embroidery aside and stood.

He shifted in the chair.

She met his gaze boldly, and nodded toward the bed. "My lord, do you wish to join me?"

His expression did not falter, though he did lift a dark brow. "I am not tired."

Fear rippled along her spine as she walked toward him, forcing herself to remain calm.

He watched her approach warily, his gray eyes intense with an emotion she couldn't decipher. Undaunted, she continued, noting that his gaze shifted over her . . . like a slow caress. Visions of the night spent in his arms raced through her mind, flooding her with warmth.

Going on her knees beside him, she rested her hands on her lap and met his gaze. "Did you have a difficult day, my lord? You seem distracted."

Reaching out, he touched her hair lightly, before his long fingers gently combed through the tresses. "You have beautiful hair, Aleysia. Like silk."

No matter how much she tried to deny it—his touch was like heaven, sending shards of pleasure pulsing throughout her. Already her body responded to his touch. Her nipples sensitive, tightening into small little buds. Even the space between her thighs grew wet and hot.

He lifted a curl to his nose and breathed deeply. "Lavender," he said with a soft smile.

She nodded, wishing he were not so handsome. How old Duncan seemed to her now. In fact, she found it difficult to conjure up her betrothed's image. Would she find the same pleasure in Duncan's arms as she had in Renaud's? Were all men the same in *that* way? She did know that Renaud's body was pleasing to look at—both with and without clothing. She could stare at his naked body for hours. For some reason she could not imagine Duncan nude. The very thought made her shudder.

"A man could get lost in your eyes." A moment later his mouth descended on hers, and the next thing she knew, he pulled her onto his lap. His powerful thighs felt rock-hard against the backs of hers.

Desire swept throughout her body as his hand moved down her throat, over her breast, cupping it through the soft material of her gown. His thumb brushed the sensitive nipple, and she could feel the hard ridge of his arousal pressed against her hip.

Resting a hand against his chest, she felt the mad thumping of his heart, matching the rhythm of her own. Feeling daring, her fingers ventured over his hard stomach and the fine line of hair that trailed down to his impressive cock. *You can do this, Aleysia.*

She gasped in surprise when he lightly pinched her nipple; the sensation was not at all unpleasant. In fact, it seemed to heighten her need, and sent a rush of heat to her groin.

Boldly, she slid her hand inside his braies, her fingers brushing over the plum-sized crown of his erection. His sharp intake of breath told her he was surprised by her actions, but he did not stop her. Rather, he guided her by laying his hand over hers, prompting her to grip his length firmly.

The velvety feel of him was in such contrast to the steely length she held, the beating of it matching the rhythm of his heart. And with each stroke of her fingers over him, he grew longer, thicker, harder. She was anxious to experience what she had only just discovered last night. Excitement rushed through her body, making the flesh between her thighs tingle.

He lifted her then, to where she faced him, straddling his thighs. His shaft rose between them—huge, the veins prominent. Her insides contracted.

And though she tried to tell herself she did this to gain his trust, she enjoyed it.

Oh, how she wanted him.

His fingers brushed over her slick, sensitive folds, then one finger slipped inside her while his thumb stroked her hidden pearl. "You're already wet, Aleysia," he said in a husky voice.

Tightening her grip on his cock, she grew more daring, her strokes faster. His breathing grew ragged and he shifted yet again. "I can wait no longer," he said, guiding her above his erection. She sank down on him slowly, inch by inch, his thick length stretching her.

His eyes closed as she settled on him, and he groaned as if in pain. She felt awkward, unsure what to do. Tentatively, she moved, shifting her hips, getting accustomed to the feel of him buried deep inside her. An exquisite ache rippled throughout her body.

Renaud suddenly opened his eyes and her heart missed a beat. His heavy-lidded gaze was so hot and penetrating, he looked as though he could devour her.

Settling his hands back on her hips, he lifted her up, then down, showing her what he wanted . . . the pace he desired.

Gripping the back of the chair for support, she started to ride him, much in the way she would ride her horse. He dipped his head, kissing the swell of her breasts before taking a nipple into his mouth, sucking through the thin material of her gown, using his teeth in a way that made her want to moan with ecstasy.

But she bit her lip to keep from crying out. The feelings raging within her intensified with each down stroke. His breathing grew rough, his fingers curled around her hips.

Abruptly, he stood, bringing her with him. He fell to his knees on the rug, and eased her onto her back. Their bodies still joined, he rose above her, his arms bracing his weight. He looked down at where his body entered hers, and her gaze followed.

Heat swirled through her veins as she watched his thick, long cock, slick with her juices, slide within her, and retreat. His hips moved fluidly, in a rhythm that had her meeting his every thrust.

His gaze found hers, and she could tell he fought to refrain from spending within her before she met her completion. Reaching between their bodies, he stroked her bud with the pad of his thumb.

Every inch of her pulsed with pleasure, intensifying to that incredible pinnacle she'd discovered just last night. "Come for me, Aleysia," he said, the words so shockingly explicit, she felt her face flush with not just embarrassment but pleasure.

How wicked she had become in such a short time.

She climbed toward the stars, the pressure in her body building—pushing toward that unbelievable high. With a hard thrust he ground into her, giving her every inch of his delicious cock, holding her hips to keep her from moving away. Climaxing, her channel tightened around him, pulsing, throbbing, pulling him in deeper.

With a satisfied groan he came, his hot seed pouring inside her. He rolled to his side, bringing her along with him. For a few silent moments she fought to catch her breath, before becoming aware of her surroundings. The wooden beams above her, the soft rug beneath her, the crackling fire behind her, and the man beside her.

He still held her, his fingers brushing lazily along her spine, but he looked toward the flames, the fire casting half his face in shadow. Once again his brow furrowed.

Silence.

His braies were still down around his knees, her kirtle up about her hips. Embarrassed at their fevered coupling and how much she had enjoyed it, she pushed her skirts down over her legs.

Going up on her elbow, she placed a hand on his chest. "What ails you, Renaud?"

He glanced at her, his troubled gaze searching her face.

She saw the hesitation in his eyes, and no longer was she worried that he had found out about the healer and the sleeping draught. Somehow she knew what his tortured gaze meant.

He smoothed her hair back from her face. "I received a summons from King William today."

The hair on the back of her neck stood on end. She sat up abruptly, and his hand fell away.

"He wants Adelstan brought to York."

She shook her head. "Nay."

"We are to leave in a fortnight."

The trembling began deep within her and drew outward until she shook like a leaf. "Nay, you cannot. William will have his head." She scrambled to her feet. "You promised!"

Worse than his silence was the simple fact he did not deny it. How could she have ever believed Renaud de Wulf would show mercy? What a fool she had been to trust him.

He would be leaving—taking Adelstan to certain death. She must get the draught. They must escape now, before it was too late. The thought of life without her brother was too painful . . . unthinkable. "You gave me your word, Renaud. You agreed to our bargain."

"And I have kept your brother safe, Aleysia."

"Aye, you did, but what now? You merely kept him alive so your king would have the privilege of killing him!"

He stood slowly, pulling his braies up and tying them. "I promised nothing."

He could not even look at her.

She shook her head, not believing her ears. She had given this monster her maidenhead, thinking she would buy them time, but he had no intention of giving her or Adelstan leniency. "I beg that you let him go. Tell William that he escaped."

Finally, he looked at her, and his eyes were full of regret. "I cannot do that, Aleysia."

She felt like her world had been ripped out from beneath her. "Why not?"

"He is my king, and I have given him my word."

"And what of your promise to me?"

His gaze shifted over her slowly. "You will stay at Braemere. I will speak to King William. Mayhap he will show mercy. In fact, I am prepared to ask for your hand."

"I would *never* marry a Norman!"

His gaze turned cold. "You would rather suffer the same fate as your brother than be my wife?"

She nodded and tears slipped down her cheeks. "Aye, I would."

He frowned and reached for her.

She jumped away. "Do not touch me *ever* again! We had a bargain and you have failed to live up to your end. I ask that you release me now. Put me in the tower with my brother, for I will not live without him."

He stepped toward her and lifted her chin with strong fingers, wiping away the tears with his thumbs, his expression softer than moments before. "I am not prepared to let you go."

She took hold of his wrist. "Then let Adelstan go, Renaud. You have the power to release him. Let him escape to Scotland. Tell William what you must—that Adelstan is dead, but let my brother live."

His finger slipped down over her throat and the pulse beating wildly there. "Release him—so he can return with Laird MacMillan to demand your freedom? I cannot take that chance." He bent his head as though to kiss her, but she pulled away so fast, she nearly stumbled back into the chair where she had ridden him moments ago.

"I do not belong to you—nor do I want you."

The sides of his mouth slowly lifted in a cruel smile. "Oh but you do, Aleysia. You want me as badly as I want you."

"I hate you!"

His jaw tensed, the nerve working there. "You will be my woman, Aleysia. You would be wise to accept that."

"I am not your woman, nor will I ever be." She ignored the warning bells in her head and slapped his hand away. "I *will* marry Laird MacMillan."

With a flick of his wrist he pulled her against him. "You are my woman, not MacMillan's. Think you he would still want you, knowing that you came willingly to my bed?"

The words were as effective as a sharp slap to the face. "I did what I must for duty's sake. Little did I know you would not hold up your end of the bargain. Duncan will forgive me."

His eyes narrowed dangerously.

A blush raced up her cheeks but she forced herself to keep his gaze. "Duncan is a gentleman and he will have me still. He loves me— and I love him," she lied.

He flinched as though she'd struck him. "And what if you carry my babe? Would he still love you then?"

Her stomach rolled, for honestly she did not know the answer. In truth, she could already be carrying de Wulf's child. She had heard of women being ostracized from their villages because they'd given birth to a bastard child. "Duncan would raise the babe as his own."

"He will not have the opportunity," Renaud snarled through gritted teeth. "And he will not have you."

"I am not your property, bought and paid for. I am a woman who can make her own decisions and I choose to return to Scotland, to my betrothed."

His fingers gripped her arm tighter. "I thought you wanted to be imprisoned with your brother?"

A sudden knock at the door made her jump. In truth, she was

thankful for the interruption. However, it appeared Renaud felt differently as he scowled at the door.

"Go away!" he yelled.

"My lord, there is an urgent matter you need to attend to," Galeran said, his tone intent.

Cursing under his breath, Renaud released her before striding toward the door. He wrenched it open.

Galeran stood with a handful of men, all wearing full chain mail. "Laird MacMillan requests your presence." The vassal's gaze shifted to Aleysia. "He says to bring *his* woman."

Relief rushed over Aleysia in waves. Duncan was here, and he would bargain for their lives! Hope stirred within her.

Renaud's lethal gaze locked with hers. There was a dangerous gleam in his eye that made her mouth go dry. "You can wipe that smile from your face, Aleysia—for Laird MacMillan will be leaving Braemere *without* you."

SIX

Duncan MacMillan was a big man. Tall and barrel-chested, with long red hair and a full beard, the Scot sat astride his horse, his hand resting on the hilt of his sword. At least ten years Renaud's senior, he looked every bit the hot-blooded Scottish laird that he was.

How Renaud hated him.

Duncan is a gentleman and he will have me still. He loves me— and I love him. Aleysia's words still burned in his ears. Did she truly love this man who was old enough to be her father? A man who would no doubt treat her like a child rather than an equal?

Their fevered lovemaking made him think not. Of course love and desire were two different things entirely. His own mother had sworn love and loyalty to his father, then left him for another. Women were devious creatures, not to be trusted.

"My lord, you know he will not leave Braemere without his woman."

Renaud glanced at Galeran, who rode beside him, along with his most trusted men-at-arms, out of the bailey, toward the field where the Scot and his army awaited. "Aleysia is *not* his woman, and he cannot have her."

Galeran's lips quirked. "I do believe she has gotten under your skin, my lord. I know it is not my place to say, but please be wary. Remember what your father always said."

Indeed. His father's words had been running through his mind from the moment Renaud had set eyes on Aleysia. The problem was, he could not purge the Saxon from his thoughts, no matter how hard he tried. She even haunted his dreams. Just this morning while he met with his men, his thoughts kept drifting to the night spent in her arms. How sweet her touch had been, setting his blood on fire, making him thirst for more. And he had received more—just moments ago when she'd ridden him in the chair, her lovely green eyes full of passion and wonderment.

He'd had no inclination to make love to her again so soon, for he knew she must be sore. Yet when she'd come to him, sinking down on her knees, he had been unable to keep his hands to himself. God's truth, he did not think he would ever get enough of her.

"Laird MacMillan looks like he could run you clean through," Galeran remarked, bringing Renaud out of his thoughts and to the confrontation ahead.

Galeran did not lie. The laird glowered at him as he approached, a murderous gleam in his eye, but Renaud felt no fear. After all, his men lined the walls of the keep and bailey, ready for him to give the signal to attack. MacMillan and his small band of men would be slaughtered.

Renaud stopped a few yards shy of the Scottish laird and nodded in greeting.

"Baron de Wulf."

"Laird Duncan MacMillan." He puffed out his chest and lifted his chin. "I have come to claim my bride. I demand her release."

He *demanded*?

Renaud's fingers tightened around the hilt of his sword. How he itched to take the man's head off with a swipe of his blade. "Aleysia and Adelstan are prisoners of the crown, and therefore they will remain at Braemere."

The Scot flinched, his gaze shifting from Renaud, to the men behind him, and up along the palisade and battlements where archers stood shoulder to shoulder, bows extended and arrows notched. MacMillan's shoulders straightened, knowing he was outnumbered. Renaud could see reservation in the laird's dark eyes when their gazes locked once more. "Do what ye will with Adelstan. I have no doubt your king is thirsty for his blood . . . but return my betrothed to me."

Disbelief rocked Renaud. MacMillan did not look at all sorry to leave Adelstan to his fate. In truth, Renaud wondered if that wasn't relief he saw in the other man's eyes. Had the Scot been jealous of the close relationship the twins shared, and therefore wanted Adelstan gone? "Why would you leave Adelstan to his fate?"

"The lad can stay in your dungeon for all eternity. He has led his sister astray, making her more into a man than the young woman she is. Mayhap with him gone, Aleysia will embrace her feminine ways."

"Aleysia is as guilty as her brother."

"Guilty of what?" the Scot asked, his rage evident by the color that stained his cheeks.

"Attempted murder of a lord of the realm."

MacMillan's brows furrowed. "My betrothed would ne'er do something so foolish."

If only he knew what else *his betrothed* had done.

"It matters not what you believe, MacMillan. I assure you, however, that Aleysia is guilty of this crime. I have the scar to prove it."

"No doubt Aleysia did what was necessary to save her life."

Irritated that the man's words rang true and that Aleysia had made the bargain to save her brother under distress, Renaud unsheathed his sword. "I have already sent word to my king that we have captured Adelstan and his twin. King William will be expecting both. I cannot arrive with only one," he lied.

"He will marry her to another!" MacMillan yelled, his face turning bright red with anger.

Everything within Renaud rebelled at that statement. "Nay, he will not, for I will not allow it to happen. If Aleysia marries anyone, it will be me. Return to Scotland, MacMillan. Cawdor's twins are no longer your concern."

The laird's eyes glittered with hatred and vengeance.

"I will pay you handsomely if you return her to me." MacMillan motioned for one of his soldiers to come forward. The soldier held a chest, which he opened to display hundreds of gold coins.

Galeran glanced at Renaud. No doubt it was more money than the young man had ever seen. "I am not interested."

"What do ye have to gain by keeping Aleysia with ye?"

Renaud lifted a brow. "Do you honestly need me to answer that question?"

The Scot's eyes narrowed and he drew his sword. All around them metal scraped against scabbards. "By God, if ye have dishonored my betrothed . . ."

"That is between Aleysia and myself."

MacMillan's fury shone bright in his dark expression. "I demand satisfaction, de Wulf."

"You cannot win, MacMillan. You know that. Take your gold and return to your beloved Highlands. Forget Aleysia."

MacMillan's jaw clenched tight. "I go now, but not because I fear ye, but because I will not have my kinsman slain by the likes of you. You have my word on it that ye have not seen the last of me, de Wulf."

"Is that a threat?"

MacMillan's lips curved into a smile that did not begin to reach his eyes. "Nay, 'tis a promise."

Aleysia watched the exchange from the bedchamber window.

She could sense Duncan's agitation as he conversed with Renaud. Strangely, she had been nervous, not only for the Scot, but for Renaud as well. Duncan was an excellent swordsman, and had a hot temper to match. Both his skill and disposition were legendary in the Highlands. But today he was outmanned, and well he knew it. Renaud's men stood at the ready, an incredible sight, weapons drawn, just waiting for their liege lord to give the word to attack.

But Renaud did not give the signal, and as quickly as the meeting started, it ended with Duncan leaving, leading his men away from Braemere. Aleysia had seen the soldier come forward with a chest, and once opened the sun glinted off the gold coin. To her shock Renaud had refused it.

Watching Duncan's retreating back, Aleysia felt a combination of sadness and anger. Worse still, all the hope she had been feeling melted away. She had hoped she and her brother would be released.

Now she must get the draught. If she failed, her brother would die and she would be alone. Her entire family extinguished. A raw ache filled her, tightening her throat. How could she live without Adelstan?

As MacMillan and his men disappeared over the ridge, Aleysia looked for Renaud. On horseback, he sat just beyond the gatehouse, his trusted vassal Galeran at his side, the army still alert, standing, waiting until Duncan and his men were safely out of sight.

Suddenly, Renaud wheeled his horse about, his gaze directed at the window where she stood. Her breath hitched, and she almost stepped out of sight. But pride made her stand firm. She lifted her chin, meeting his gaze head-on, hoping he saw her fury.

To her surprise there was no triumphant smile on his handsome face. No gloating. In fact, he showed no expression at all as he stared at her. Then Galeran said something to him and he turned to his vassal, the moment gone.

What had Renaud said to Duncan? Had he told her betrothed that he had taken her maidenhead? Knowing the truth now, would the laird return in force, or would he consider her not worth the effort or risk? No doubt he thought her soiled goods. Shame rippled through her. If only her body had not betrayed her. Then she would have no reason to feel guilty.

She stepped away from the window, her mind racing. Yes, she must get the draught from the healer and leave Braemere before Renaud took Adelstan to York.

Weary, Renaud climbed the steps to the bedchamber where Aleysia awaited him.

He had seen her watching from the window, knew that she had seen the exchange between he and MacMillan. Her fury had been evident even from a distance, and he wondered what to say to her now. In his heart he knew MacMillan would return, but he was not about to tell her that.

Still he was stunned that the Scottish laird had not wanted Adelstan's release.

And what would Aleysia say if she knew MacMillan had so easily left her beloved twin to his fate? Would she still love him then?

Considering how fiercely loyal she was to her brother, he would think not.

A maid stepped out of his bedchamber just then. "My lord," she said, nodding to him as she passed by, the candle fluttering, casting shadows upon the stone walls.

He nodded and entered the warm chamber where a fire blazed in the hearth. He closed the door behind him and looked to the bed where Aleysia lay.

Wearing only a fine linen chemise, she lay on top of the furs, her back to him. He could sense her sadness and her anger by her rigid posture.

He had never been good at comforting . . . having himself never sought his mother's touch for any ache or pain. Always the task felt awkward and unnatural, yet now he felt compelled to ease Aleysia's ache somehow. If only he knew how. Trying to think of something to say, he sat on the edge of the bed and reached out to her, his hand settling on her hip.

She froze at his touch, but did not pull away. He could feel her skin beneath the sheer material—and his body responded, his cock hardening.

"What did he say?" she asked, her voice barely above a whisper. He could hear the pain in that question and it tugged at his heart.

How easy it would be to tell her that her loyal betrothed had not wanted Adelstan at all. That he had seen the jealousy in the Scot's eyes, toward a twin who had taken excellent care of his sister, keeping her out of harm's way for all these years, when he could so easily have used her as a pawn. But he could not hurt her again. She had suffered enough with the news of Adelstan's being summoned to York. "He asked for you, but I refused."

Regret filled every inch of him. If only she were not Saxon, and her brother had not killed de Pirou. How could he take her brother, her only living family member, to certain death? If he were honest with himself, he would admit that he admired the young Saxon, who had taken a fief back from the devious de Pirou. Renaud would have done likewise if his parents had been killed. Aye, it was a shame Adelstan was Saxon, for Renaud would be honored to have such a knight in his ranks. As it was, he could not trust the young, clever man. The boy was simply too dangerous.

Plus, King William expected Adelstan at York by month's end. Renaud's mind raced, knowing William would not show the Saxon mercy. Mayhap if Renaud convinced the king that Adelstan could, with proper training, become a trusted vassal and a fearless knight? Yet would Adelstan agree to such a life?

More important—would William allow such leniency, especially given the extremity of the crime?

In his heart he knew the answer.

Already the heads of Saxon leaders sat atop pikes along York Castle, a message to all that King William was in England to stay.

"What else did he say?"

Renaud shook away the gruesome image of the pikes on the battlements at York. "He asked only for your release."

She rolled over, her gaze locking with his. Her eyes were reddened and puffy from crying. "And what of Adelstan?" Her voice broke.

How lovely she was. Amazingly beautiful, fiercely loyal. She was the kind of woman a man would kill to protect. A woman *he* would protect. Oddly enough, he had not been swayed by the coin MacMillan had offered. Many in his place would have taken it and offered the fortune to William in order to gain favor, but Renaud had not been tempted in the least.

Her eyes narrowed as he continued to stare, reminding him that she had asked him a question and awaited his answer.

Not wanting her to hurt more than she did already, he nodded. "Him, too."

Tears pooled in her eyes, and when she blinked, they slid down her cheek, onto the sheer material of the chemise.

He lifted her chin with his fingers, brushing away the tear with his thumb, but she jerked away. "Aleysia, you know if I could change this, I would."

Her eyes searched his, and with a moan of despair she turned away, onto her side, lifting her knees toward her chest, her sobs wracking her body.

A stab of guilt pierced him as he helplessly watched her. He had done this. Made this beautiful creature cry. And she had suffered so much already. The death of her parents, the loss of her home—and shortly, the loss of her beloved twin.

Feeling wretched, he removed his boots, chausses, and tunic, and lay down on the bed beside her.

Her sobs tore at his heart. How he ached to comfort her, to pull her into his arms and just hold her. Tell her everything would be all right.

But it would be a lie.

And they both knew it.

His gaze slid from her quaking shoulders, down her slender back, over the curve of her hip. The chemise hugged her body, outlining its perfection. Her bent knees pulled the fabric tight, emphasizing her buttocks and long legs, and his body responded to the sensual sight.

He could feel his heart pounding, hear the crackle of the wood in the fire, burning, much like the blood within his veins.

She shivered, so he pulled a blanket over her, tucking it around her, relieved it covered her curves, for he desired her greatly—and seeing her in the thin chemise aroused him nearly as much as if she lay naked.

Within minutes her breathing evened out and he realized she had fallen asleep. Going up on his elbow, he looked down at her. How solemn she looked, almost angelic, save for the tears.

Resisting the urge to brush them away, he instead lay back on the bed, staring at the canopy above him. He wondered if he'd have been better off rejecting her bargain. Mayhap he should have sent her back to Scotland.

SEVEN

The healer's small hut sat alone in a wooded area east of the village. Smoke curled from the chimney, filling the air with a strange scent.

Aleysia remembered her mother telling her when she was a child that the healer's hut had sat apart from the village because the old woman needed to be near the forests, where she grew her potent herbs. She had also heard that many of the villagers feared the healer, claiming her to be a witch, but Aleysia did not believe the dear woman to be evil. Nay, she had always been incredibly kind, and though she must be one hundred years old, her mind was still sharp.

Aleysia looked over her shoulder to make sure she had not been followed. Thankfully, Renaud was busy with his troops, wielding swords and practicing archery. She had managed to slip away from the guard who had fallen asleep beside a large oak, while she had been busy picking berries.

It had been nearly a week since she'd visited Adelstan in the tower. In that time she had done nothing to raise Renaud's suspicion, doing what he said, and making no argument. She had even cuddled close to him at night, but not once since Duncan's departure had he made love to her.

In truth, he seemed to be spending more time in the great hall with his men. And last night he had not come to the chamber at all. Aleysia had awoken in the early morning hours to find herself alone, and experienced a moment of frustration while she wondered where Renaud had slept.

She had noticed how the female servants watched him, particularly the big-breasted servant who had wanted to rub his back—and no doubt more than that—when he had bathed that first night upon taking Braemere. Aye, it seemed all the women wanted him, making eyes at him, hoping to catch his interest. Had he spent the night in another woman's arms? The thought made her stomach tighten painfully.

She had seen him this morning in the great hall. He looked well rested and in good spirits, completely ignoring her as she made her way to his side. He had merely nodded at her in greeting, a soft smile on his handsome face, before turning to converse with Galeran.

Shaking away the memory, she refocused her attention and took a quick glance over her shoulder to make sure she had not been followed. Seeing no one, Aleysia knocked on the door. A moment later, the healer opened the door and smiled.

"I was expecting you, my dear. Do you have time for tea?"

"I am sorry, but I must return before the guard awakes and realizes where I am." Aleysia glanced over her shoulder once more, before handing the healer the note she had written earlier, when she had stolen a few moments alone. "I fear I must ask another favor of you, and when you have done so much already. I have written a letter to Duncan MacMillan, the Scottish laird who was here not long ago. I am hoping your grandson can deliver a message to him. I know it is a dangerous task, so I will give him this," Aleysia said, removing a ring from her finger. The ring had belonged to her mother, a gift from her father. How she hated to part with the treasured piece, but she knew the risk was great for the young man. The least she could do was sacrifice something for his effort.

The old woman's eyes lit up. "'Tis beautiful, my lady. But surely it is worth too much for a simple errand."

"Nay, take it. 'Tis a dangerous journey I send him on, and in such uncertain times."

"I will see he gets it the moment you leave, dear." The healer placed a small pouch in Aleysia's hand and closed her fingers around it. "A pinch in a drink will put them out for the better part of the night. You must be very careful and stir it well, for there is a bitter taste to it."

"Thank you," Aleysia murmured, and kissed the healer's wrinkled cheek before stuffing the draught into the pocket of her gown. She hurried back toward the orchard, where thankfully the guard still slumbered, his snores loud.

Renaud had given her some freedom these past two days, allowing her out of the castle and the stuffy chamber that had made the days far too long. Glad to have the chance to wander at her leisure, she had not balked when he sent a guard with her. Now she picked the berries hurriedly, aware that if she were caught by Renaud or his men, it could mean disaster for her plans to escape.

She quickly filled her basket with berries, and not too soon, for the guard opened his eyes. He blinked several times, then guiltily scrambled to his feet. "Are you ready, my lady?" he called, and Aleysia nodded.

On their way back to the castle, they passed by Renaud and his men, practicing in a meadow of wildflowers. Bare to the waist, the Norman shouted encouragement as two of his men battled with swords. Each clash of metal made a ringing sound, one that was nearly drowned out by the soldiers' yells.

Obviously frustrated by what he saw, Renaud shook his head, and taking up his sword, approached Galeran, who drew his blade. The vassal brushed back his golden hair with a swipe of his hand and grinned mischievously at Renaud. What followed was a display of physical agility the likes she had never before seen.

Aleysia found herself entranced by the sight as Renaud cast blow after blow, his muscles bunching beneath his dark skin with the effort it took to hold off Galeran's answering parry and thrusts. Sweat beaded on his skin, a sheen that emphasized the thick, hard planes.

As she watched, desire rippled throughout her, swooping low into her belly, causing a deep throbbing ache between her legs. Her body's reaction disturbed her greatly. Why did she desire him so much—this man who was the cause of all her grief?

But Renaud truly was a magnificent-looking man, his powerful frame impressive. His dark, long hair was held back by a band, drawing emphasis to the chiseled features of his face. Her nipples hardened remembering the feel of those shoulders beneath her fingertips, as she held on while he had filled her with his rock-hard cock.

Renaud whipped his wrist and unarmed Galeran, sending the sword flying through the air, toward Aleysia. She ducked out of the way just in the knick of time.

Heart pounding, she stared at the sword just a few feet from her, in the exact spot where she'd been standing. Thank God she had regained her wits and stepped aside in time, or the blade would have impaled her.

She looked up to find Renaud rushing toward her, concern and something that resembled anger flashing in his silver eyes.

Dropping the basket, she stepped toward the sword and using both hands, pulled it from the earth. She rotated it, feeling its weight. It was far heavier than her sword, and Galeran had swung it as though it were as light as a bag of feathers.

The guard who had been watching her, held his hand out for the sword, expecting her to hand it over. She shook her head and was amused to see the wariness in his eyes. Did he actually fear she would use the sword and hurt him, or even kill him? The thought amused her almost as much as it disturbed her.

Renaud, having motioned the guard away, ran a hand through his hair. "God's breath, woman, you could have been killed."

She lifted a brow. "And would that be so terrible?"

He frowned. "Aye, it would."

Surprised by the declaration, for it looked like he meant it, Aleysia shifted on her feet. "Would you like to fight, my lord?"

"With you?"

"Are you afraid?"

His lips curved slightly. "I fear no man, but I refuse to fight a woman."

She swung the sword up and around, catching him off guard, and he faltered back a few steps. His brows furrowed. "Aleysia, I am in no mood for games."

"This is no game, my lord," she replied, taking a step forward and swinging again, this time with all her might.

He held her off, not swinging back, but using his sword to block each blow. Her hands shook with the power it took to hold the heavy sword, the muscles in her upper arms burning with the strain. She was well used to handling weapons, though never one this large.

Seeing the irritation in his eyes, she almost smiled, but refrained, knowing it would only anger him. Meanwhile, Galeran laughed loudly, watching with fascination—as did the rest of Renaud's men who had gathered around.

"Aleysia . . ." There was a warning in Renaud's voice, one she ignored as she swung yet again.

But this time he did more than block the blow. He used force, then brought his sword around to unarm her, so fast she did not have time to blink.

She rushed for the sword, but he grabbed her arm and brought her up against him, trapping both her hands behind her back with one of his own. "Aleysia, stop this."

"Why—are you afraid to be bested by a woman?"

He grinned then, his white teeth flashing, and to her horror her stomach coiled tightly. "You would not win."

"Then why will you not let me try?"

"Because you are a lady, and ladies do not wield swords." Gray eyes flashed with humor, but Aleysia found no humor in his words. It was a slight against her, and though she knew she should not take the words to heart, she did. No doubt his betrothed would never have worn men's clothing, nor would she use weapons as Aleysia had her entire life. She knew that aside from embroidery, which her mother had insisted she learn, she would always prefer the sports of men. She loved the feeling of holding a bow taut, notching an arrow—the pride in hitting a mark, in bringing down an animal. She had always enjoyed wearing men's clothing over pretty gowns, and that would never change. Even now she yearned for her breeches and loose-fitting tunic.

Her father had often said he felt like he had two sons, rather than a son and a daughter, and that had never bothered her—until today. She suddenly felt foolish and unfeminine, and for whatever reason, she wondered again where Renaud had spent last night. Visions of him wrapped in a buxom woman's embrace came unheeded and she pushed them away with a shake of her head.

Why should she care where and with whom he slept? In truth, she should be relieved he had already grown weary of her and slated his lust with another. Furious at herself and de Wulf, she tried to pull away, but he held firm.

Unable to keep his intense stare for fear he would read the jealousy in her eyes, she let her gaze fall to eye level. A huge mistake, for the golden skin that covered his defined chest made her remember him as he'd been the first time they'd made love. His chest heaving as he fought for control to keep from climaxing before she found her release. The sweat that glistened there now—that had glistened then, in the light of the fire.

Her body throbbed, remembering the feel of his long, thick shaft within her. To her chagrin, her cheeks warmed from the memory. "If I am so unladylike, then you will not care if I find other quarters in which to sleep, my lord. Or perhaps you would like to make things easier and return to the very place you spent last night?"

She glanced up at him to find his lips slightly quirked. Why had she voiced her thoughts aloud? She sounded like a jealous wife and now he knew how hurt she was. Damn him!

Renaud's grip on her tightened, and she could feel every hard inch of him pressed against her stomach. To her horror her body responded to him, her nipples hardening into sensitive buds. His masculine scent surrounded her, making her lightheaded. He leaned down and whispered in her ear, "Did you miss me last night, Aleysia?"

His breath was hot against her ear, stirring her hair. She tried to jerk away from his iron grip, but failed. "I most certainly did not!"

Still holding her wrists with one hand, he tipped her chin up with the other, his fingers gentle. "Aleysia, look at me."

The others had left them, returning to their drills, and she was glad. She was relieved they could not see her flushed cheeks, her fury—or her body's obvious response to this man who both infuriated her and excited her at the same time.

His eyes softened as he looked at her. "I was not with another woman, Aleysia."

Despite the immense relief she felt at those words, she replied, "I do not care where and with whom you sleep."

He lifted a brow. "Is that so? Then you do not mind if I sleep with another tonight?"

How she yearned to lift her knee and injure him where it would hurt most. She swallowed past the lump in her throat. "Nay, I do not care. Just as I am certain you do not care with whom I spend the night. In fact, do not expect me in your bedchamber tonight, my lord." She managed a coy smile. "I have other plans."

All humor left his eyes and his hand tightened about her wrists. "You will not be *sleeping* anywhere other than my bed, Aleysia. You belong to me. Is that understood?"

The possessiveness in his tone shocked her, and surprisingly pleased her, too. She lifted her chin high. "I belong to no man."

"Not even Laird MacMillan?" The words were little more than a whisper, but she could hear the fury in his tone.

Though part of her wanted to say that she did belong to the Scottish laird, she remembered her plan to release Adelstan and escape, and in order for the plan to work, she must gain Renaud's trust. Angering him would not help her cause. "Nay, not even Duncan."

He stared at her for a long moment, his gaze searching hers before shifting to her lips. Her pulse skittered, for she knew he meant to kiss her.

Worse than the horror of him kissing her within sight of his men and anyone else who cared to see was the simple fact that she *wanted* to kiss him. To feel his touch on her again. The softness of his lips, the taste of him as he possessed her completely. She craved it. How she had missed him this past week.

Furious with her response, she quipped, "Will you be taking a bath this evening, my lord?"

He dragged his top teeth against his bottom fuller lip, a gesture that would make most men appear vulnerable, but all she could think of was how incredibly sensual he looked and how she'd like to bite that lip herself. "Why do you ask, Aleysia?"

Ripping her gaze from his moist lower lip, back to his, she wrinkled her nose. "You are dirty and sweaty, my lord."

"Do you not like me dirty and sweaty?" he asked, his voice low and husky, making her believe that his words held another meaning altogether.

An image of him standing before her naked, his body sleek with sweat, his large cock rising above his navel, came to her, leaving her breathless and her body aching. For a moment she could not even remember the question. The sides of his mouth lifted a little as he awaited an answer. It was as though he knew how much he flustered her. "Nay, I do not like you dirty and sweaty, my lord," she blurted, grateful that the question had come back to her in a rush.

A clash of swords reverberated throughout the glen, reminding Aleysia where they were, and that they were far from alone. Renaud must have been jarred as well, for he abruptly released her, and took a step back, but not before brushing a stray hair out of her face, and over her ear. "Even your hair will not be tamed," he said, a soft smile on his lips.

The touch surprised Aleysia, and she felt it all the way to her toes. Oh, how she desired him.

"I shall see you tonight then." He grinned boyishly and to her horror, her heart gave a hard tug.

"Tonight," she said, and grabbing up her basket, she rushed toward the castle.

EIGHT

Aleysia reached for the pouch of herbs in her pocket, her thumb brushing over the soft velvet bag. Already the great hall filled with men, women, and children, their voices rising to the wooden rafters. The smell of venison en frumenty and elderberry wine permeated the space, making her stomach rumble and her mouth water. If only she wasn't so nervous; but how could she not be? Tonight she would escape!

She had arrived early for dinner, freshly bathed and wearing a gown made of fine linen and dyed a light green that flattered her coloring, or so the maid had said. She wondered if Renaud would notice.

She did not want to do anything that would warrant suspicion. So much depended on the coming hours. She must, without fail, drug Renaud and his men. The best way to distract him from Adelstan and the journey to York was to show him that she had accepted her place in his bed. Since he had not touched her for days, she thought perhaps she could entice him tonight. They would make love, drink wine, and God willing, he would sleep like the dead.

Once he fell asleep she would escape into the night. She had watched closely the routine of the past few nights, and knew that a servant made her way up the tower stairs to bring the guards a glass of warm wine shortly after supper. Tonight, Aleysia would make sure she would be passing the servant, and offer to take the wine herself.

And she would pour the draught into the drink, stirring it so the bitterness would be hidden, before delivering it to the guards. She would wear a cloak, hoping to hide her identity. If the healer was true to her word, then the guards would soon be fast asleep. And shortly after, Aleysia would give the wine to Renaud in his bedchamber. God willing, they would all sleep soundly for hours.

At least that was the plan.

The voices quieted, and Aleysia looked up to find Renaud entering the hall. His hair was damp, no doubt from the bath she had requested he take. Aleysia's heart skipped a beat and she shifted on the bench. His gray tunic matched his eyes but conflicted fiercely with his dark hair and skin, and the black braies clung to his powerful thighs.

With a start, Aleysia noticed the woman on Renaud's arm, and felt a sinking feeling in the pit of her stomach.

The woman, a statuesque brunette with large breasts and womanly curves smiled up at Renaud. Her gown, made of exquisite blue silk and covered by a lighter blue gauze, floated as she walked, the material not at all disguising her long, slender legs. Wide sleeves embroidered in silver matched the silver in the girdle that rode low on her curvaceous hips.

Aleysia, though dressed in her finest gown, complete with leather girdle, felt quite plain in comparison to the other woman's cool beauty. Then a horrible thought struck her, making her even more ill at ease. Dear God, was the woman Renaud's betrothed? The familiarity between the two was obvious. Even now Renaud laughed at something she said, and the woman actually went so far as to playfully rest her head against Renaud's shoulder.

Something resembling jealousy rushed through Aleysia, and she sat up straighter. What in the world was wrong with her? Why should she care if this woman was Renaud's betrothed? If anything, she should feel relieved.

Because you desire him, Aleysia—and you resent any other woman who would share his bed.

Renaud pulled out a chair for the woman, who sat down and looked directly at Aleysia with a charming smile. To Aleysia's dismay the woman was even more beautiful up close. Her eyes, an amazing blue-gray were large and framed by long, thick lashes as dark as her hair. The woman glanced at Renaud and smiled, exposing small, white teeth. "You're right. She is lovely."

Aleysia did not know how to take that statement. How odd for a man's betrothed to offer sentiments about his mistress. Or did she know the truth? Mayhap Renaud had told her Aleysia was someone else's woman.

A servant poured a pitcher of warm water into the bowl where Renaud and his guests washed their hands before drying them on a cloth.

The woman dried off her dainty hands, then her gaze shifted past Aleysia. "Galeran, is that you?"

Aleysia turned to Galeran, who sat to her right. "Indeed, Lady

Elena. What a pleasure it is to see you again." And it was obvious he meant what he said. Galeran grinned from ear to ear, raking a hand nervously through his golden locks. She had never seen the soldier so lively.

Lady Elena? Was that the name of Renaud's betrothed? Her mind raced, trying to remember, but she could not recall. But the woman was French, her accent thick, despite her command of the English language.

"You have grown into a man. The last I saw you, you were but a boy." Her gaze shifted over Galeran in a way that suggested more than words could ever say. Aleysia watched Renaud closely, gauging his reaction, but he seemed not at all bothered by the exchange. In truth, the slight smile on his lips made her think him amused by the banter going on between the pair.

Lady Elena laughed under her breath. "Indeed, you were my brother's page when last we met. You were rather small back then."

Her brother's page? Then realization came to Aleysia in a flash. This woman was not Renaud's betrothed, but his sister. She ignored the exhilaration rushing throughout her. Aleysia glanced at de Wulf to find him watching her closely. Did he guess at her uneasiness, and could he sense the vast relief she felt knowing this beautiful woman was not his betrothed? To her dismay, she could not help the smile that came to her lips.

Renaud smiled, too, and Aleysia's pulse quickened.

"I am no longer small, nor am I a boy," Galeran said, his tone intent. His fingers curled around his goblet as he brought it to his lips, watching Lady Elena over the rim.

Elena pursed her lips. "No, you are *much* larger. Every inch a man."

Galeran choked on his wine, his cheeks blazing crimson.

Renaud laughed, and Aleysia smiled, pleased at the deep, rumbling sound.

Aleysia reached for her goblet, knowing she could use the wine's effect to calm her.

But it seemed Galeran was not finished. "Are you at Braemere for an extended stay, Lady Elena?" There was no mistaking the hope in his voice. Though the young knight could not be much older than herself, it was clear to Aleysia by the fine lines around the woman's eyes that Elena was at least ten years his senior, perhaps more. However, those lines did nothing to diminish Elena's beauty.

"Aye, I am." Elena's eyes twinkled with an inner fire, and Aleysia wondered if perhaps she was not witnessing the beginning of a liaison. Would she one day wear her emotions openly like this woman did, and flirt outrageously while in the company of others? She doubted she could ever be like this strong woman, who seemed not to care who heard or saw the exchange.

"I am sorry to hear of your husband's death, Lady Elena," Galeran said sincerely before drinking deeply from his goblet.

"You are the only one then, Galeran."

Galeran choked again on his wine, and Renaud shook his head.

Once Galeran was again breathing right, Renaud turned to his sister. "Father always said you would be the death of Lorange."

"He was right. That is what father deserved for marrying me off to an old man." Elena shrugged. "Enough of me and my best-to-be-forgotten past. I would like to know more about Aleysia. Since my rude brother has failed to introduce us, I shall have to take it upon myself to do so."

"Forgive me," Renaud said apologetically.

"Elena, meet Aleysia. Aleysia, this is my outspoken sister Elena."

Elena nodded. "A pleasure to meet you, my dear. Now tell me something of yourself."

Aleysia, having felt secure in listening to the banter going on about her, shifted uneasily. She always hated talking about herself, preferring to listen to others instead. "I fear there is little to tell, Lady Elena."

"You are Saxon, yet my brother tells me you have lived with the Scots for some time? How did that come to pass?"

Aleysia tried to ignore the burning gray stare of the man at her side, but found it difficult. "When Baron de Pirou killed our parents, we decided we could not stay at Braemere. My brother and I traveled to Scotland to live with my father's good friend, Laird MacMillan. We have been there these past three years."

Elena lifted a fine dark brow. "And this MacMillan is your betrothed?"

"Aye, he is."

"*Was,*" Renaud blurted.

Elena smiled knowingly, her gaze skipping to her brother before returning to Aleysia. "Do you love this man? This Scottish laird?" She shuddered, as though truly horrified. "I have heard the men from the north are positively barbaric!"

Though Aleysia had half a mind to make a comment about Norman barbarians, she refrained, not wanting to anger Renaud, his men, and sister.

Aleysia's cheeks turned warm under the other woman's intent stare. She swallowed hard, choosing her words carefully. "I admire Duncan, and have come to care for him."

"But you do not love him?"

Aleysia remembered well her words to Renaud the day Mac-Millan had come to Braemere. "He was a dear friend of my father's."

"Then we are kindred spirits, for I was forced into marrying my father's good friend." She took a sip from her goblet. "I assure you, Aleysia, that you do not love this man, but you agreed to marry him because of your father's wishes. You are an obedient daughter, just as I was." Elena reached across her brother to touch Aleysia's hand. "Be glad that you do not love him. The only reason I am grateful for my husband at all is that he managed to give me two beautiful sons. They were, and remain, my saving grace."

"You are a mother, then?" Aleysia asked, unable to keep the surprise from her voice.

"Aye, and I can see by the brightness of your smile that you desire children as well."

Aleysia nodded, doing her best to ignore the man sitting beside her. She felt his steady regard—and it unnerved her, especially given the current discussion. "Aye, Duncan has children already, but he desires more."

Renaud's jaw clenched tight, but he stayed silent.

"Did your children travel with you?" Aleysia asked.

Elena's smile faded. "My sons are in Sicily with their uncle, my husband's brother, acquiring lands for their future. I know they are safe with their uncle, but I miss them horribly."

"I can only imagine."

"They miss their uncle Renaud as well," Elena said, smiling at her brother. "They hope one day to serve in your army."

Aleysia realized in that moment how very little she knew of

Renaud de Wulf. She had learned more in the past few moments with his sister, than during a full week in his company. Ironically, she wished to know everything about this man who had come storming into her life. What he was like as a child. His likes. His dislikes.

His loves . . .

"And one day they shall, sister," Renaud replied with a wink. "I look forward to that day."

Aleysia felt her cheeks grow hot as Renaud turned back to her and stared. "Are they grown then?"

Elena's gaze dipped from Aleysia to Renaud, then back to Aleysia, a knowing smile on her lips. "Morgar is five and ten, and Renaud is two and ten."

Aleysia turned to Renaud to find him watching her closely. There was a softness in his eyes as he watched her. "Your nephew shares your name."

He nodded. "Aye, he does."

"I feared my brother would not live long enough to have sons himself, so I selfishly named my youngest after him," Elena said, rubbing her brother's forearm. "Mayhap I was wrong in doing so."

Renaud turned to Elena and took hold of her hand. "Nay, sister. I am honored that you would name your beloved son after me. God willing, I will have a son, and when I do, I will give him a name different than my own, so that I do not make my wife crazy with confusion."

"You were always wise," Elena replied, before turning back to Aleysia. "What of your brother, Aleysia?"

Aleysia set her goblet down with a trembling hand. Apparently,

Renaud had not informed his sister of Adelstan's whereabouts. "What of him?"

Elena smiled. "Is he as beautiful as you?"

Flattered by the compliment, Aleysia replied, "Thank you for your kindness, and yes—women have always favored my brother. It is sad that he rots away in the tower as we speak."

Elena frowned. "You jest?"

"Nay, I do not."

Thankfully, the pages approached with large trenchers of venison, mutton with dried peas, and beans. The smells of garlic and onion filled the space, and everyone's attention turned to eating.

Aleysia reached for her goblet and drained it, ignoring Renaud's sideways glance. She rarely drank wine, not liking the effect it had on her mind, but she needed to steel her nerves for what lay ahead this evening. Tonight she would be leaving Braemere, forever. She had to remind herself that the beautiful fief was no longer her home, that it had stopped being so the moment her parents had been killed. She would return to Scotland with Adelstan, and live the rest of her days in peace.

Away from this man and his dangerous beauty. Feeling too warm all of a sudden, Aleysia moved over a little, away from Renaud and closer to Galeran. The young knight glanced her way and smiled. He then looked at Renaud, and abruptly returned his attention to the food before him.

Supper continued, and Aleysia ate heartily, knowing it might very well be the last meal for her in a while. She had hidden away in a canvas bag some fruit, cheese, and bread for the journey.

By the time the musicians began to play, filling the high-ceilinged room with the sound of lutes and harp in concert, Aleysia's nerves were on edge. Time was of the essence. She must get back to the tower before the servant took the wine to the guards.

She glanced over at Renaud, who watched the musicians play. Catching her gaze, he turned and smiled.

Her heart pounded loudly as she stared at him, memorizing each feature, each line on his face. The beautiful shade of his eyes, the scar on his cheek that marked him as the warrior he was. She doubted she would ever meet another man like him for as long as she lived.

He tilted his head a little and frowned. "You stare, Aleysia. What displeases you so?"

Did he actually believe she found him lacking? If only he knew the truth. She leaned forward to where her lips were just inches from his. "Nothing, my lord. I am going to retire."

"So early?" The words were low, husky, his eyes dark with a fire she recognized.

Her blood burned for him as well. "It has been a long day, and I am tired." She dropped her gaze from his for a moment in an effort to steady her nerves. "Would you like to join me?" she asked, meeting his gaze once more. She knew he would certainly stay in the hall for a while with his sister. It would be rude to leave now since she had only just arrived.

The sides of his mouth curved. "Aye, I would, but I must make my sister welcome. Mayhap you can keep the bed warm?"

She smiled, relieved. "Aye, I will."

"Then I will be along shortly."

"I will be waiting, my lord."

NINE

Renaud entered the darkened bedchamber. Aleysia sat on a chair before the fire, a fur wrapped about her slender frame. As he closed the door behind him, she looked up and met his gaze.

His heart skipped a beat. Her hair had been brushed out until it glistened like fine silk, the soft blonde curls falling all about her like a veil. He pushed the door closed and removed his boots.

She watched him intently, her gaze shifting over him slowly. One would never guess by looking at her that just days ago she had been a virgin. Not by the way she stared at him now, her light green eyes boldly wandering over his body.

Desire coiled within him, warming his veins, making his cock throb and his balls ache. It had been days since they had last made love. He had not had the heart to touch her after MacMillan's visit, when she had cried. Her sobs had torn at him, and though he wanted to make love to her every day since then, he refrained, too afraid that his father's words would ring true.

Plus, Renaud could not afford to forget his focus, and that was securing Braemere, along with the rest of the north. Only when that task was completed would he have time to pursue other things, like marrying and having children.

Yet Aleysia had already worked her way under his skin, and he could not afford to lose himself in a woman. Not now, when there was so much to be done.

He removed his tunic and tossed it aside, then worked on his chausses and braies. Her light eyes seemed lit from within as she watched him, her cheeks tinged a flattering shade of pink.

She stood, letting the blanket fall, and he let out a breath.

Her trembling gave her nervousness away, but to her credit, she did not try to cover her naked form. Instead, she straightened her spine, her shoulders arched just enough to push her breasts out. Her rose-pink nipples crinkled into hard points.

His gaze shifted lower, over her flat stomach, to the blonde triangle of hair between her legs. Memories of her tight channel gripping him made his cock harder and longer. She noticed his arousal, for her brows lifted as she stared boldly, and she licked her pink full lips.

That stare had him crossing the room to reach her, but he stopped a few feet from her. He wanted her to be the aggressor tonight.

She took a step, and then another. Next her arms looped around his neck, and she lifted her chin. He didn't have long to wait for her kiss—a soft peck that ended far too quickly. His fingers curled about her hips, pulling her closer, encouraging her.

Her tongue stroked the seam of his lips and he opened. She sighed as her tongue stroked his, slowly, parrying with his, experimenting as her arms tightened about his neck.

Her hard nipples brushed against his chest, and for a second he forgot about letting her take control. He rubbed his cock against her belly, showing her what she did to him. She moaned low in her throat, and he smiled against her lips, pleased by her response.

His hand slid down her belly, lower to the soft curls that guarded her femininity. Parting her, he stroked her hot, slick flesh with his fingers. Her breath hitched in her throat and she stopped kissing him back. Instead, her head fell to his shoulder, her breath warm against his chest. Then her lips were there, pressed against the pulse now beating wildly. Using his foot, he pushed her feet farther apart and continued stroking her, inserting a single finger into her slick, molten core.

While he pleasured her, she in turn kissed the lobe of his ear, his jaw, his chin. With heart pounding nearly out of his chest, he looked down at her, and what he saw took his breath away. Her eyes were bright with a passion he had not seen before. And he realized with a start, that she wanted him as badly as he wanted her. Her gaze shifted to his lips once more, and he lowered his head, capturing her mouth with his.

Velvety soft, and tasting of mint, her tongue danced with his. Her fingers wove through his hair, pulling a little. He felt her desperation to the very depths of his soul.

Lifting her in his arms, he strode toward the bed, where he gently laid her down on the covers and stared at her for a long moment. He would never forget the image for as long as he lived. The desire in her green eyes. Aye, she was perfect in every way, this little enemy of his.

She lifted her arms, and he joined her on the bed, crawling between her thighs. His fingers returned to her heated core. He swallowed a groan as he slipped one finger within her, then another. She was already so wet, so hot, her honeyed walls gripping his fingers tight.

Moaning, she bit into his lower lip as his thumb brushed against the sensitive knot of flesh nestled between her folds. She arched her hips against his hand, and when he rubbed the pleasure spot inside her inner walls, he was pleased when she moaned again, the contractions squeezing his fingers.

Reaching between them, her fingers slid down his rigid cock and up again. He couldn't remember a time he'd been so hard, or his need so great, and he feared he would spend himself if she did not stop.

Her fingers curled around his cock, making a tight fist, moving in a frantic rhythm. In truth, her awkward strokes excited him more than had she known exactly what to do. His balls tightened and with a low-throated moan he grabbed her wrist, halting her. She reared back, her brow furrowed. "You do not like my touch?"

How wounded she looked and sounded. He smiled to ease her mind. "I like it too much."

Comprehension came over her slowly, along with a relieved smile, before she kissed him once more. With hand on his chest, she pushed him onto his back and straddled his hips, surprising him yet again with her boldness.

Her long hair tickled his thighs and belly. How beautiful she was, her full breasts, the nipples erect, begging to be suckled. His gaze lowered to her flat stomach and the patch of pale curls at her damp womanhood. Her musky scent aroused him even more. She was a vixen who was fast learning her power.

Her gaze shifted to his chest, where she splayed her hands and touched him. Her fingers grazed his nipples before moving down over his stomach, which tightened at her touch. His cock rested against his navel, and she bit her bottom lip as she stroked him, her fingers teasing the plum-sized head. How determined she looked. When her gaze met his, he was shocked and pleased at the heat he saw in their light-green depths.

"Ride me, Aleysia," he coaxed.

She went up on her knees, and sank down on his cock, taking him slowly into her. Though he yearned to thrust and bury himself in her womb, he refrained and let her take control, even if it tested his strength of will like never before.

Once she settled on him fully, he clenched his jaw as her sheath gripped him like a hot glove. Buried to the hilt, she rotated her hips in a small circle. He reached for her, cupping her breasts with each palm. She arched her back, giving him better access.

Sitting up, he took a nipple into his mouth, sucking it lightly. Her arms encircled his neck, her fingers weaving through his hair, pulling him tighter to her breast. She moved slowly, up and down his length, finding her own rhythm.

Sweat beaded his brow, and he forced himself to contain his climax, keep it at bay until she was ready to come. He tried to think of other things—anything but being buried within her sweet body, but failed time and again. Then he felt it at the same time Aleysia gasped and bit into his shoulder—the tiny contractions grew stronger, her sheath pulsing around his length as she came.

His mouth left one nipple to service the other; his fingers stroked the one he'd just suckled, pulling it lightly, pinching it softly over and over again. His other hand moved down her back, over the high arc of her buttocks, slipping between the cleft there.

Her breath hitched a little and he smiled, cupping her ass, pulling her tighter against him.

Her pace increased as he suckled harder. Nails raked across his shoulders as she came again, her sheath tightened around him, squeezing and coating his cock with her honey.

He fell back onto the mattress, grabbed her waist, and lifted his hips.

With her faint tremors still pulsing around him, he took control and rolled her onto her back, his thrusts long and fluid. The bed rocked, pounding against the wall with the force of his strokes. The slap of skin against skin reverberated in the room.

Sweat poured off him, but he refrained from coming until he brought her to climax again. He wanted her crying his name. Her breasts bounced with each thrust, and he spread her thighs wider, tucking his hips to go as deep in her as possible.

Her fingers slid around the headboard above her head. She opened her eyes, and the need he saw there made him even harder. "Renaud," she said on a moan.

Her inner walls clenched his cock like a vise, drawing out his seed. He came with a loud, satisfied groan.

He rolled until she lay fully on him. She smiled against his lips, her breathing labored, her heart pounding hard against his. Lord, he would never be able to release her. It would be impossible. His fingers slid up and down along her spine, loving the silky-soft feel of her skin against his rough hands.

The pounding of her heart eased as the minutes ticked by, and still she lay on him, not moving. With his free hand, he brushed her hair back from her face, caressing a silky strand between his finger and thumb.

He could get used to times like these, lying about with a beautiful woman. A novelty for him, a man whose mind always seemed to be on other matters that required his attention. Yet now, even wild horses couldn't drag him away from this woman, who lay so still and content in his arms.

Just the thought of being separated from her made him uneasy. It was too new, these emotions he felt, not to mention confusing. How could he feel them so quickly, especially for a woman he had not even known existed a fortnight ago?

Lust, plain and simple, his better judgment said, nothing less, nothing more.

Whatever the case, this brave woman had worked her way into his soul. She had lost so much in her tender years. In truth, she would lose the one man who meant most to her by month's end. Then she would have no one.

But she would have him.

Yet would it be enough?

"My lord, would you like a glass of warm wine?" she asked, rolling off him.

Surprised by the request, since she had never brought wine into the chamber before, he nodded and watched as she slid from the bed and walked over to a table where a tray with two goblets sat.

He liked that she made no effort to cover herself. Her long legs were sheer perfection, her ass high and tight. The softly curved hips and slender waist.

Already his cock stirred.

She spilled some of the wine and smiled sheepishly. "I am so clumsy."

"It matters not, Aleysia," he replied, thinking how much he would like to lick the wine from her body. Mayhap she would not mind such an exercise after they rested awhile.

She returned to the bed, and handed him a goblet, her long blonde hair falling about her, a pink nipple visible behind the pale strands.

He reached up and stroked the small bud with his fingers and she sucked in a breath. "My lord, have you not had enough sport for one night?"

"I cannot help it. You are so beautiful. Already I want you again."

She glanced at his growing erection and grinned before she sipped the wine.

He lifted the goblet to his lips and stopped, smelling the faintest hint of a strange, bitter scent. Disbelief rushed over him, along with a sick feeling. She had tainted the wine, but with what—poison?

She watched him intently—almost expectantly? He pretended to take a long swallow, and then set the goblet on the side table. She looked over at the goblet, instantly wary. "You did not drink very much, my lord. Do you not like the wine?"

"Would you like some?" he asked, reaching for the goblet.

"Nay," she said, her cheeks turning pink as he stared. "I have my own."

And he knew in that moment that she had done exactly what he had feared. She had seduced him into bed. Coaxed him to drink the poisoned wine, so she could escape with her brother. No wonder she had been so agreeable these past days, not asking to see Adelstan. He had thought it odd, but dismissed it, thinking mayhap she might be coming around now that she knew her brother's fate had been decided. Instead, it was clear she meant to leave him by way of killing him or drugging him.

How innocent she looked, her eyes wide, her smile soft and angelic. Had the entire night been an act then, he wondered, remembering her coyness during supper, or the way she had let her inhibitions go tonight while they made love. If it had been pretend, she had become quite an actress.

He forced a smile. "I have nearly drank the entire cup, my lady. I was thirsty after such sport."

She looked relieved then, and set her goblet aside as she snuggled up against him. "I am so tired," she said, yawning and stretching at his side, before settling down and closing her eyes. "Good night, my lord."

"Good night, Aleysia," he replied, glancing over to where her dress lay draped over a chair, and beside it her boots and stockings.

Aye, she was leaving. Clever, devious woman.

His father had been right.

He should never trust a woman.

TEN

Aleysia's heart thudded hard against her breastbone. Renaud's breathing had been even for over an hour. After drinking the wine he had fallen right to sleep, and she had lain in his arms, too afraid to move for fear he would wake.

Ironically, she felt guilty. Tonight she had planned to seduce him, and instead he had seduced her, making love to her, bringing her such pleasure she had nearly wept with joy. Each climax had been stronger than the one before it, leaving her sated and content. Any woman would desire such a lover in her bed.

Sadly, she would never know such pleasure again.

She stole a glance toward her gown, draped over the chair, her boots and cloak nearby. Everything was ready, and she must leave now if she hoped to rescue Adelstan from the tower and escape the castle before dawn. Hopefully, the healer's grandson had left earlier today with the message for Duncan.

If the young man made good time, then Duncan should be able to catch up with them soon enough, since Aleysia and Adelstan would be on foot. They could break for the border and never look back.

Ignoring the deep ache in her heart, she looked at the door. She had no time to lose. Slowly she eased away from Renaud's side, moving only inches at a time, waiting, praying he did not wake. The fire had died down and the room was so cold, her breath formed fog in the air. She glanced at Renaud in the warm bed she'd just left, wishing to be back there, safe and warm in his arms. If only things could have been different for them. They could have married, had children, and raised their family on the same land where she had grown up.

Pushing the thought aside, she ran her hands up and down her arms to warm herself. She'd best get used to the cold, for there would be many cold nights before they reached Duncan's village.

On the tips of her toes, she made her way across the chamber and dressed quickly, checking over her shoulder to make sure Renaud did not stir. If he woke and saw her dressing, he would know the truth and all her efforts would be for naught.

But he had drunk the wine and she trusted the healer. Nay, Renaud *would* sleep for hours. God willing, by the time he woke, she and Adelstan would be well on their way for the border.

Tying her cloak tight about her shoulders, she grabbed the canvas bag filled with enough provisions to get them through the days ahead. Aleysia spared one more glance toward the bed.

Renaud's chest lifted with each breath, his head turned toward the other side of the chamber.

She ignored the pain in her chest at leaving, confused at her feelings about this man who had turned her life upside down in such a short time. This man who had taken her virginity by way of a bargain. A bargain he had reneged on.

Stop it, Aleysia!

She should hate him and be rejoicing that finally she was escaping, never to return.

Focusing on her anger served her better. Without a backward glance, she pushed open the door, relieved to find no guards present. She quietly shut it behind her, and started up the stairwell. Her heart pounded so hard, it was a roar in her ears. Calming herself, she started up the dark stairwell, praying that when she got to the top she would find the guards sound asleep.

The flame of the torches fluttered as she passed by, and in the wavering light she imagined someone right behind her, which hurried her along. Hopefully, Adelstan's shackles had been removed since her last visit. If the healer had been called in, then chances were they were still off—unless Renaud had requested otherwise. She would know soon enough, for she had reached the tower, and heard the soft snores of the guards.

Relief rushed over her at the sight of the guards' limp forms slumped over. She went down on her haunches beside one of the armed men who lay sprawled near the door, the keys slightly under him, a dagger in hand. One false move and he could kill her.

Heart in her throat, Aleysia gently nudged the big man aside. He smacked his lips loudly, and for a heart-stopping moment she feared he would open his eyes and find her hunched down beside him. However, luck was on her side, for he rolled into the other guard, leaning just enough for her to get hold of the keys.

Aleysia stood and tried to fit one of the keys into the lock, but it was not a match. One of the guards muttered under his breath, and she fumbled with the heavy ring, nearly dropping it in her haste, but caught the ring just before it hit the floor.

Forcing herself to remain calm, she glanced at the guards, relieved to find them both still asleep. Trembling, she tried another key in the lock. She winced as it clicked loudly, and waited a moment before pushing on the heavy door.

Suddenly, a large hand covered her mouth and pulled her up against his hard body. His hand brushed hers away from the door and ripped the keys from her grasp.

Fear coursing through her body, Aleysia kicked her assailant hard. He grunted but did not release her. No matter how hard she tried to jerk or pull away, it was no use. His arms were like steel bands about her. She was abruptly lifted into the air and flung over a bare shoulder.

Her head jarred against his hard back with each step he took down the spiral staircase. Then a door to a chamber opened, and he kicked it closed once on the other side. A moment later she was tossed unceremoniously onto the bed.

Aleysia scrambled to her feet.

"Do not move an inch," Renaud said between gritted teeth, his chest rising and falling with his fury. He wore just his braies, nothing else. His eyes held no warmth whatsoever.

She had never seen anyone look as fierce as he did in that moment, and she feared for her safety. How could he be awake after drinking the draught? "Let me leave, Renaud."

"I will not!" He swore loud enough to wake the dead.

"Release us. Please have mercy, my lord."

"Have mercy?" He ran a trembling hand through his hair, his jaw clenched tight. "Your pretty words will not save you. I should have known better than to trust you."

Who was he to speak of trust? "I trusted you, and look what you did to me. You tell me you will keep Adelstan safe, and instead you take him to his death."

His eyes narrowed. "You tried to poison me."

"Poison?"

The side of his mouth lifted in a snarl. "I smelled the herbs, Aleysia. How do I know they were not deadly?"

"It was a sleeping draught, not poison. Certainly, you cannot believe that I would kill you?" she asked, offended he thought her capable of such a deed.

She saw the confusion in his eyes, but she also saw the mistrust. "Either way, you sought to escape."

"I told you before that I would do anything to save my brother—anything short of murder."

"Aye, you did warn me. But I did not believe you would go to such lengths. Tell me, is that why you pretend to enjoy my touch? Is that why you moan and sigh, playing the whore every time I take you to bed?"

Though she wanted to refute what he said, she did not. He didn't need to know the truth—that she burned for him, and wanted him all hours of the day and night. That she had not needed to act one bit, because he had brought her immense pleasure, the likes she may never experience again. It was her shame, for theirs was a future that could never be. Let him believe what he would, because nothing she could say or do would make up for it now.

She came to her feet and walked toward him. He put up a hand. "Do not come near me now, Aleysia."

She ignored his demand, her gaze shifting over him, his broad chest, the corded muscles of his abdomen, the huge bulge at the base of his thighs that the braies could not hide.

Arousal flooded throughout her body, making her nipples hard and her woman's flesh damp. Even his scent excited her, and now as his gray eyes stared into hers, so untrusting, she yearned to have him.

She went up on her toes and kissed him.

He was unresponsive, so repulsed, that he even went so far as to step away. "Do not touch me, Aleysia."

She removed her gown, letting it slide to her feet.

His jaw clenched and he looked away.

She took the step that separated them, and wrapped her arms around his neck, her body pressed flush against him. Every muscle in his body tightened, his hands still at his sides.

She kissed his neck, and felt the hair on his body stand on end. Her tongue flicked the lobe of his ear, sliding inside, then along the ridge.

His cock jerked against her stomach and she hid a smile. She caressed him through the material of his braies, his hard length growing longer, thicker with every second. He could say he did not want her, but his body betrayed him.

With a growl he pushed her back on the bed, flipped her over, and pressed his cock against her opening. Her heart pounded loud in her ears as he slid into her slowly, filling her completely, stretching her. She gasped at his size, at his fierce strokes, pushing her into the mattress with each thrust. Nothing at all gentle, but she found it exciting, her hands clenching into the bedding at her sides with each hard stroke.

She lifted her buttocks higher, shocked how full she was in this position. So deep, so satisfying.

Renaud's balls tightened, his seed ready to spew. A part of him wanted to punish her—this woman who had betrayed him so. Bring her to the brink of climax and then withdraw, leave her wanting and aching.

He would never trust her again.

When her breathing increased, he knew she was close to climax.

Trembling, he pulled out and she arched her back, trying to follow him.

Her scent permeated his nostrils, the musky fragrance making his cock that much harder. He brushed the head of his rock-hard cock along her wet, swollen folds.

She looked over her shoulder at him, her green eyes dark with passion and frustration. Good, he wanted her hurting. He cupped her breasts, weighing them in his hands, playing with her nipples, rolling them between his fingers and thumbs, pulling, pinching. "Renaud," she whispered, the word a plea. "I need you."

She arched her back while a deep-throated moan escaped her full lips.

His cock rested against the cleft of her ass, probing against her hot, wet slit. "What do you want, Aleysia?"

"I want you to take me."

"Take you where?"

"You know."

He could hear the frustration in her voice, the desperate need. Releasing one breast, he brushed his fingers down her stomach, through the dewy curls of her sex. Two fingers slid into her heat, and she sighed, moving her hips against him.

He toyed with her button and she cried out, moaning, her inner walls contracting around his fingers.

"Please," she said, and he could wait no longer. He put them both out of their misery by sliding his cock into her slowly, his cock head brushing against her womb.

It only took a handful of strokes and he came, flooding her passage with his thick cream.

They stayed connected for a second, her slender back rising and falling as she fought to gain her breath.

The pleasure he had known earlier when they had first made love was no longer there. Instead, the reality of what she had done, and what she would do in the future, had him up and out of bed. He pulled up his braies and walked toward the door.

"Where are you going?" she asked, now sitting on the edge of the bed, her hair shielding her breasts. She looked like an angel.

So innocent.

So beautiful.

So devious.

"I am going to check on my prisoner, but I shall return."

She opened her mouth, then snapped it shut a moment later. He could see her disappointment. Did she think that a quick tumble would change anything?

"My father was right. A man should never trust a woman. I will never again trust you."

He tied her to the bed.

Aleysia could not believe Renaud had gone to such lengths to make sure she did not escape, but he did. He had left the chamber for only a few moments to check on Adelstan, and when he returned, he'd tied her up—her arms and legs bound to each corner of the bed by strips of silk. She had tried without success to loosen the knots, but it seemed her efforts had the opposite effect and drew the material ever tighter.

Thank God she had put on an under tunic before he'd returned. Being tied up naked would have been even more humiliating.

"Surely you do not intend to leave me like this?" she asked Renaud, who was busy testing the binds.

Silence met her question as he moved to the end of the bed and tried the bind there.

"Why do you pretend not to hear me?"

"I choose not to hear any more of your lies."

"Do you intend to leave me like this?"

He shrugged. "I have not decided yet, but for now, this should hold."

"For how long?"

"For as long as I desire."

"I will scream."

"And I will shove a rag into your mouth." He crossed the room, opened a chest and rummaged through it. "Ah, this will do." He pulled a beautifully embroidered kerchief from the chest and proceeded to roll it into a ball.

God's breath, he was actually going to do it! "I will not scream. Do not stuff that in my mouth, Renaud. We will never return to Braemere. I swear it!"

"What am I to do with you?" he asked, almost to himself, as he tossed the kerchief aside and planted hands on his narrow hips. His gaze traveled from hers, slowly down her body and up again. Her nipples tightened under his regard, sending an ache straight to her swollen lower lips. Even her core tightened in anticipation of his long cock stretching her.

How fine he was, his body in profile, half his face cast in shadow, his hair still mussed from their lovemaking. The man was sex personified. The hair on her arms stood on end, remembering the feel of his hard length within her. How strong, powerful, and desirable he was.

His gaze found hers. How tortured he looked, this man who could bring grown men to their knees. A man whose name caused an entire Saxon army to flee for safety.

A man, who, for whatever reason, desired her. "Release me, Renaud."

The sides of his mouth lifted in a wolfish smile. "So you can betray me again?"

"I will not betray you."

"Will you not?" He laughed without mirth. "You would as soon I was dead than sleep with me."

"Nay. That it is not true."

"How do I know that, Aleysia? You lie so prettily. You give pleasure, then drug me within the same hour . . . only to use your body to make me lessen your punishment."

"I will not do so again. I swear it, Renaud. If you let me go, I shall do whatever you say."

His gaze shifted over her. "Whatever I say?"

The tone of his voice was silky soft yet dangerous.

"Aye," she replied.

He stepped toward the bed, his fingers brushing along the inside of her bare ankle, up toward her knee, bringing her gown up as well.

She swallowed hard and licked her lips, which had gone suddenly dry. Her traitorous body thrilled at his touch.

"I could do whatever I wished to do," he said, his fingers climbing higher, along the sensitive skin of her inner thigh, dangerously close to the folds that grew wetter by the second. "What do you think of that, Aleysia?"

"I did not take you for a man who was prone to rape."

He smiled wolfishly. "I have no need to rape a woman. They come to my bed most willingly."

The words made her angry and extremely jealous. "You are quite arrogant."

His fingers slipped over her folds, along her sensitive button, causing her to gasp aloud. She tested the binds, which held her fast. "You have me at a disadvantage."

To her horror her body reacted to his caress, her insides growing hotter. His touch grew more intimate, his thumb working in tandem with his fingers that spread her folds, a long finger slipping inside her tight heat.

"You are so wet, Aleysia. Could it be that you desire my touch, after all?"

She shifted, the movement drawing his finger in deeper. She bit the inside of her cheek to keep from moaning.

He added another finger, moving them slowly in and out. His thumb brushed her tiny nub again and again.

She closed her eyes, unable to look at him or the knowing smile on his lips.

Yet her body betrayed her as she grew closer to climax, his fingers working faster, stroking, until she was arching her hips.

She heard sounds outside the door, and for a moment thought it might be her heart, until she felt Renaud's fingers slip from her.

"No," she said, twisting against the bonds, her need so great that even the feel of her tunic over her sensitive flesh made her bite her bottom lip.

He held out a hand as he listened, and then as the sound of footsteps passed by, he returned to the foot of the bed. It seemed she was not the only one aroused.

Untying the cord of his braies, he stepped out of them. She swallowed hard, staring at his long, thick cock, which seemed to grow as she stared.

He touched himself, his long fingers wrapping around the girth, sliding up and down again, over the round, plum-sized head, which filled with blood, the color a deep purple. Then down they slid, over and over again.

Watching him made her skin burn and her heart pound.

She shifted on the bed, trying the bonds again.

Licking her lips, she watched as he climbed onto the bed, directly between her thighs, still stroking himself.

She could not believe it when her insides clenched. She had been so aroused from when he had touched her, and now watching him had pushed her over the brink. She needed release—needed his cock buried deep inside her.

He leaned over her, his long hair brushing over her stomach as he licked a nipple. How soft and velvety his tongue was, so smooth as it laved first one, then the other. Meanwhile his cock brushed against her cleft.

She arched against the binds. "Release me."

"No," he said, sucking hard on a nipple while playing with the other.

"Renaud, I need you to take me. I need you inside me."

He looked up at her, a pleased smile on his lips.

"Not yet."

Placing a kiss on each nipple, he moved down her stomach, kissing her there before moving further down. Her breath caught in her throat when his tongue flicked over her clit. Over and over again he worked the tiny bud, the perfect amount of pressure that had her begging for him to take her.

"Renaud, please. I need you."

He looked up at her, his gray eyes intense.

"Please."

He went up on his knees and grabbed her beneath her buttocks, pulling her against him. Taking his cock in his hand he guided the huge head into her opening, moving inch by inch inside her, all the while watching as he sank slowly into her heat. Her muscles tightened around him, and she spread her thighs as much as possible against the binds, pushing her hips up in order to take him deeper.

She sighed when he thrust home.

Seconds later Renaud slid in and out of her, his strokes sure and even. She came immediately, and cried out, wishing she was free of the binds, but instead she was helpless as her body rode out the pleasure.

Renaud watched Aleysia's breasts bounce in tandem with his strokes. Her moans were music to his ears and he could hardly believe when she came over and over again.

Her juices coated him, her inside like molten honey. So hot he grit his teeth. He untied her arms, giving her that freedom, and she clung to him, her fingernails biting into his shoulders.

Though she infuriated him, he kissed her, and was shocked as she kissed him back so passionately, her tongue mating with his in a frenzy, like she could never get enough.

His balls lifted and he held her hips tight as he pumped furiously within her, grinding against her pearl, until the familiar fluttering of her climax squeezed the seed from his cock.

ELEVEN

It had only been one day since Aleysia's attempt to flee Braemere with Adelstan, but it felt more like a fortnight. She had not said a word to Renaud, refusing food or drink of any kind. True, he had tied her to the bed, but what did she expect after she drugged him and his men? For him to let her run free? Plus, after they had made love, he had untied her and she had snuggled beneath the covers, and had fallen straight to sleep.

He had heard her cry, even though she had fought to hide her tears.

She had failed in her attempt to save her brother, and there had been nothing he could do to ease her pain. If only he could give her what she wanted. If only they had not been enemies. If only her brother had not been one of William's most wanted Saxons.

He had hoped Elena would speak to her on his behalf, but his sister seemed to have a different agenda. She obviously enjoyed Aleysia's company, and the two were as tight as long-lost friends.

Just as they were now, sitting on a blanket in the meadow, their heads bent as they spoke. Close by, four of his most trusted men watched, standing guard.

"She is a lovely woman."

Renaud glanced at Galeran, who was busy polishing his sword. The man trusted no one else to shine his blade, insisting they could not do better than he, and Renaud would have to agree. Renaud had even requested his squire learn Galeran's technique, but the young knight had not been forthcoming with the information. "Indeed."

"I am surprised she remembers me."

Renaud realized then that it was Elena he spoke of and not Aleysia, and he smiled for the first time all day. "She is a good deal older than you, my friend. Perhaps too old?"

Galeran raised a brow, clearly offended. "She is not old. In truth, I believe her even more beautiful now than when she was younger. There's a wisdom in her eyes that I like very much and I enjoy how she speaks her mind. 'Tis refreshing."

"Aye, she is quite outspoken." An understatement if ever there was one.

"Indeed, and spirited. I like my women with a bit of experience."

Renaud frowned. "She is a widow, that is true, but you would do well to remember that she is also my sister. Forget that for one minute, and I will snap you in two."

Galeran laughed under his breath, his blue eyes flashing with good humor. "Spoken like the overbearing brother you are, my lord. Aye, it is hard not to remember she is your flesh and blood when you growl like that." He sobered a little. "I would never hurt her, my lord. Ever. I would sooner rip my heart from my chest than hurt either of you."

"Now you are frightening me, Galeran," Renaud replied with a sardonic smile. In all honesty, he was more concerned with Elena hurting Galeran than the other way around. His young vassal, aside from nightly trysts with whores and serving wenches, had never been involved with a woman. His sister, on the other hand, was well experienced in the art of love. She had remained faithful to her much-older husband, but after his death rumors of her sexual exploits had traveled throughout the French court. He had tried, without success, to curb the rumors. But it seemed Elena did not care what others thought. She felt it her right to have the sexual freedom most men took for granted. "When last you met, she was a woman full grown, and you a child. Remember that she has lived longer and knows a great deal more than you."

Galeran made busy rubbing his sword with a soft cloth. "Aye, she is older, and perhaps experienced, but I am certain I could show her a thing or two."

Renaud thunked him on the back of the head. "Do not speak of my sister as you would a common whore."

"My apologies, my lord. I meant no disrespect," Galeran said with a frown, rubbing the back of his head. "Even as a boy, I cared for Elena. I will never forget her kindness." He winked, his good humor fast returning. "Methinks back then she fancied me. Mayhap she knew that one day our paths would cross again. Mayhap that is why she came to Braemere—because she knew I was here."

Renaud laughed under his breath. "You are quite confident, my friend. I suggest you be a bit more wary or she might break your heart."

Galeran flashed a devilish smile. "She fancies me. I know it."

Though he had been taken aback by his sister's boldness toward Galeran, she was two years older than Renaud and an experienced woman of the world. If she wanted his vassal, then so be it—as long as the flirtation did not interfere with Galeran's duties.

"Think you I should ask her to go for a stroll?"

Renaud shrugged. "Do as you like. Knowing Elena, she will not refuse you. But again, be wary, my friend, and remember this warning— if you hurt her, I will kill you."

Galeran grunted. "I will remember. And I shall gather the men for drills."

As his vassal walked away, Renaud looked toward the meadow where Aleysia and Elena sat. No longer was it just the two women. Now they had been joined by a man. Renaud recognized the soldier as one of his sister's men who had come over with her from France. The young soldier, a man close to Aleysia's age, and nearly as fair as she, but with light brown hair, was down on his haunches beside her.

Elena laughed at something the man said, and Aleysia joined in, her shoulders shaking with good humor. It had been the first time she'd laughed since she'd tried to escape, and it irked Renaud fiercely that it had taken this young man to do so.

Renaud felt like he'd been socked firmly in the stomach as he watched the soldier charm Aleysia. By God, was that a flower he handed her? His blood ran cold. To make matters worse, Aleysia lifted the pink blossom to her nose and grinned warmly at the younger man.

To further his dismay, the boy sat down beside her, no doubt at Elena's invitation. Damn Elena! Did she not realize that Aleysia was his lover? Of course she knew. Everyone knew. How could they not, when he looked at her as he did now with such longing? God's breath, he behaved like a lad of two and ten.

And even worse, every time he caught one of his men so much as looking at her, he felt a jealousy that rocked him to the core. He had never been a jealous person . . . before he had met Aleysia.

Mayhap it was because she had gotten under his skin and wedged herself there.

If only he could grow tired of her and send her packing.

That day will never come, and well you know it.

Elena's laughter rang out, pulling him from his unsettling thoughts.

Elena had forever enjoyed playing matchmaker, even from an early age, but she went too far by introducing her soldier to Renaud's mistress. True, she did not know about the bargain. Even his spirited sister might be shocked to discover that truth.

But he would not have her encouraging one of her foot soldiers to court Aleysia. Nay, he would put a stop to this immediately!

Renaud's fists tightened at his sides, and though he knew he had much to do to prepare for his upcoming trip to York, he walked toward the small group.

Another thought struck him as he approached. He could be in York for more than a week's time. Perhaps a fortnight or longer, for William was known to keep his favorites near. And in the interim, this charming younger man with a flare for the romantic would be here at Braemere, along with Aleysia, no doubt wooing her with flowers and poetry. Renaud had never wooed a woman in his life. He had never had to, nor had he felt inclined to—until now. *He* wanted to give Aleysia flowers, buy her things. Spoil her.

For a moment he thought of taking Aleysia with him to York, but if he did, he would run the risk of William taking her for someone else's bride . . . just as Duncan had warned. He had heard of his king doing so before. Spoils of war, Saxon princesses married off to his most noble of knights in a way to appease the old Saxon nobility. And though Renaud was in his king's favor, and had been promised Braemere if he could overtake her, he was not sure his liege would award him Aleysia for a bride. Especially, when Baron Comte', another of William's favored knights, was hunting for such a prize. One look at Aleysia and Comte' would ask for her hand. No, she would have to stay. It would be too risky to take her with him. Plus, how could he take her, knowing William would sentence Adelstan to death?

Renaud must be very careful. One false move and he could lose everything. Even a bride. All it would take was one baron in favor to win the hand of a beauty like Aleysia. Any man who saw her would want her.

He weighed the risks of taking her and decided the safest thing to do was to leave her at Braemere with someone he trusted explicitly.

Nay, his trusted vassal would not be happy with the news since he had not left Renaud's side for the past thirteen years. But he needed someone, other than his sister, looking after Aleysia. Galeran would make sure that no one touched her while Renaud was away. Though the man was young, he was wise to the ways of the world. An old soul, Renaud's father had once said.

At his approach Elena looked up. "Ah, Renaud, your ears must have been burning."

Renaud forced a smile. "How are you this fine afternoon?" he asked, glancing at Aleysia. Dressed in a yellow gown with floral embroidery at the neck and wrists, he noted she wore no shoes. They lay nearby, as did his sister's. Mayhap Elena was not the best influence, after all?

The soldier seemed to notice Aleysia's lack of footwear also, for his gaze kept slipping to her dainty feet.

Aleysia did not acknowledge Renaud in the least. Rather, she spoke to the soldier, her smile wide, her hand mere inches from his on the blanket. The soldier seemed so taken with Aleysia, he still had not bothered to look up.

Until Renaud took a step closer and the soldier noted the shadow that fell across the blanket. The boy glanced up, his brows furrowed into a frown—until he recognized Renaud and scrambled to his feet.

"My Lord. I apologize. Please excuse my insolence. I fear Lady Aleysia's beauty has distracted me." He gave a bow. "I am Philip Maley of Anjou."

Unfortunately, the soldier was even more handsome at closer range, his eyes a clear blue, his face free of blemishes—or scars. It seemed Aleysia had taken notice of the man's charms, for her cheeks were stained a delicate shade of pink. In truth, she appeared smitten. "Mayhap you would like to join my men for practice this afternoon, Maley?"

"I would be delighted," the soldier said, glancing at Elena, who nodded her approval.

"Good, I shall meet you in the armory, posthaste."

"Very well, my lord." Philip nodded, then turned to Aleysia. He reached out for her hand and brought it to his lips, completely unaware of the murderous thoughts racing through Renaud's mind. "It was a pleasure to meet you, Lady Aleysia. I look forward to seeing you soon."

The boy's accent was thick, much as Renaud's own had been on his arrival in England three years ago. Apparently, Aleysia understood him well enough, for she smiled warmly. "As do I, Philip."

Philip's face glowed at Aleysia's use of his Christian name, and he nodded. "Until then, my lady."

Aleysia sighed heavily, her fingers stroking the flower's stem as her gaze lingered on the man's backside. Renaud was not sure whom he felt more like strangling—Aleysia or Philip.

"He is quite handsome, is he not?" Elena asked, stealing a glance at Renaud.

Aleysia nodded. "Indeed, he is."

Renaud's nails bit into his palms. "I leave at week's end and will need extra men for the journey to York. If Maley proves to be an able soldier, would you be willing to relinquish him from his duties and allow him to come with us, Elena?"

To her credit, Elena tried not to smile, but failed miserably. Renaud had not blushed since he was a lad, but trapped by his sister's stare, he felt his ears turn red. She always seemed to know his mind, and now she sensed his jealousy, for she gave him a conspiratorial nod. "I do not see why not, but do you not have enough men already, brother?"

Apparently, she was not about to make it easy for him. Worse still, Aleysia watched him with lifted brow, waiting for his answer. "I do have many men traveling with me, but as you know these are dangerous times, and I cannot be too careful. I felt Galeran would be of more *service* here."

Elena's eyes widened and her lips pursed. "Well then, you are more than welcome to take Philip. He is still quite young and no doubt under your tutelage he could learn a great deal."

"I thought you would have a change of heart, dear sister."

Elena nodded but remained silent.

Renaud glanced at Aleysia, whose face had gone from pink to pale in seconds. No doubt, talk of the trip to York had reminded her of her brother. He had not realized how insensitive he was being. God's breath, would he ever learn?

"My dear, are you all right?" Elena asked, putting a motherly hand to Aleysia's brow.

"I am fine," Aleysia said, brushing away Elena's hand and coming fast to her feet. "My lord, may I have a word with you in private?"

Renaud glanced at his sister, who in turn nodded. "Oh go ahead, I shall be fine. But do not be long. We would like to return to the hall in time to change for dinner."

Relieved that Aleysia was actually speaking to him again, he walked beside her until they came to a meadow of fruit trees. "We have walked far enough, Aleysia," he said, grabbing her wrist. When she turned, her eyes were filled with tears that she was trying hard to blink away. "Will I see my brother before you leave for York?"

Seeing her in pain unsettled him immensely. He wanted to comfort her, but he refrained, her body language telling him to stay at arm's length. "I do not think it is wise."

Her eyes narrowed and a tear slipped down her cheek. He ached to wipe it away, but instead watched as it fell on the bodice of her gown. "Why?"

His gaze returned to hers. How he yearned to pull her into his arms and tell her all would be right. But how could he promise her anything, especially when he could not give her the one thing she wanted most of all? "Because, Aleysia, you have undermined me at every turn. You conspired against me and very nearly succeeded."

She caught his hand between her small ones. "Renaud, he is my brother, and we both know that he will not be coming back to Braemere." Her voice hitched and more tears slipped down her cheeks. "If it were you in that tower, and Elena were here, would you not expect the same from her?"

Renaud glanced at his sister, who watched them intently. He nodded. "Aye, I would."

"Then will you let me see him?"

Her eyes, so bright with tears, tore at his heart. Though his better judgment told him he was a fool, he could not deny her this one wish, for he knew she would never forgive him if he declined her request. "Tonight I have a meeting with my men-at-arms. You may visit Adelstan during that time, but I will not be gone long. I am trusting you, Aleysia. I am trusting you not to make another mistake."

She smiled then and even shocked him by giving him a hug. "Thank you, Renaud." Feeling her soft breasts pressed against his chest made his stomach coil and hot need rush straight to his groin.

"Return to the hall with Elena and prepare for dinner and your meeting with your brother."

She wiped away her tears with the sleeve of her gown. "Yes, my lord."

TWELVE

"Repeat what you just said?"

Galeran, who had already secured his helmet, glanced at Renaud. "I heard it plainly from Philip's mouth, my lord. He said and I quote, 'How I would love to squeeze Lady Aleysia's full tits—as ripe and sweet as melons while I skewer her with my rod.'"

Renaud gripped the reins in his fist.

Galeran laughed under his breath. "My lord, mayhap you should allow me to take the men through their drills while you ease your temper."

"And miss the fun? There is not a chance in hell. Nay, Galeran, I will show someone a lesson he will not soon forget. I promise you that the cocky young bastard will be regretting those words."

Renaud and Galeran crested the hill where the men were ready, lined up in regimented rows, all wearing chain mail. Usually, he did not insist that his men wear armor while practicing, but the Saxon threat was so great, he wanted them in peak condition. Tonight they would all rest well. "Philip, come forward," Renaud called, ignoring Galeran's laugh.

Renaud slid his helmet on and motioned to his squire to bring him a lance.

Philip's eyes widened in alarm, but he followed suit, and put on his helmet. He swallowed hard and took up the lance the squire handed him.

"Maley, you will ride over to that line of trees. When Galeran nods, we will rush each other. You will try to unseat me, and I you."

Maley's cheeks were bright red. "My lord, I—" As though just now realizing he was surrounded by experienced soldiers who would not let him live it down if he bowed out, Philip stopped in midsentence and with a tentative nod, brought about his horse and galloped toward the tree line.

Galeran laughed under his breath. "My lord, he is but a boy."

"That *boy* is no younger than you. Methinks he must learn to curb his tongue."

"Very well, my lord. Good luck!"

Without another word, Renaud kicked his horse into a gallop. His men shouted their encouragement as he passed, and finally he took his position across the field from Philip. He waited for Galeran's nod and immediately shot forward, straight toward Philip, who already looked in danger of falling from his steed.

The blood pumped through Renaud's veins, memories of the younger man's hot stare on Aleysia, coupled with his crude remarks, fueling his anger.

Renaud adjusted the lance as he closed in on the younger man.

A second later Renaud knocked the soldier from his horse and onto the hard-packed ground. Feeling a good deal better already, he rounded back and looked down at Philip, who still had not moved. The helmet had flown off his chestnut-colored locks and lay a good ten yards away. The boy blinked rapidly, clearly dazed, his chest heaving as he fought to catch his breath.

Renaud smiled inwardly as he dismounted. "You must block the blow next time, Maley. Your enemy would kill you with such a hit."

Philip opened his mouth but no words were forthcoming.

Renaud turned toward his men, who applauded their liege lord, grunting their approval.

Galeran strode toward him. "Well done, my lord." He shared a smile with Renaud before reaching out and helping Maley to his feet.

Philip stood and faltered, almost falling back down, making Renaud feel a bit guilty for having hit the boy so hard. He could have tried for a lesser blow that would have been nearly as effective without stealing the boy's breath.

"You have much to learn, Maley. But I am impressed," he lied. "So impressed that I would ask you to be part of my entourage when I leave for York."

Philip looked from Renaud to Galeran, as though he did not fully believe his ears. Galeran looked equally puzzled, and made no effort to hide his surprise.

Maley nodded. "I would be honored to ride with you, my lord."

"That is welcome news, especially when I am in need of another sword while I am away, especially since Galeran will be staying at Braemere."

"My lord!" Galeran blurted, his shock clearly evident to everyone around them. "Are you mad?"

Renaud had expected a strong reaction from his vassal, but not this strong, and not in front of his soldiers. He frowned at Galeran and lowered his voice. "Nay, I am not mad. I simply need you here. Have you forgotten MacMillan's threat?"

Galeran, realizing he had spoken out of turn, shifted on his feet, his jaw clenched tight, reminding Renaud of the boy he'd once been—always eager to please and wearing his heart on his sleeve for all the world to see. "There are others who can look after the fief, my lord. I do not understand why I must stay."

Renaud had injured his friend's pride greatly, but he could not back down now. A good leader never gave in, especially in front of his men. With each second of silence Galeran's cheeks reddened, and Renaud did not know if it was from embarrassment or anger. He gathered the latter as Galeran's jaw locked, the nerve working there.

"Galeran, my sister is here now, and I must be assured of her safety, as well as the safety of Lady Aleysia. I trust you with my life, but more important, I trust you with my sister's and Aleysia's lives. Do you understand why I ask this of you, and *only* you?"

The words seemed to appease Galeran a little, but Renaud could still see the hurt in his eyes. "I would be of more service to you riding by your side. The English could have ambushes set along the road to York, my lord."

Touched by his friend's concern, Renaud laid a hand on Galeran's shoulder to calm him. "I know you would be of great service on this journey, Galeran. You would take an arrow for me. In truth, there is not a man I trust more than you. That is why I ask you to stay."

Galeran released a heavy breath and shifted on his feet.

"We have only just secured this fief. Defend Braemere for me. Do not let my sister or Aleysia out of your sight. I need the peace of mind to know they are in *your* capable hands."

Galeran swallowed hard, but nodded. "Aye, my lord. I shall do as you ask."

Renaud paced before the two women in the solar.

Elena sat in a chair, beside her a young wench whose eyes were red and puffy from crying. She turned to the girl and in a kind voice said, "Heathra, tell my brother what you told my man last night."

The girl looked absolutely terrified, and kept her gaze averted. "My Tom left the village two days ago with a note to be delivered to the Scot."

Renaud stopped pacing. "What Scot?"

"The same who came to Braemere that day."

His stomach turned over. "MacMillan?"

"Aye, that would be the one," the girl said, shifting in her seat.

"And what did this letter say?"

"For the Scot to come back to Braemere. That Aleysia was freeing her brother, and they would find their way back to Scotland. She asked him to meet her and give her safe journey back to Scotland."

Renaud could not believe his ears. "And Aleysia gave him this note?"

"She gave it to the healer, who is Tom's grandmother." The girl looked terrified. "I pray you do not punish either of them. They have known Aleysia all their lives and have always been loyal to her family. Please, do not hold it against them."

Furious, Renaud ran his fingers through his hair. "She is the same woman who gave Aleysia the sleeping draught. 'Tis treasonous what she has done."

Heathra turned to Elena, panic in her eyes.

"Are you certain of this? It was Aleysia?"

"Aye, I have the ring to prove it."

The servant opened her fist, showing a slender gold ring, much like the one he had seen on Aleysia's hand when they first met.

"You may go, Heathra," Elena said, waiting until the servant had closed the door before turning to Renaud.

"Aleysia is desperate, brother. She knows what will happen when you bring Adelstan before King William. We all know his fate."

Renaud shook his head, furious with himself and with Aleysia, re-membering her watching him today, pleading with him to let her see her brother. That image mixed with another—her naked in his bed after making love, prompting him to drink the tainted wine. She had played the part well. "She is a witch, that one. And I forever am falling under her spell."

"She is but a woman, Renaud. A woman who has lost much and is about to lose the one person she loves more than life. He is her twin, her flesh and blood, and she knows that he is on borrowed time."

"Why do you defend her?"

"I do not defend her as much as understand her and ache for her. Knowing her plight, even you must pity her."

"Do you think me a fool for keeping her with me?"

"Never," Elena said, taking his face between her palms. "You care for this girl. I know you do, and you feel protective of her. I see it every time you look at her, Renaud. It kills you to have to bring Adelstan before William."

He nodded. "It does. Never have I questioned my king. I have always done what I was told, and gained my riches because of it. And here when I have Braemere within my grasp, I am wondering at what cost will I win her?"

"When you say 'her,' of whom do you speak—the fief or the woman?"

He shrugged. "Both."

"And I can give you no reassurance. I do not know the answer. Who of us can see the future?"

"Do you know what she asked of me earlier today?"

Elena shook her head.

"She asked if she could see her brother tonight for the last time."

"And you said yes?"

He nodded. "Aye."

"Then you should allow her to do so. She does not know that you are aware of the message."

"But how can I trust her?"

"Renaud, she is under constant guard. What can happen? Act as though nothing has changed between you. You are leaving in a few days' time, and well she knows it. Allow her to see her brother, spend an hour or so, and then that will be the end of it. You will go to York and she will be here on your return."

"You're right. There is nothing I can do now, but hope that the message never makes it." He stepped away, toward the windows, taking in the fresh air.

"Do not be too harsh on her, brother. I would do the same if it were you in that tower. I would die trying to get you out."

"I know you would, Elena. And I would do the same for you."

She walked to him and put a gentle hand on his shoulder. "She will never forgive you if her brother is killed, and we both know he will be. Mayhap it would be best if you hand her over to the Scot."

"I will not!" The words echoed inside the chamber, surprising even him with their force. It apparently shocked his sister as well, for she laughed lightly.

"Then there is your answer, brother. Perhaps William will listen to reason and spare Adelstan. Will he pledge homage to William, do you think?"

"I think not. He is as stubborn as his sister. Perhaps more so."

"But if he were given the choice of homage or death?"

"I do not know."

"Mayhap you should ask him?"

Renaud was surprised at Adelstan's appearance. The young man appeared gaunt, his skin a grayish color. He knew Adelstan had been fed, but wondered if the boy had eaten any of the food that had been prepared for him. Renaud guessed not, for he had lost a stone during his short imprisonment.

It would be so much easier if Adelstan were not Aleysia's twin. In truth, had Adelstan not been Aleysia's brother, then he would not be here now, asking a Saxon traitor to make a pledge to King William. But the eyes staring at him now with distrust and venom, mirrored his sister's, unsettling Renaud. "We leave for York by week's end."

Adelstan took a deep breath and released it, but showed no emotion.

"I have come to give you an opportunity."

Adelstan's eyes narrowed. "An opportunity?"

"Aye, it could spare your life."

"Go on."

"Would you swear homage to King William?"

Silence filled the chamber and for a moment Renaud thought Adelstan had not heard him.

Running a hand through his straggly blond hair, Adelstan replied, "Nay, I would not."

"Even if it meant your life?"

The Saxon nodded. "Even if it meant my life. I will not become Judas to my people. Not after all that we have fought for."

"Think you they would deny this opportunity if given the chance themselves?"

Adelstan nodded. "Aye."

"You know King William will remain in power."

Defiance shone brightly in the young man's eyes. "I know *your* king will continue to burn the north, leaving not a soul alive, not even an animal. He would oppress the entire country to retain his power, and that to me is not a king. Your king is a tyrant. What kind of man would want to swear allegiance to such a man?"

The boy's treasonous words angered Renaud, but he did not let Adelstan see it. Instead, Renaud's mind raced, wondering what he could do to change this young man's fate. "For Aleysia's sake, will you consider it?"

At the mention of his twin, Adelstan flinched and Renaud knew he had found the boy's weakness: Adelstan's love of his sister. "She will be alone, Adelstan."

Adelstan swallowed hard, his jaw clenched tight. "Duncan will come for her."

"He has already come and gone."

"When?"

"Days ago."

Adelstan frowned. "I heard no fighting."

"There was no fight."

"He left? So swiftly?"

"He did. He brought a small army who could not stand up to my men. It would have been suicide."

Disbelief came over the Saxon's features, and for a while he said nothing. He ran a hand down his face. "Aleysia remains at Braemere?"

"Aye, she does."

Adelstan cursed under his breath. "I cannot believe Duncan left without her. Did he offer money?"

"He did."

"And you refused?"

"I did."

Renaud did not want to hurt Adelstan any more than he was already hurting, but he felt like he owed the young man the truth. "Adelstan, MacMillan asked only for Aleysia's release. He said you could remain in Braemere's prison for all eternity."

The young Saxon fell silent for a moment, his gaze searching Renaud's so intently as to be uncomfortable. It was clear he did not believe him. "He did not ask for my release?" he asked in disbelief.

"Nay, he did not."

"And you say this as a man of honor, and not as a means to coerce me into swearing allegiance to King William?"

"I swear on my honor, Adelstan. MacMillan told me to do with you what I would. He wanted only Aleysia."

Adelstan took a step back as though he'd been struck. "The bastard! To think my father had depended on this man to protect us to the death. He must be pleased to know that soon my body parts will be scattered across England."

"I am sorry, Adelstan."

He shook his head. "I always knew he disliked me. I could see it in his face whenever I was around."

"Does this change your mind about swearing homage to King William?"

This time Adelstan was not as quick to respond. He looked down at the floor, his brow furrowed. Silent moments passed, but Renaud did not push him for an answer.

Adelstan rubbed the back of his neck. "I cannot swear fealty to your king. I cannot. Too much blood has been spilled because of him. Look at what he has done to the north. It is now a barren wasteland. Why would a king do such a thing to his own lands and his own people?"

"Such is the way of war, Adelstan. You do what you must in order to survive. William was given this land by Edward because he believed William would strengthen it."

"By stripping Saxon nobles of their lands and titles? By marrying off its daughters and widows to lusty Norman barons who have no use for them after they bear children?" Adelstan laughed sardonically. "What would my father think—or my people, if I bowed to such a king?"

"That you saved yourself, and your sister. You have avenged your parents' deaths, and done far more than most men. Your parents would be proud of you. I know it, just as your sister is proud of you. Aleysia needs you, Adelstan. Think of her happiness."

Adelstan shook his head. "I cannot swear allegiance to him. Not even for Aleysia."

Renaud nodded. "I wish things were different, Adelstan. I would have been honored to have you amongst my ranks." Unable to stand the haunted look in the boy's eyes, Renaud left.

CHIRTEEN

Aleysia sat on the high dais, a few seats down from Renaud, who conversed with his guests: three soldiers who had fought with him years ago and had secured their own fiefs in the north. He seemed in a fair mood, though he barely touched his food, his thoughts clearly somewhere else.

Elena sat to Aleysia's right and leaned close to her. "Aleysia, see Galeran there. Do you know that woman to whom he speaks?"

Aleysia, shaken from her thoughts, followed Elena's line of vision to where Galeran stood talking to a servant girl. The woman, a little younger than Aleysia herself, laughed innocently and blushed profusely at something Galeran said.

"He is taken with her. Look at him. He even blushes," Elena whispered so no one else could hear them, but there was no mistaking the jealousy in her voice.

"You fancy Galeran, do you not?"

Elena turned and smiled. "Indeed, I do. Do you think that silly? Me, a woman who is old enough to be his mother?"

"Nay, I do not think it is silly at all . . . and you are not that old."

"I am three and thirty."

"You do not look it, and what does age matter? Look how old your husband was, and none seemed to be concerned at the difference in your ages."

Elena laughed without mirth. "'Tis different for men. They can marry anyone they wish, and age does not figure into it. But for women, we are considered old by the time we have met our twentieth year. Used, discarded, and once you have children, men often look elsewhere. It is the curse of our kind, I suppose."

"It is most unfair."

Elena nodded. "Aye, 'tis a man's world, my dear. It always will be."

"I wish I had been born a man."

"I love your spirit, dearest Aleysia," Elena said, laughing. "Nearly as much as my brother loves you."

Aleysia's heart jolted and her cheeks burned. "Your brother does not love me."

Elena took a sip of wine. "He cares for you. You have crept beneath his skin. Something no other woman has done. Love. Lust. It is all the same in the end."

"Is it really? I thought there would be a difference."

"Lust is when you want a person so badly that you think you might perish if you do not get him. Or when your heart pumps nearly out of your chest when he enters a room," Elena said.

Aleysia knew that feeling well. Ironically, it seemed that a room would light up when Renaud entered, and that same light extinguished when he left. "What of love?"

Elena lifted a dark brow. "Love is when you care so much for another, you cannot imagine life without them. It's all consuming. You love everything about him, wonder about him when he's not with you. Trust me, Aleysia. You will know when you are in love."

"Have you ever been in love?"

The sides of Elena's mouth curved. "Once, a very long time ago. I was a little younger than you when I fell in love with a groom."

"Did he love you as well?"

Elena smiled softly. "Aye, he did. I will never forget the first time he kissed me. 'Twas heaven."

"What happened?"

"My father discovered our liaison. I think it was one of his soldiers who told him, a man who secretly coveted me for his own. Unfortunately, the groom was sent away, and I never saw him again."

"I'm sorry. How devastated you must have been."

Elena shrugged. "I cried myself to sleep many a night, but the heart often heals itself in time, and I survived it."

Aleysia stole a glance over at Renaud, relieved to find him deep in conversation with one of his men-at-arms. "What of his betrothed?"

Setting her goblet down, Elena leaned forward. "Morgana was a spoiled, pampered woman. A beauty, yes, but she cared nothing for others. I was never fond of her, and well she knew it."

"I understand she was furious when she heard of Renaud's leman."

Elena grinned coyly. "Her pride could not stand that Renaud wanted another, especially when he was to wed *her*, the most sought-after woman in the French court. It didn't matter that his leman had been his lover long before his betrothal, or that she was one of Renaud's many mistresses. Nay, Morgana could not bear the humiliation."

"So she attacked Renaud?"

"Aye, she did that, but there is more. Feeling slighted, Morgana took a lover, certain she would win back Renaud's affection out of jealousy alone. Unfortunately, she became pregnant with that man's child and tried to pass it off as Renaud's—thereby trapping him into marriage. Thank goodness her lover came forward and admitted the liaison. That was when Morgana attacked Renaud. It caused quite a scandal, I must say."

"So he never did love her?"

"Nay."

How relieved Aleysia was at that simple word.

"He has never loved anyone. But you, my dear, might just be the one to change all that."

"I will never love him," Aleysia blurted, feeling stupid and childish the moment the words came out.

"Sometimes our minds and hearts conflict, but perhaps one day they will collide and you will feel differently." Elena glanced over at Galeran again, who still spoke to the servant girl. "Do you know that the only reason Renaud asked Philip along to York was because he did not want him near you?"

Oddly, the knowledge that Renaud was jealous of Philip pleased her. "Nay, I thought him a good soldier."

"I heard on good authority that he nearly killed Philip in practice. Indeed, see for yourself. There, to the right. Philip is sporting a bruised face."

Aleysia found Philip amongst the other soldiers, and he indeed looked battered and bruised.

"You see, Aleysia, as women we do have some power over men. Think you Renaud would have paid Philip any mind if he hadn't been conversing with you earlier? Also, it did not help that Philip gave you a flower. It is up to us to use that power to our advantage."

"How?"

"To make men jealous. To make them want us. To burn for us, until they can no longer contain their desire. Watch. You see how Galeran speaks to the servant wench? Though it seems like he is intent on everything she says, I believe he is watching us from the corner of his eye." Elena took the shawl from her shoulders and let it fall beneath the table, where she then kicked it off the high dais and onto the floor below. With a wink, Elena turned to the man at her right. "Richard, is it?" she asked the brawny soldier, who appeared surprised by the sudden attention. "I have dropped my shawl. Would you be so kind as to fetch it for me?"

The man smiled widely. "Indeed, my lady."

As the soldier went after the shawl, Elena watched his every move, as though she could not take her eyes off him. "Now tell me, is Galeran still speaking to the servant, or is he watching me?"

Aleysia glanced where Galeran had been, and found him instead heading their way, or more specifically, toward the shawl. "He is heading for us."

Elena grinned. "You see?"

Galeran beat Richard to it. The older man did not look at all pleased as Galeran snatched up the shawl.

"And just as I have made Galeran jealous, you, too, have the same power over Renaud. And I know just the man who will make him sit up and take notice." She nodded toward Philip. "Go ahead, flirt with him. Even if it is just a tilt of your head. The slightest nod."

"But Renaud will not notice. He has been conversing with those men since he arrived in the hall." Aleysia sat back in her seat, took a sip of wine, and looked in Philip's direction. To her dismay the younger man did not even glance her way, but it seemed his friend next to him had noticed her staring, for he nudged Philip, who in turn looked at Aleysia. With a wide grin, the young Frenchman lifted his goblet in mock toast. She did the same, took a drink of her wine, all the while keeping eye contact with the young man.

Elena leaned forward and whispered, "Excellent. Renaud is positively furious. Now be discreet, and every once in a while look at Philip while you eat. No lingering stares, but rather quick peeks. Mayhap flash a smile and then look away. Flirt a little."

Aleysia grinned at Philip again, and the young man smiled, and then added a wink.

At her side Elena laughed under her breath. "My brother is coming out of his skin."

Cheeks blazing, Aleysia stole a glance at Renaud. His eyes were narrowed as he watched her intently.

"Now lift your glass to your lips, take a sip, and watch Philip over the rim. After you set the wine down, lick your lips and then look away."

She did exactly as Elena said, though not quite as delicately. But the move was effective: Renaud was already walking toward her.

Elena covered her laughter with a false cough as her brother exchanged seats with the person directly to Aleysia's left.

"My lord," Aleysia said with a curt nod.

"Aleysia." His voice was harsh.

"Do you not care for the venison, my lord? You barely touched your plate."

"I am shocked you noticed." Again his tone was clipped and curt.

Aleysia wondered if perhaps making him jealous was unwise. After all, didn't she want to gain his trust? "I am not very hungry," she said, managing a bite of venison.

He watched her as she chewed, his gaze on her lips. "And why are you not hungry, my lady?"

She wiped her fingers on a cloth. "Because my brother is leaving me on the morrow, which saddens me greatly."

"You do not appear sad to me."

"Perhaps I hide it well."

"You cannot be in too much pain if you are flirting with a mere stranger."

So he had indeed noticed Philip. "Stranger? Whomever do you mean, my lord?"

Renaud's jaw clenched. "I saw the exchange between you and Philip."

"I was not flirting, but merely thanking him for the flower, my lord. Plus, he is not a stranger, but a friend."

"Do not encourage the boy, Aleysia."

She took a sip of wine, enjoying the warmth as it slid down her throat. Setting the goblet down, she asked, "Why?"

He shook his head as though confounded by the question. "You are my woman, and I will not have you flirting with every man that crosses your path. 'Tis not right to promote a liaison, especially in the company of your lover."

Hearing the word *lover* from his lips made her insides burn. Such an intimate word—one that conjured up one wicked image after another.

The possession in his eyes took her aback, but the jealousy she saw there even more so. She had never understood before that she could have such power over a man. Especially a man such as Renaud de Wulf. It was both frightening and exhilarating.

She looked away and saw that Galeran sat on a bench beside Elena, shoving the other knight's food away in his haste to make room. Renaud shook his head, obviously aware of the bond that was forming between Elena and Galeran. Elena, whose shawl was firmly on her shoulders, glanced at Aleysia and smiled.

One of Renaud's guests stood and clapped his hands, until the entire hall fell silent. "To show our appreciation for your fine hospitality, de Wulf, we have a gift for you. One we hope you will all enjoy."

The sound of drums and pipes played in a seductive tune, which carried up to the high ceiling.

Four dark-skinned men entered the hall, all wearing red vests embroidered with gold. Following them were six women, wearing cropped, sleeveless chemises made from a sheer cloth threaded with gold. All around them, men clapped loud, their voices raised in praise for such a spectacle. Aleysia sat up straight, conscious that Renaud's attention was fully on the women, their skirts a combination of blood-red to bright orange that floated around their slender legs. Golden chains encircled their hips and golden bracelets with bells encased small wrists and dainty ankles, causing a melodious tune with every movement.

Many of the women at the lower tables took their leave, obviously not enjoying the spectacle, some pushing stunned children toward the door, while others sat intrigued. Indeed, most of the men shouted their praises loudly.

Aleysia herself felt a sudden desire to leave, and even moved to stand, when a hand clasped her wrist. It was not Renaud, but Elena who leaned forward and whispered, "Stay. Watch. You may learn something. Watch how they use their bodies, particularly their hips. Does it remind you of something else?"

Aleysia felt her cheeks burn. No wonder men enjoyed watching such a display. In fact, strangely enough, she felt aroused watching the men and women dance to the pounding rhythm.

Sparing a glance at Renaud, she noticed his attention focused on a large-breasted blonde. Her breasts were so large, the cloth barely covered her nipples.

Her hips were wide and womanly and as she rotated them from side to side in a circular motion, the men around the hall yelled their approval.

The blonde smiled seductively as she twirled, the motion sending her skirts flying up, giving everyone a view of her long legs and firm buttocks.

Aleysia scanned the hall to find every man focused on the one woman. To her horror, she felt jealous that they all wanted her, this woman who danced for money, and no doubt did far more for the right price.

Mayhap Renaud wanted the big-breasted blonde in his bed tonight? The very thought made her furious.

She watched him from the corner of her eye. Damn! He certainly was entranced; taking a sip of wine, he watched the woman over the rim of the goblet. Aleysia glanced at Philip, hoping Renaud would catch her flirting, but even Philip had become distracted by the dancers.

The music picked up in tempo, and so did the dancers. They fell into a straight line, directly in front of the high table. The blonde gypsy danced in the middle, right before Renaud. The whore's light eyes were outlined with black kohl, her lips stained red. Her long, straight hair, darker than Aleysia's, fell past her hips, like a shimmering veil of silk.

Her hips moved fast, back and forth in a way Aleysia had never before seen. The men applauded and she moved faster, rotating her hips harder. With every second that passed, Aleysia found herself more irritated, and she dug her nails into her palms.

What was wrong with her? Why should she care that Renaud looked like he was ready to jump over the table, grab the woman up in his arms, and take her back to his bed?

The same bed where he had taken her virginity!

Aleysia took a long drink of wine. She could feel Renaud watching her, which surprised her since she thought he hadn't taken his eyes off the wench who was still undulating before him.

Elena whispered in her ear, "Play the game, Aleysia. Remember that there are more than women here." She motioned to one of the dark-haired gypsies, his skin glistening with oil.

His gold eyes shone brightly in the dark room, and as he flung off his vest, she saw how strong his body was. Not as powerful and muscular as Renaud, but still appealing. He came closer to the high dais and lifted one of the women up in his arms, to where she stood on his shoulders. His muscles bunched with the strain and Aleysia smiled when he glanced at her. The young man smiled in return, flashing white teeth, before turning his attention back to the woman on his shoulders.

Aleysia jumped when she felt a hand on her thigh. She looked down at where Renaud's hand rested, then up at him.

He smiled as their eyes met, and before she knew what she was doing, she placed her hand over his, her fingers sliding between his long ones.

Strangely, relief washed over her, along with a heat that settled low into her belly.

His gray eyes searched hers and she could see the pleasure there.

The music stopped abruptly and everyone around them came to their feet, applauding loudly. Aleysia lifted her hands to do likewise, but Renaud held the one hand firmly. "Are you ready to see your brother, Aleysia?"

Excitement rushed along her spine and she nodded. "Indeed, my lord. I am."

FOURTEEN

They walked the stairs in silence. Neither one had said a word since the gypsies had left the hall. Aleysia had been sick to her stomach when she heard Renaud invite the guests to stay for an extended time, fearful the gypsies would stay, too. The blonde-haired gypsy had not been able to hide her excitement or her desire for Renaud, whom she kept watching under thick lashes. The woman had to have noticed that Aleysia and Renaud held hands beneath the table. A clear sign they were lovers, but as Elena had said, some women did not care if a man was taken or not. If they desired that person, then they would stop at nothing to get him in their bed.

Aleysia had never hated another woman so much in her life.

"You are meeting with your men so soon?"

"I have matters to attend to beforehand."

Aleysia wondered if that *matter* wore a gold top and a red and orange skirt.

"Will you come for me after your meeting, my lord? Or do you wish me to sleep elsewhere this evening?"

He frowned as he stared at her, and then she saw him comprehend the question for his lips curved just the slightest bit. "Why do you ask, Aleysia?"

"I thought perhaps you would want to spend time alone with your guests."

"I consider all three barons my good friends, but that does not mean I desire to be alone with them."

She frowned. "You know I was not speaking of the men."

"I did not invite the gypsies, Aleysia."

"Did you not, my lord? It seemed you were well acquainted with at least one of them."

"Which one would that be?" he asked, stopping and taking a lock of Aleysia's hair, wrapping it about his finger.

She looked down to where his thumb and finger stroked the strands, remembering the feel of those long, strong fingers in her slick passage. "The wanton dancing before you."

"I saw no one dancing for *me*. They danced for all of us."

"Then you must be blind, for she was doing everything she could to gain your attention." Aleysia lifted her arms over her head and mimicked the gypsy's movements as best she could.

Renaud's hand fell to his side, and he leaned back against the wall, his arms crossed over his chest as he watched her.

"Does that not look familiar, my lord?"

His gaze slid from hers, making a slow path down her body, stopping at her breasts for a moment before moving farther down.

She turned in a circle, just as the wanton had, swaying her hips to and fro. When she faced Renaud again there was no mistaking the lust in his eyes—which stopped her cold.

What had Elena said? To watch and learn. How smart her new friend was. The look in Renaud's silver eyes made her nipples harden and gave her a tingle right between her legs.

Renaud moved toward her and pulled her into his arms, kissing her hard.

His cock pressed against her belly and he pulled up her skirts.

She stepped away, looking up into his passion-filled eyes.

"I want you now," he said, his words low and husky, kissing her jaw, her neck.

"Here? Are you mad?"

He kissed her again, then lifted her in his arms. He took the steps two at a time, and pushed open the door of his chamber. A moment later they were inside the room and Aleysia's back was against the hard door. He lifted her gown with one hand while untying the cord of his braies with the other. "I need you. Now," he said, as he lifted her legs. "Lock your ankles behind my waist."

She did as he asked, and gasped when he thrust inside her, surprised how hard he was. He filled her so completely, stretching her hot walls in a deliciously painful way.

Footsteps sounded outside in the hall, but it did not deter Renaud, who thrust, the action sending her back up against the door, making a knocking sound. "Someone will hear."

"I do not care," he said, cutting off any more protests with a kiss. His tongue delved past her lips, tasting her, teasing her.

Her channel tightened around him, growing wetter with each stroke. His lips left hers, nipping at her earlobe, sucking gently. Her nipples ached, stabbing against his chest. As though sensing her need, he covered one breast with his hand, his fingers plucking at the sensitive nipple, pinching it, pulling it.

Still holding her up with one hand, those fingers tightened on her buttocks, fingers brushing against her cleft.

The first quivers of climax came, her breathing quickening as she rocked against him. He followed right behind, moaning low in his throat as he filled her with his seed.

A minute later, her feet once again on solid ground, he led her over to the bed. She still trembled from the force of her orgasm, her legs feeling weak. "Renaud, I must see Adelstan."

"Aye, and you will. But the least I can do is clean you before you go."

She frowned, not wanting to take a bath when she could be spending precious time with her brother. But when Renaud took a rag and dabbed it in rose water, she understood his meaning and held out her hand. "I shall clean myself."

He held the rag back. "Nay, I will clean you. Hold your skirts up."

Her cheeks burned with embarrassment. "Renaud."

"I have seen every inch of your body, Aleysia."

Doing as he asked, she held up her skirts while he washed her gently. The touch of his fingers against her heated flesh aroused her yet again. She could not think clearly when in his presence, particularly when he touched her so intimately.

Finished washing her, he next used a soft drying cloth. Brushing over her bud, the little bit of pressure sent a delicious ripple throughout her body.

When he continued long after he had dried her, she swatted his hand away.

He laughed lightly and took her hand. "Come, we had best be on our way. There will be plenty of time to attend to you later. 'Tis a cold evening. Bring your cloak."

They walked the tower steps in silence. Two guards stood on either side of the door, and one turned to unlock the door. "I'll return for you in a few hours," Renaud said, already heading back down the stairs.

"I will see you then," she said, entering the room. The guard shut the door.

Adelstan, who had been lying on the cot, stood.

Aleysia rushed toward him and hugged him tight. Tears clogged her throat and she clung to him, knowing it might be for the last time.

Finally, he put her at arm's length. She saw that his wrists and ankles were not shackled and had been bandaged recently. However, he had lost a good deal of weight.

A bowl of stew and a loaf of bread sat next to his cot, untouched. "Why do you not eat?"

He smiled then, taking her hand in his. "I have had no appetite."

"But you must eat for strength."

"They take me to York." She was shocked to see defeat in his eyes. He had given up and accepted his fate.

"I know they do."

"I am sorry you have suffered."

Her cheeks felt hot. If he only knew how little she had suffered.

"When I am gone, you must try to make peace with the Norman."

She brushed the tears from her eyes. "I will never have peace."

"King William is here to stay, Aleysia. Do what you must in order to stay alive."

"I hate him!"

His lips curved slightly. "King William or de Wulf?"

"Both."

His brows drew together. "You do not hate de Wulf, sister."

She was struck silent by the observation. How could he think she liked Renaud?

Unable to keep eye contact, she dropped her gaze. "I do hate him."

"Yet your eyes tell a different story," he said, his gaze shifting to her neck, where Renaud's rough beard had scratched the delicate skin there.

It was no use lying to her twin, as embarrassing as it was. He knew the truth. "It is wrong to care for him."

"Who says it is wrong?" Adelstan cupped her face with his hands. "Look at Father and Mother, she a Dane and he a Saxon. Enemies, born to hate each other, but even they found love. It is not so different for you now, save for de Wulf is Norman. Just remember, he is not the man who killed our parents."

"Aye, but the Normans took everything from us, even our family. They are the reason for all our suffering."

"You cannot blame one man for all of his countrymen's sins, Aleysia."

"But that makes him no less a murderer. He is taking you to York."

"He does so because it is his duty. Think you that he wants to do this?" Adelstan's lips curved a little. "Nay, he does not. If he could save you the pain, he would do it. I know it, Aleysia. I have seen it in his eyes, and the eyes do not lie."

"How can you defend him? He is the reason for all our pain."

Adelstan laughed under his breath. "Aleysia, de Wulf is only guilty of doing his duty to his king. He could have killed us both and not thought of us again. If the tables were turned, I am not sure if I would have shown such mercy."

"Mercy—you call taking you to York mercy?"

"We all die sometime. I have lived this long only because de Wulf favors you." He shrugged. "And it is that same favor that will save you."

"You know what will happen at York. We have heard the rumors for months, and many have seen the truth for themselves. They will take your head, Adelstan." Her voice broke, and he hugged her tight.

"Aye, they will swipe my head from my body, but they will never have my soul."

The image horrified her and she shuddered. "I cannot bear it."

"I will not have died in vain, sister."

"They will torture you."

He lifted her chin with gentle fingers. "I am not afraid to die."

She shook her head. "I can not sit by and do nothing." Lowering her voice, she said, "I have a plan."

His brows furrowed. "Did you get the draught?"

"Nay, Renaud caught me, and so close was I. Just at the chamber door there."

"We will never escape. There is not enough time."

She untied the cloak and let it slip from her shoulders. "Put on my kirtle and cloak."

He laughed under his breath. "You speak madness."

"We are twins, Adelstan. Who will know?"

His gaze searched hers intently. "You *are* serious."

"Indeed."

She could see his mind working, the denial . . . then slowly, the hope. "But what will de Wulf do when he discovers your betrayal?"

"I do not care."

"He might bring you before the king."

"I go willingly."

"You risk too much."

"Renaud will not hurt me, Adelstan. I know that. Now is your only chance. He will not let me come to visit you again before you depart for York. He is in a meeting with his men, and not expected back for hours. If you go now, then you might make it to Scotland . . . to Duncan."

"Duncan?" He frowned.

"Aye, Duncan will protect you."

Adelstan shook his head. "Did de Wulf not tell you?"

"Tell me what?"

"Duncan did not ask for my release. Rather, he told the Norman he was well to be rid of me."

Aleysia could not understand why Renaud had kept that information to himself. What other reason than to keep her from hurting more than she already was? She remembered asking him what Duncan had said, and he had wiped away her tears, saying nothing negative about the Scot.

She felt physically sick. What a fool she had been—sending Duncan a letter pleading for him to rescue them. She prayed the letter did not make it.

"I have faith in God that we will see each other again one day."

Five minutes later Aleysia, dressed only in her chemise, looked at her twin, hoping their masquerade would work. Knowing he would not have time to stop, she made him eat the cold stew and bread, and he washed it down with the warm ale.

"You look convincing," she said, trying without success to keep the sadness from her voice. They would both die if he were caught.

He rolled his eyes. In truth, with the wimple over his head, and the cloak secured tightly about him, he could easily pass as her. She gave him a handkerchief. "Now, dab at your eyes as you pass by the guards. Cover that square chin. They will think that I am too distraught to stay. Meanwhile, I will lay upon the cot with my back to the door, pull the blanket over my head, and God willing, they will not check to see if it is you."

"Are you certain about this, Aleysia? De Wulf might keep you locked away in the tower once he discovers I am gone and you are the one who helped me escape."

"I have never been so certain of anything in my life. It is the only way, Adelstan. Do not feel sorry for me. I will be fine."

He hugged her tight. "God be with you." He put her at arm's length. "I *will* see you again."

She blinked back tears. "God keep you, Adelstan."

She slipped onto the cot and smoothed the blanket over her while Adelstan opened the door. She heard the guards mutter a question and then the chamber door closed with a hard *thud*. She waited, holding her breath, her heart pounding so loud it was a roar in her ears.

The key turned in the lock, and only then did she release her breath.

Saints be praised! They had done it.

FIFTEEN

Renaud ran a hand down his face. He was so tired, but there was still much to do. If only he could sleep the night away in Aleysia's arms, feel her heated skin against his own, take her beneath him and bury himself deep within her and forget that he was taking her brother to his death.

"What if MacMillan returns in your absence, my lord?"

Renaud glanced to his right, where Galeran sat, drinking ale from a goblet. His vassal had not said a word all night, apparently still angry he was being left behind. Renaud had been embarrassed to tell his men that someone had sent a message to Duncan, and that the message could already be in MacMillan's hands. He refrained from naming the culprit, but given his men's knowing looks, they all guessed the traitor to be Aleysia. "I am hoping I will return before any trouble begins. It would take him time to build his army."

"Aye, my lord."

"You will know what to do, Galeran. Plus, I do not think MacMillan will strike this soon."

"What if he need go no farther than the borders? There are clans that are his allies."

Galeran had a good point; it was one he had worried about since MacMillan had left Braemere. What if MacMillan did bring an army along with him while Renaud and a good number of men were away? MacMillan could break through Braemere's gates and take Aleysia, and Renaud would never see her again.

Again he thought of taking Aleysia with him, but he could not. There was too much to risk, plus it would only make her parting with Adelstan even more difficult.

Concluding their business, Renaud made his way through the hall. He walked across the bailey, up the bridge, his gaze straying to the tower's uppermost chamber where Aleysia and her brother were saying their final good-byes.

If only he could give her what she wanted most.

In truth, he was prepared to ask William for leniency when it came to Adelstan. It didn't help that Adelstan refused to pay homage. His liege lord would be shocked that such a request would come from Renaud, and William would look upon said request as a weakness. In his heart Renaud knew his liege would never allow such leniency. Whether Renaud liked it or not, his hands were tied, which meant Adelstan would die.

Renaud would ask for Aleysia's hand though. He wanted her—nay—he *needed* her by his side. Hers was the first face he wanted to see each morning, and the last face before he closed his eyes. He wanted her round with his child. She would be an amazing mother, with the same defensive streak that she showed with her brother.

Then he remembered his mother and her deceit, and an image of Aleysia as she smiled at Philip, the too-pretty soldier, came to mind. Aleysia was a passionate lover. Mayhap she yearned to make love to the younger man?

The thought rankled.

He took the tower steps two at a time, his need to see Aleysia so great. The guards came to attention seeing him. "My lord? What is it?"

"I am here to escort Aleysia back to her chamber."

The guards shared a confused look. "Lady Aleysia left over an hour ago, my lord. Not long after she arrived."

Renaud frowned, surprised she would leave her brother before he came for her. He had envisioned her complaining that she had not had enough time. "Was she upset?"

"Aye, she was quite distraught, my lord. Crying, she was."

Of course she would be upset. How could he blame her? The only family she had left was being taken from her.

He nodded and went straight to their bedchamber, thinking of what he could say to ease her sadness.

The room was dark, save for the fire that cast shadows against the walls. His brow furrowed at finding the chamber empty.

His mind raced. Surely, she had not come to the hall? He would have seen her on his way. Yet he had made haste. Mayhap she visited the chapel to pray for Adelstan's fate, or perhaps she had gone in search of Elena?

Renaud backtracked, his steps long and hurried. After checking the chapel and finding it empty, he strode toward the great hall to find

Elena sitting before the large fire, Galeran across from her, playing a game of chess. Galeran stood at his approach. "My lord?"

"Have you seen Aleysia?"

Galeran shook his head and looked at Elena. "Nay, I have not seen her since dinner," she said.

"Would you like me to search with you, my lord?" Galeran asked, but Renaud shook his head.

"Nay, finish your game. I shall see you both on the morrow."

Renaud next checked the bailey, and as he passed the gatehouse a guard called out, "My lord, do you look for the woman?"

Renaud stopped in midstride. "Do you speak of Lady Aleysia?"

The soldier nodded. "Aye, my lord. She passed this way over an hour ago. Said she needed to go to the healer, to assist with a difficult birthing, and said that she had your permission."

His stomach twisted. "She was alone?"

"Yes, my lord."

With a curse, he raced back up the bridge, to the tower, taking the steps two at a time, his fury growing with each step. The two guards jumped at his approach. "My lord, what is amiss?"

"Open that door!"

One of the nervous guards fumbled with the keys, dropping the chain once before slipping the correct key into the lock. Renaud pushed open the door and entered. He closed it behind him, and the body on the cot jumped.

His heart pounded harder with each step that brought him nearer. A sliver of light shone through the high window. The blanket covered the form that lay there, now still as could be. Renaud reached down and ripped the blanket off.

He cursed loudly. Wearing only a thin chemise, Aleysia didn't move. But she was awake. She trembled and he doubted it had anything to do with the cold.

He shook with fury. He should have known. Aleysia had given her brother her clothing. What a fool he was. His father had been right about women being untrustworthy, and was probably rolling over in his grave. To care for a woman meant to lose one's wits, and he most assuredly had lost his wits to let Adelstan disappear right beneath his nose, along with the help of the woman who had been sharing his bed. The woman who had sent a message to her betrothed in Scotland to come wage war on Braemere. She had betrayed Renaud at every turn. He should never have trusted her after her last deceit.

It burned to know that all along she had been planning Adelstan's escape.

"What have you done, Aleysia?" he asked, his voice strangely calm, considering the fury that raced within him.

She rolled onto her back, her green eyes locking with his. There was no triumph there, no gloating. "I had to, Renaud. He is my brother, and without him I would die."

Her eyes were red and puffy from crying, and he wondered if she cried because she knew the trouble she was now in, or because she still feared for her brother.

"I trusted you, Aleysia."

Tears welled in her eyes. "Let him go, Renaud. I beg you. Just let him go—"

"I cannot do that."

She sat up, and the chemise fell off her shoulder, exposing the swell of one ripe breast. "Why not?"

Even now, when he was furious with her, he wanted her. Damn her! Her neck still bore the rash from his whiskers when they had made love so frantically in their chamber. They shared the same lust and passion. What a shame they were, and always would be, enemies.

He pulled his gaze from the creamy expanse of her neck and firm breasts, back to her face. "We have been through this more times than I can count. King William expects Adelstan at York, and I *will* bring Adelstan before him."

"I will never forgive you if you go after him."

"I must."

She reached for him, catching his hand within her own. "Renaud, let him go. I beg you."

"Is there more I should know, Aleysia? Any more treasonous acts you wish to tell me about before I find out on my own?"

"Nothing, I swear it!"

"You swear it?"

She nodded, her fingers tightened around his. "Renaud, please believe me."

His blood boiled in his veins. How innocent she looked. He lifted her hand. "What of the ring you used to wear?"

She turned pale. "I can—"

He took the ring from his pocket and slid it back on Aleysia's finger.

She swallowed hard, but said nothing.

"I will *never* trust you again."

Her fingers tightened around his.

It was the hardest thing he had ever done, but for his own sanity he jerked his hand away. Without another word, he turned on his heel and left.

Renaud and a handful of men had been riding for hours when they came upon a cloaked figure in the distance. A lone rider, moving at a steady clip for the Scottish border. They had traveled most of the night, and now with the gray of dawn upon them, they had finally caught their man.

Adelstan. There was no question it was the Saxon, for Renaud recognized Aleysia's cloak.

"Congratulations, my lord," Galeran said triumphantly. "You have found your man. We will be back at Braemere before the sun sets."

Renaud waited for the exhilaration he normally felt when capturing a Saxon prisoner, but this time it did not come. Instead, a part of him was disappointed that Adelstan had not escaped. "Give me a moment alone with him," Renaud said to Galeran and the other men, who shared puzzled looks.

"Are you sure that is wise, my lord? He could have a weapon." Galeran asked, concern in his eyes.

"Aye, I am sure. I will be but a moment."

Galeran nodded, and Renaud rode ahead toward Adelstan.

To Adelstan's credit, he did not try to outrun Renaud. Instead, the Saxon turned to Renaud, a slight smile on his lips, as though he'd expected him all along. In that moment he looked so much older than eight and ten—tired, defeated . . . as though he had already given up.

His eyes, so like his sister's, stared back at Renaud. "I am surprised it took you so long, de Wulf."

Renaud smiled at the young man's wit. "I am surprised you did not try to outrun us, Adelstan."

"My horse is already laboring with the pace we've set thus far. I did not feel it fair to ride him to his death when he has served me so well." Adelstan ran a hand over the horse's neck. "He is weary . . . just as I am."

Renaud could only imagine how exhausted the young man was. The past few weeks, not to mention years, must have aged him immensely. "You know I must take you to York."

Adelstan nodded, looking past Renaud to the outlying hills, where the sun was just getting ready to make its appearance. "Our mother always loved to get up before the sunrise. She often would wake us, take us by the hand, and together we would watch it rise in all its glory." His lips curved. "Aleysia would lean her head back, close her eyes, and smile." He glanced at Renaud. "She continued to do the same after our parents were killed. She said it gave her hope to see the sun rise each morning. That each new day was a new beginning full of limitless possibilities." He laughed without mirth. "If only I had her faith."

"You must have had faith to get this far in life."

"True, true. But my sister is the stronger of us. She is a willful woman. Sometimes she knows not her place, but she is loyal to the bone."

"I know. She loves you very much, Adelstan. She has risked much to see you live."

"I hope you do not punish her. It was my idea to escape, after all."

168

"I doubt your sister is as innocent as you claim," he said, running a hand through his hair. "I must set an example, else word will carry across the north that I have been manipulated by a woman."

Adelstan frowned, anger in his eyes. "She cares deeply for you, and still you would punish her?"

The words shocked Renaud, yet pleased him. "She has told you as much?"

His lips quirked. "We are twins, and we feel each other in a way that I cannot explain. I often know what she's thinking before she even opens her mouth, and likewise."

"I have heard it said that twins share such a bond."

"Such is the case between my sister and I. You had made a bargain with her, de Wulf." He twisted the reins about his fist. "I know what that bargain was, and now I ask you to make a bargain with me."

Renaud frowned. "I can make no promises, Adelstan. I have a duty to my king."

"This is a promise from one man to another. From a brother who loves his sister more than life itself." Adelstan swallowed hard and Renaud could see he fought to keep his emotions in check. "I ask that you never leave her. Though she has proven resourceful when need be, she is not accustomed to being alone. And I would hate to think—"

"I will marry her, Adelstan. God willing, I will take her as my wife, and she will never be alone again. I will protect her with everything that I am. You have my word on this."

Adelstan smiled and Renaud's stomach coiled, for he saw Aleysia in that wide grin.

And in that moment he realized that he could not, with good conscience, take this man to York to certain death.

King William would be furious with him. Perhaps strip him of his titles and lands, nor would his men understand—but he could not live with himself if he killed Adelstan, for taking him to King William was the same as slitting the young Saxon's throat.

Renaud glanced over his shoulder at his men who watched intently before turning back to Adelstan. "I release you, Adelstan. Go now, before I change my mind."

Adelstan's brows furrowed. "You are letting me go? Do you jest?"

"Nay, I do not jest. But I give you fair warning. If you return with MacMillan to Braemere, I will not be so forgiving."

"MacMillan has betrayed me, and I will never trust him again. You have my word that I will not return with him, but I do hope to return to Braemere one day—to see my sister. God willing, we will both live to see that day."

"I pray it is so."

"You do me a great service, my lord." Adelstan extended his hand. "You are a man of honor, de Wulf. I shall never forget your kindness toward me."

"Go, make haste to the border—before I change my mind. God be with you, Adelstan."

"And you." Adelstan nudged his horse and off they rode, toward the border.

Renaud waited until Adelstan was but a spot on the horizon before wheeling his steed about and heading toward his men and Braemere.

SIXTEEN

Dear God, what was taking them?

Certainly Renaud and the others would be back by now. It had been a couple of days since Renaud had left Braemere. Had they rode straight to York after capturing Adelstan?

Aleysia pushed the tray of cold pottage away. A guard had brought the food to her, frowning at her and cursing beneath his breath all the way. No doubt the young soldier had received a fierce tongue lashing, or more, from Renaud for not seeing through Adelstan's disguise. *Let him be angry*, she thought to herself, for by damned she would not apologize to him . . . or to Renaud.

Aleysia heard the sound of spurs on the stone steps outside the chamber and her heart raced wildly. The lock clicked and Galeran stepped in. Disappointed, she chewed on her bottom lip and glanced past his shoulder, hoping Renaud would be on his heels, but no one followed.

The handsome young knight's gold hair was matted to his head, evidence that he had only just returned. His ice blue eyes beheld no welcome. Rather, his lips were in a flat, firm line, his jaw set. "My lady, I am here to escort you to your chamber, where you will find a bath and clean clothing."

"Is my brother at Braemere?" she blurted, needing desperately to know the answer.

The young soldier gave her a black, angry glance. "I come by my lord's request. I am to tell you that your imprisonment in the tower has come to an end. I will show you to your quarters, where several guards will be stationed outside. Come, let us not dally."

Galeran motioned for her to exit the chamber, and he followed. It was clear he was in no mood for conversation, so she refrained from speaking at all.

She stopped outside Renaud's bedchamber but the soldier said, "Nay, my lady. Your bedchamber is elsewhere."

She frowned, not sure why she should be surprised Renaud had removed her from his chamber. He had told her to her face that he did not trust her—that he never would again. Lord only knew what he had planned for her now.

She heard voices coming from the room—one voice Renaud's, the other clearly female. Mixed feelings surged through her, among them jealousy and rage. To her horror, she had half a mind to throw open the door and confront him. The woman on the other side of the door laughed again, and Aleysia dug her fingernails into her palms.

"Come, my lady," Galeran said, taking her by the arm and escorting her down the stairs. Though his hold on her was not at all tight, she felt very much like a prisoner.

He needn't worry. She would not flee. She had nowhere else to go now that she knew the truth about Duncan.

The chamber where she was being held was dark save for the single light that shone in from the tall, narrow window. A bath had been poured for her before the fire, and she had lingered in it until it grew cold—as cold as her heart felt. She wanted answers. She desperately needed to know what had happened to her brother.

And, she wondered what her own fate would be.

An hour later, freshly bathed, wearing a clean yellow kirtle, Aleysia took Galeran's arm and he escorted her downstairs to the great hall. She did not bother initiating conversation, certain his anger had not dissipated in such a short amount of time.

The normal joviality of the hall had diminished and silence welcomed them as they entered. Aleysia wouldn't be surprised if they stoned her to death.

At a glance she knew a good number of men were missing, and Renaud was not on the dais as usual. Dear Lord, had they already journeyed to York? She suddenly remembered Renaud telling Galeran he was to stay behind in order to keep an eye on Braemere.

Elena was already seated at the high table. As the two of them approached, the older woman waved them over.

Thank God she had one friend amongst all these enemies. Tears burned the backs of her eyes and Elena must have seen her distress, for she stood and hugged Aleysia.

"You look pale, my dear," Elena said, brushing the tears from Aleysia's cheeks. "How about some warm wine? That ought to help soothe your nerves."

"That would be nice. Thank you."

"Sit," Elena said, motioning for a page to come forward and pour the wine. The sound of a lute filled the high-ceilinged room, and Aleysia was reminded of the gypsy girl who had danced so provocatively. She did not see the barons who had been visiting the other night, and hoped that they had left, along with their gypsy friends. Or mayhap that's who had been in Renaud's chamber with him? The gypsy girl. The thought did not help her mood and though she tried to relax, she found she could not, and picked at the duck that had been set before her.

Galeran and Elena flirted throughout the meal, and from time to time the beautiful woman would try to involve Aleysia in the conversation. Aleysia realized with a sinking feeling that she would probably never know what it was like to share such times with Renaud.

Finally, when she could stand it no longer, she asked, "Elena, is your brother at Braemere?"

Elena glanced at Aleysia, her brows drawn together. "Aye, I would have thought he had spoken to you by now."

Aleysia's pulse skittered. "He is still here, then?"

Which meant that Adelstan must be here, too.

Renaud stared into the flames. A tray sat on a nearby table, untouched, the smell enticing, despite the fact that he had no appetite. He had not been able to eat since arriving back at Braemere.

Even more, he could not make sense of his feelings where Aleysia was concerned. Nor could anyone else, his men included.

His vassals had been silent from the moment they had left Adelstan at the border. Still, he could not forget the looks on their faces when he told them they were not bringing Adelstan back to Braemere. Galeran had even reminded him of his duty to William, and the repercussions for allowing Adelstan to escape. Finally, Renaud had told him to be quiet, and they had ridden back to Braemere in silence.

All his life he had been loyal. A loyal son, a loyal vassal, a loyal friend. Always, his God came first, and then his king. But now he had defied his king . . . and he knew he would pay. At what cost remained to be seen. Perhaps everything—even his lands and titles in Sussex. Everything he had spent a lifetime attaining, gone.

Upon entering Braemere's gates, his gaze had gone to the tower where Aleysia was imprisoned . . . unless she had outsmarted his men yet again. He would not put it past her.

Why had he made the damnable bargain with her to begin with? Had he just thrown her in the prison alongside her brother, his future would not now be in jeopardy.

But he had let his lust guide him. Rather than allow Aleysia to become a pawn of King William's, he had instead made her his leman and now he would lose everything because of it.

Though he was angry with her, he was even angrier with himself and the desire he still felt for her. Aye, he should ship her off to Scotland, back to her betrothed. Trouble was, he had no desire to rid himself of her, despite all her lies and deceit.

Yet he had been the one to let Adelstan go, and he and he alone would suffer for it. Not his men. Not even Aleysia, who could very well still become William's pawn. He feared what his king had planned for her. Would he give her to another baron, for he had little doubt Braemere would be handed to another since he had let Adelstan go?

When he should have been furious at her for having let Adelstan escape to begin with, he instead worried if she had suffered in the past two days. Had she been warm enough with just her chemise and threadbare blanket? Had she enough to eat? The guards would be angry with her for outwitting them, and though he had told them to treat her as they would any other traitor to the crown, he realized too late that the treatment might be too harsh for a woman.

While the questions raced through his mind, the walls around him seemed to close in, and everywhere he looked he thought of Aleysia. Aleysia standing by the window in her male attire, furious and angry with him, and no doubt herself, for offering her body for her brother's safety. Then she had stripped off her clothes, and he had taken her that first time. He remembered the way she had responded to his touch, how she had fought herself and her feelings.

Even now he could see her as she stood before the fire, her body bathed in the warm light as she nervously awaited him. The way she bit into her bottom lip, her light green eyes full of questions she was too proud to ask. If only she knew how she had gotten into his blood.

He stood with a curse, upending the chair in his haste. It seemed no matter how hard he tried, he could not escape her. He ran a hand through his hair in frustration. Would this madness never end?

Leaving his chamber, he headed for a place where he could clear his head. In the bailey he could hear laughter, his men in high spirits, no doubt drinking heavily of the ale that flowed so freely here at Braemere. He had never been one to abide drunkenness—for it dulled one's wits, but tonight even he was tempted to drink until he no longer felt the cold ache in his chest.

Seeking solitude, he made his way to the ramparts, to the place he first met Aleysia.

The wind hit him full in the face, and he welcomed the cold chill, inhaled deeply of the fresh breeze. There was not a cloud in the sky, the stars twinkling down on him, the full moon bathing the English countryside with its glow. How he had coveted this keep and the lands that went with her. So beautiful—much like her mistress. He had held both in his grasp, and let them slide through his fingers like sand. "What have I done?" he asked aloud, as though he expected his father to answer. No doubt he would be horrified at what Renaud had given up.

And all for the sake of a woman.

Weak, he would say, his voice heavy with disappointment.

"My lord, I am sorry to disturb you."

Shocked he had not heard Galeran's approach, Renaud turned to find his vassal and Elena, and directly behind them, Aleysia, who stepped out from behind the two.

His heart gave a fierce tug. How fragile she looked, dressed in the pale yellow gown that emphasized her full breasts, the bodice too tight. Her hair shone brilliantly under the moon's rays, recently washed and falling in curls to her hips. Lavender with a hint of vanilla drifted to him, and he smiled. He would always associate the scent with her.

"May I have a word with you, my lord?" Aleysia asked, taking another step toward him, looking nervous yet determined as she lifted her chin and made direct eye contact.

Renaud glanced at his vassal, who dropped his gaze between them, then up to his sister, who watched him intently. He knew his sister well enough to know she had coerced Galeran into bringing Aleysia with him. "We will be nearby, brother, if you have need of us." Taking Galeran by the hand, the two left.

Aleysia shifted on her feet and looked ready to bolt. "Where is my brother?"

How exasperating this woman was. "I do not know."

Her brows furrowed. "What do you mean?"

"I mean just that. I know not where Adelstan is."

"Do you jest?"

"I never jest, Aleysia. You should know that by now."

"You never found him?"

"Nay, I found him."

She crossed her arms over her chest. "I do not understand."

"Do you not?" How beautiful she was, even with her brows drawn together, confusion written all over her face. Though his better judgment told him it would be best to walk away from her here and now, he could not help himself. He brushed his fingertips along her jaw, over her lips, his thumb caressing the fullness there. "I let him go, Aleysia."

She gasped, and pulled away as though he'd pinched her. "Why?"

"In truth, I do not know, especially when I had every intention of bringing him before King William. He was at the border, and he did not try to outrun us. I think he was as surprised as you are that I released him."

She looked bewildered. "He lives?"

He dropped his hands to his sides. "I pray it is so."

"Aye, as do I." Tears filled her eyes, and then she shocked him when she took the step that separated them and hugged him tight, her arms encircling his neck, her cheek flush against his chest. "Thank you, Renaud. Thank you."

He shook with the need to embrace her in return, but he didn't trust himself to. She sniffled and looked up at him, her cheeks stained by her tears.

"Why do you cry? I thought this news would please you."

Her lips curved into a smile that made his heart miss a beat. "Because I am happy that my brother is well and free. I will forever be indebted to you, my lord."

She went on the tips of her toes and kissed him. 'Twas a gentle kiss, soft, swift. To his shock, her fingers wove through his hair and she deepened the kiss.

The blood coursed hot through his veins, his body completely aware of the woman kissing him, her fingers tightening in his hair. His cock strained against his braies, hard, throbbing. He brushed against her stomach and she felt it, for she gasped against his lips.

But she did not pull away.

In fact, she deepened the kiss, her tongue thrusting against his lips, seeking entry. And when he opened, she moaned low in her throat, her arms tightening about his neck.

Knowing he could wait no longer, he pulled away from her. "What do you want, Aleysia?"

"I wish to go to your chamber, but only if the woman is gone."

He frowned, not sure what she meant by such a remark, then he remembered the servant who had scrubbed his back when he had bathed earlier. The woman, twenty years his senior, was beautiful, yet happily married to the blacksmith, but Aleysia need not know that. Her jealousy rather pleased him. "I assure you, my lady, there is no one there now."

"Yet what of later? Will she return after I have gone?" she asked mockingly.

"Gone where, my lady?"

"To my new quarters. Is it far enough away from you, my lord? If not, mayhap I could find a room in the barn with the horses. Or perhaps in the armory, or even in the hall with your knights. At least that way they could keep an eye on me."

"Do you wish to return to my chamber, Aleysia?"

Her gaze searched his, as though she did not trust herself to answer.

"Do you want me to?"

"I asked if you wanted to."

She lifted her chin a fraction. "Aye, I do."

Everything within him screamed to be wary of this woman, who had tricked him time and again, but his heart won out. Taking her by the hand, they hurried down the steps, passing by Galeran and Elena, who were kissing in a small alcove but jumped apart the moment Renaud and Aleysia were upon them. Elena did not look embarrassed by the indiscretion, but Galeran's cheeks were considerably darker than they'd been moments before. He cleared his throat. "May I be of assistance, my lord?"

"You are free of your duty this night, Galeran. Enjoy. I shall speak to you on the morrow."

Impatient to reach his chambers, Renaud lifted Aleysia in his arms. They passed by two servants, who quickly got out of their way. The two women giggled and Aleysia hid her face in the crook of his neck.

SEVENTEEN

Renaud opened the chamber door, then set Aleysia on her feet. The fire had died a little, the flames not as fierce, yet the room was warm. Aleysia smoothed her gown, her fingers trembling.

How nervous she was! Kicking off his boots, Renaud made quick work of his tunic, chausses, and braies. Her gaze fell from his, drawn slowly downward. His body responded, as though she touched him. The fire in her eyes could not hide her desire and he reveled in it, his cock lengthening, thickening with the need to possess her.

She walked toward him, lifting the gown up and off, tossing it aside. With a growl, he pulled her against him, kissing her, his tongue parrying with hers as his hands slid down the smooth skin of her back, cupping her buttocks, pulling her up against his erection.

He buried a hand in her hair, holding her by the back of the neck, kissing her harder as his need grew stronger. She sighed as his other hand caressed her breast, his fingers playing with the hardened nipple before moving lower, over the soft swell of her stomach, and finally through the curls of her womanhood.

Her breath hitched as he parted her, his thumb stroking her clit, his fingers finding her moist, heated center. He inserted one finger, following with another.

"Renaud," she whispered against his lips.

"Yes?"

"I want . . ."

He pulled away just enough to look into her eyes. The light green orbs were dark with passion and desire. "What is it you want?"

She licked her lips, her breathing growing shallow as his fingers and thumb continued to stroke her. "I want to feel you."

Her hand slid from his ass to his cock, her fingers caressing him in a practiced rhythm.

Soon he was the one breathing hard, right along with her.

He brought her down on the rug, pushing open her thighs as he settled between them. She lifted her hips, coaxing him to take her.

He leaned down, kissed her, his tongue stroking hers, rubbing his cock against her weeping core as she wriggled beneath him.

He could feel her frustration. Just as she would find him, he would pull away, teasing her, wanting her to ache as he did.

Bending over her, he took a nipple into his mouth, and her fingers threaded through his hair, holding him tight to her breast, as though she would never let go.

Aleysia looked down at Renaud, watching as he pleasured her, his lashes thick against his cheekbones, his tongue long and so skillful as he suckled her, using his teeth just enough to have her panting. She arched against him, urging him to take her, to bury his long, thick length within her. She burned for it.

And he knew it.

Her fingernails scraped along his shoulders as she released a loud sigh.

His cock brushed against her bud, and that slight pressure had her body throbbing, pulsing. A delicious sensation, making her wetter and hotter. She groaned low in her throat.

"That's it, my love," he said, knowing she was ready to climax, knowing she still ached for him.

When she had had her release, she coaxed him over onto his back. He frowned a little, but said nothing as she went on her knees between his thighs, lowered her head and took his length into her mouth.

His satisfied moan filled the chamber, bringing her intense pleasure. He was so large she could only take so much of his impressive length in her mouth. She suckled lightly, taking care, just as he had with her nipples, being sure to not use her teeth or to hurt him in any way. Instead, she licked, stroked, sucked, learning as she went, gauging her progress with each sigh, intake of breath, and satisfied moan. She found she enjoyed being in control.

He reached out to her, taking her breasts in his hands, but she pulled away, wanting him to receive pleasure for once.

She spread her fingers on his thighs, her thumbs drawing little circles on the sensitive flesh there. "Ride me, Aleysia," he said, the words torn from him.

He lifted her, and with knees on either side of his hips, she sat down on his huge cock, taking him within her, inch by delicious inch. He groaned, caressing her breasts, teasing her nipples as she started to rock.

Making no move to help out, he lay back, watching her through lowered lids. "You're so hot, Aleysia. So wet."

The words excited her, and the more he played with her nipples, the wetter she became, sliding along his hard rod, her pace increasing with each stroke. "You make me wet, Renaud."

The sides of his mouth lifted, and he leaned forward, laving her nipple with his silky tongue.

She rotated her hips, and he bit down the slightest bit, the sensation not at all unpleasant.

Renaud's blood coursed through his veins, his balls tightening with each down stroke. As he continued to suckle her, her rhythm increased. Her fingers bit into his shoulders, and her sheath contracted hard, pulling him in deeper as her climax rocked her body.

He held her hips tight as he thrust deeper, filling her with every last drop of his seed.

Aleysia watched Renaud, who had left the bed moments ago to stoke the fire. She stared, memorizing every detail of his beautiful strong, body. The fire had cast his form in shadow, the planes emphasized, the muscles bunching beneath the golden skin she longed to touch again. She would never tire of looking at him.

She knew he was to leave for York in the morning, and hated the thought of parting, especially since she felt they had come so far this night. He did not trust her, and with good reason, but she hoped in time that would change.

Perhaps they could have a future together? She still could not believe he had let Adelstan go—and at what cost? How would William react when Renaud arrived at York without Adelstan?

From what she had heard of William, and from her experience, she knew he would be disappointed in Renaud. He had been such a loyal vassal.

As though sensing her perusal, Renaud glanced over at her. He smiled, flashing white teeth, and she could not help but grin. How safe she felt with this man who weeks ago she had not even known existed. How strange fate was.

He climbed back into bed, and she snuggled against his hard length, her fingers wandering over his chest, a finger sliding over a long scar there.

She was accustomed to men and their scars, knowing that in a time of war there would be many battle wounds. But now she yearned to know the story behind each of Renaud's scars. "How did you get this?" she asked, before she could stop herself.

He glanced down at her, and then at the scar. "At the Battle of Hastings. A Saxon about twice my age came at me with a battle axe. I had never seen such a weapon, particularly at such close range."

She laughed at his expression. "You must have been terrified."

"Yes, though I struck him before he could do further damage," he said with a cocky grin.

She looked down along his ribs. "And this one?"

He seemed amused by her curiosity but humored her. "I was quite young. Still a page, and in my haste to bring my knight his armor, I slipped on horse dung and fell. The shield left a nasty, jagged wound, as you can see."

Aleysia's heart clenched envisioning a young Renaud so eager to please, much like Galeran still was. "You jest."

"I never jest," he said, repeating his words of earlier that day. "Though I wish it had never happened, particularly in front of nearly fifty men."

She laughed softly, and kissed the scar on his chest before pulling the blanket aside to find more battle wounds. Lower, along his belly, next to his navel was a short scar, about an inch in length. "And this one?"

"I was two and twenty. A battle along my father's lands. The other man suffered far more than I."

"What did you fight about?"

"They grazed their cattle on our lands."

"Such a silly reason to fight."

"Many battles are fought over things that seem frivolous. But if you allow such acts, then people will push you further. You must stand your ground, always."

She kissed the mended wound and moved down his thigh, to a long scar. "And this one?"

"While hunting a boar."

"I am surprised the boar got you."

He grinned. "Aye, but I got him back."

She kissed the scar and moved to his other leg. "And this?"

"That would be compliments of Galeran."

"Galeran?" she asked, shocked that his friend had maimed him.

"Aye, he was practicing bow and arrow, and I apparently had been standing too close to the target."

"I bet he was horrified."

Renaud laughed, the sound making her smile. "Aye, he was. He turned as pale as the bed linen. I do not think he will ever forget it, or forgive himself."

"He is a loyal vassal."

"Aye, he is."

"What of your other scars?"

His brows drew together. "You did not kiss that one."

She leaned down and kissed it, noticing his cock was no longer flaccid, but had taken interest in this new game. "Roll over, my lord."

His eyes narrowed slightly. "Why?"

"So I may see all your scars."

"You will not drive a dagger into my back, will you?" Though there was humor in his eyes and in his tone, she realized that he might actually mean it, and again she knew she had a long way to go before she earned his trust again, if ever.

Hurt, she tried to hide her gaze, but he reached out and lifted her chin. "I know you would not hurt me, Aleysia. Not knowingly."

She smiled, relieved at his words. "Thank you, Renaud."

He rolled over then, his arms outstretched to his sides. Desires rippled through her. A tingling between her thighs began, deep in her woman's core. How beautiful he was. His strong back, his narrow hips, the tight globes of his ass, his long, muscular legs. She resisted the urge to lay on him and feel her body stretched across his hard length. Instead, she continued her quest and started at the scar behind his left knee. "This one?"

"A battle in Normandy."

She kissed it. "And this?" she asked, running a finger along a horribly long scar across his lower back.

"Ah, that one nearly killed me. I was but nine and ten. Not much older than you. My first real battle. A very angry Spaniard who wielded a nasty blade. I have never seen a man move so fast in all my days. Like a blurring of the eyes. Fate smiled upon me that day, for I got him with the first strike, but he did not go down without a fight. He fell to his knees and I made the mistake of turning my back. I felt a horrible pain in my back a moment later."

"It seems all your life you have been at war."

"Such is the life of a knight."

No wonder he was such a fierce warrior. He had to be, in order to survive. It was not a life she was used to. In truth, before the coming of King William, aside from the constant threat of Danish invasion, she had known little of war. It seemed that Renaud had known nothing but war. "How old were you when you left your home to become a knight?"

"I became a page at the age of six."

She gasped, horrified that a child would be sent from his family at such a young age.

"Some boys are sent even earlier."

"I cannot imagine sending my son away."

He glanced over his shoulder at her, his gray eyes intent. "A boy needs to find his own way. He cannot depend upon his mother his whole life. It will only weaken him."

"Weaken him? Nay, a son can learn much from his mother."

"Such as?"

"Loving, caring. Life is not all about war and defending one's things, my lord."

"Is it not?"

"Aye, I will never send my son away at such a young age. I could not."

"That is why you should hope for peace, my lady. Hope for peace so that you can always stay safe, and your children as well."

Not liking the talk of war, for it reminded her of their differences, she kissed the long scar, then moved to the one at his shoulder, which was still pink and puckered. The scar she had caused.

"That one came by way of a witch," he offered.

She gasped and slapped his ass.

His lips curved. "Aye, a witch with beautiful light green eyes, luscious long, blonde hair, and an aim that would make any soldier proud."

Pleased at the description, she leaned over and kissed the scar.

"And this one?" she asked, touching the scar on his cheek.

The playful smile disappeared. "A woman. A true witch."

"Indeed, and who was this witch?"

He rolled over, his hands folded behind his head, his cock semi-hard. "She was my betrothed."

Her stomach tightened. "And where is she now?"

"I do not know. Nor do I care."

"In truth?"

He nodded. "And what of you, Aleysia? What of your betrothed?"

"I do not love him, Renaud. You know that."

"Then why did you send for him?"

She twisted the ring on her finger guiltily. "I did so to save Adelstan. I had no idea Duncan had not asked for Adelstan when he came to Braemere. I swear on my life, Renaud, I would never have written that note had I known the truth."

He watched her a long time, searching her face and she held his steady gaze. "I swear on Adelstan's life."

He pursed his lips. "But you would marry him still?"

"I do not wish it." She sighed. "Since my parents died, my entire life has been full of uncertainty." Feeling awkward under his keen regard, she asked, "Have you ever loved anyone other than your family?"

"Nay."

How relieved she was to hear that single word.

He watched her for a long moment, and then pulled her into his arms, to where she lay full against him, her head against his chest, his cock firm against her belly. "You will stay with me, Aleysia. Forever."

He rolled her over, and went up on his elbows, staring down at her. His silver eyes shone brightly as he looked at her.

She reached up and brushed a strand of dark hair from his face. Turning his head, he shocked her by kissing her palm. "I want to stay with you, too."

He lifted a brow. "Forever?"

She nodded. "Yes, forever."

The sides of his mouth lifted before he kissed her.

She loved the feel of his body flush against her own. The powerful muscles that played beneath her fingers as she ran her hands down his strong back, and over his high, firm buttocks. Her insides coiled as his rock-hard rod pressed against her.

Her tongue traced the seam of his lips and he opened, kissing her gently. He slipped inside her and she gasped against his mouth, but did not pull away. Instead she chose to enjoy it, to give herself freely.

He made love to her so tenderly, so gently, and as he brought her quickly to orgasm, she wondered if the day would ever come that she could walk away from this man. Or God forbid, death take him from her.

EIGHTEEN

"My lady, would you care to join me for a game of chess?"

Aleysia jumped at Galeran's question. She had entered the hall only moments before, her thoughts on Renaud, who had left a few days before. She hated to admit it, but she missed him horribly, and everywhere she went in the castle she was reminded of him.

She recalled the morning he had left for York. He had been dressing and she had stared unabashedly, wanting to memorize every line, every muscle, of his body. He had looked up to find her staring, and still she remembered the softness in his eyes, in his smile. What a beautiful, desirable man he was. No wonder things had been whispered about him. There probably wasn't a woman alive who did not want him.

"Aleysia?"

Pushing away the thought, she replied, "Of course," and followed

Galeran toward the fire where two chairs and a table sat, a chessboard atop, the figures well worn from years of use. Her father's trusted servant had lovingly carved each piece and presented it to him on his fortieth birthday. It was one of the few items of her parents de Pirou had not destroyed.

She watched Galeran settle into the chair. The soldier reminded her of Adelstan. Of the same age, and of quick wit, he had proven to be as loyal to his liege as her brother had been to his.

"You do not like being left behind?" she asked, settling into the chair.

He looked up at her and shrugged. "I do not mind doing my duty. I just am not used to being idle for so long."

"You would rather be with Renaud?"

He nodded. "Aye, I would, even though I know he feels I serve him better by staying at Braemere."

"How did you come to be his squire?"

"Our fathers were friends, and when Renaud became a knight, my father asked Renaud if I could serve under him."

"You must have been young."

"Aye, seven."

"Did you miss your home?"

Galeran's lips curved a little. "Very much, but his lordship was kind and always kept me busy. Many thought him too soft toward me. He was not, though. He treated me more like a brother."

"Did you always get along as you do now?"

He pursed his lips. "Aye, I served him faithfully, and I still do."

There was no denying the pride in his expression and voice. "And what of Elena?"

The Bargain

Galeran's gaze dropped, instantly flustered. "I have known her since she was a young woman."

"She is beautiful."

A blush rose from his neck to his cheeks. "Indeed, she is."

"What was Renaud like when he was younger?" Aleysia asked, sensing how uncomfortable he was with the current line of questioning. Also, she was curious about the man who had come rushing into her life. A man she could not purge from her thoughts, no matter how hard she tried.

"His father was a huge man, who had a penchant for fighting and telling far-fetched tales. His mother was Austrian, and what a beauty she was. Hair as black as night, and eyes as gray as the rain-filled clouds."

"Much like Renaud's and Elena's?"

His white teeth flashed. "Aye, indeed, much like Renaud's and Elena's."

"Are his parents still living?"

"Nay, both are dead."

"How sad. I know what it is to lose one's parents."

"His father's death hurt him greatly."

"But not his mother's?"

Galeran took a sudden interest in setting the board. "Nay, she was not a good wife, or mother."

"In what way?"

"What do we have here?" a feminine voice said, and Aleysia looked up to find Elena watching the two of them.

Galeran stood so fast, he nearly upended his chair.

"My lady, please join us."

195

"I do not wish to interfere," she said with a coy smile, even as she took a seat. "I was hoping we would hear news from York. This waiting is agony."

Aleysia nodded. "Indeed, it is."

Elena frowned, concern in her eyes. "I fear by allowing Adelstan to escape, that Renaud stands to lose everything."

Aleysia's heart skipped a beat. "You mean Braemere?"

Galeran dropped his gaze to the chessboard, and remained silent.

"Certainly, William would not strip him of Braemere after securing her?"

"Aye, but his duty was to secure Braemere and bring Adelstan before William in York. True, he secured Braemere, but William expects absolute loyalty. He will not be happy to learn that Adelstan is free and therefore still a threat."

"What if he is stripped of Braemere? What becomes of the fief?"

Elena brushed out her skirts. "I fear it could be given to another baron. One who has found favor with William." She forced a smile. "Do not fret so, Aleysia. My brother has lands in the south of England. All is not lost."

But the south of England was not Braemere.

"And what of me?"

Galeran looked at Elena. "Enough," he said, the words barely above a whisper.

"'Tis only fair. Would you not want to know your fate?" Elena lifted a dark brow. "She should know what might await her, Galeran."

With a curse, Galeran folded his arms over his chest.

Elena ignored him. "You could be given to the new lord of Braemere."

Aleysia gasped. "Nay."

"'Tis true." Elena lay a gentle hand on Aleysia's shoulder. "It has happened all over England. It is William's way to make peace with the Saxons. You must prepare yourself for the worst."

"I will not marry a Norman."

"Not even my brother?"

Aleysia opened her mouth to deny the words, yet she found she could not. It was odd, but she didn't look at Renaud or even Galeran as her enemy anymore.

Elena's lips curved. "God willing, you will not be given to another. I pray that William shows Renaud leniency. I hope that my brother will return and Braemere will still be in his possession."

A shiver rushed through Aleysia at the prospect of lying in a stranger's bed. "I would rather die than marry another."

"What of your Scot?"

What of Duncan? She no longer felt the same way about her father's friend. He was not to be trusted. No longer someone she could depend on. "I do not trust him. Not after he denied Adelstan."

"I admire your brother," Elena said. "Though I never met him, the stories I have heard speak of a proud, fiercely loyal man."

Aleysia smiled at Elena's analysis. "Aye, but he also has a huge heart."

She laughed, the sound like music. "Much like my brother."

Aleysia had never thought of Renaud de Wulf as having a huge heart.

"You think not?" Elena queried.

"I have not known him for very long, but I do know he can be kind."

Elena's gaze shifted to Galeran. As the young soldier glanced at Elena, Aleysia feigned a yawn, wanting to give the two time alone. "I think I shall take a nap before supper. I did not sleep well last night."

"Sleep well, my dear," Elena said, looking not at all sorry to see her go.

As Aleysia started for her bedchamber, she wondered what Renaud was doing and if he thought of her even a little. She hoped so, for the days seemed endless without him.

Three guards followed her to the tower and up the stairs to her bedchamber. She had grown accustomed to their presence, and actually felt protected with Renaud gone. Nothing would happen to her, she knew that much.

She lay down for a while, but sleep would not come, so finally she picked up her embroidery out of the basket. She looked down at the likeness of Braemere castle on the fabric. She hoped that she could stay here with Renaud. She closed her eyes and said a silent prayer.

Aleysia worked only for a few minutes and stuck her finger twice. With a frustrated oath she set the embroidery aside and sucked on her injured finger. No matter what she did, she could not keep her mind from Renaud and William's decision. Perhaps that was why he had been detained.

Though dinner would be ready soon, she stayed in her chamber, in no mood to converse when she was in such a sullen mood. Instead, she stared at the flames in the hearth, wondering what had become of the two men she cared for most in the world. God willing, her brother had found a safe place to stay.

And he had that chance because of Renaud. Her heart swelled. She realized with a start that she might actually love Renaud de Wulf.

A knock sounded at the door, making Aleysia jump. No doubt it was Elena, come to see if she would join her for supper.

She opened the door to find two men staring back at her. Both wearing cloaks, their faces hidden in shadow. She heard a moan behind the men, and realized too late what had happened.

She opened her mouth to scream, but one of the men moved fast, and shoved a rag inside her mouth. The other tied her hands behind her back, and then she was lifted into the air.

Kicking and flailing with all her might only got her a smack to her bottom. Every step down the stairs made her head jar, and she tried to squirm again.

"Stop it, Aleysia. We have come to take you home."

She stopped squirming, wondering if she had heard him right. Mayhap Adelstan had rallied a small army and they had come to her rescue? Her mind raced. Thank God he was alive and well!

Cold air enveloped her, and then the man was running, the ground racing past Aleysia.

Finally, she was set on her feet. They had made it outside the bailey, into the forest without being seen. At least, she had not heard any of the guards yell out. In the distance, she could make out the silhouette of at least four dozen men. No doubt Adelstan would be among them.

One of the men helped her onto a mount, and climbed on behind her. She searched the awaiting crowd, anxiously looking for her brother.

The closer they came to the group, the more nervous she became. She did not see Adelstan, and knew he would have made himself known to her by now.

Then she recognized one figure, a tall man astride a horse, the dark helmet hiding his features. But she would know him anywhere. Her heart sank to her toes. Duncan.

She looked toward the castle, hoping someone was in pursuit, but there was no one. No signal, no sign of anyone at all.

Her mind raced, wondering what to do. She could never outrun the men, for they were all on horseback. Nay, the only thing she could do was make Duncan believe she wanted this. After all, she had sent the letter asking for his help.

Her heart slammed against her ribs as they approached Duncan, who took off his helm—his dark eyes traveling over her in a way that made her shift in the saddle. She did not like the possessiveness of his gaze one bit.

He brought his horse alongside. "She will ride with me," he said gruffly, and the Scot who had been riding behind her immediately dismounted and helped her onto Duncan's horse.

Aleysia settled in front of Duncan, her back ramrod straight as not to touch him.

But he would have none of it. He wrapped a beefy arm about her waist, pulling her tight to him, to where she could feel every inch of the front of him, even his rigid manhood.

She shuddered.

"It is time to go home, Aleysia," he said, his lips brushing against her ear. "You are safe now."

NINETEEN

"Galeran, you have grown quiet. Is something amiss?"

Galeran, who had been staring off into the distance, looked up at Elena. The beautiful widow's blue-gray eyes mirrored the concern in her voice, and he smiled to put her mind at ease. "I apologize for being such a poor dinner companion, my lady."

She placed a hand on his thigh, her long fingers brushing up and down, coming dangerously close to his cock. "Do you miss my brother?"

In truth, he had been thinking of Renaud . . . until her hand had touched his thigh. He did not like being left behind, nor had he imagined it would take Renaud this long to complete his business in York. No message had been sent, which worried him immensely. He had very nearly dispatched a man to journey to York Castle this morning, just to inquire, but reconsidered, knowing Renaud would be furious.

He knew he should not worry so, and though Renaud had not marched off to battle, these were dangerous times and anything could happen. "Aye, I do."

"You are a loyal vassal," she whispered, her warm breath stirring his hair. How beautiful she was. Her skin like porcelain, her hair like silk. How he yearned to see it down, falling about her hips in thick waves. Oh to run his fingers through the shiny, rich brown locks.

"Thank you, Lady Elena."

She laughed. "Such formality between us, Galeran. Please, call me Elena."

He swallowed past the lump in his throat. "Very well, Elen—uh," the last cut off as her hand brushed against his erection.

Her lips curved in a coy smile. "I know something that will keep your mind off of my brother."

His gaze fell to her lips. They were full and red, and he ached to feel them beneath his own. She must have sensed his need, for she leaned forward and whispered, "Come to my chamber." Before he could blink, she had walked away.

He looked guiltily about the hall, grateful to find everyone busy conversing. Perhaps no one would miss him for a short while?

His heart pounded loudly in his ears with every step that brought him closer to Elena's chamber. He knocked, and immediately the door flew open and he was pulled inside.

Elena kissed him, her tongue slipping past his lips to taste him.

His arms came around her, and he was shocked to feel bare skin beneath his hands. He moved to put her at arm's length, wanting to see her, but she held him too tight. Sensing she might be just as nervous as he, he held her and she relaxed.

A few minutes later his hands moved down her body, over her slender back, full hips, and over her rounded bottom. Growing more daring, he took hold of that luscious bottom and squeezed. She gasped against his mouth, and her lips left his, drawing a path downward, along his throat while she pulled his tunic up and off him, flinging it aside.

He caught a glimpse of her full breasts with dark-rose nipples and the triangle of dark hair between her thighs, before her lips continued their journey down his body. His breath left him in a rush when she went to her knees, kissing his navel while untying his braies.

His hands tightened on her shoulders as she looked up at him, her beautiful eyes framed by long, thick lashes. "You have the body of a god," she said, causing his cock to lengthen and thicken.

A delicious thrill wracked his body as she leaned forward and took him deep into her mouth. His stomach tightened as she sucked, nibbled, and continued to pleasure him in a way he'd never been pleasured before. Her fingers drifted along his thighs, and along his ballocks, where she stroked him, while her hot mouth continued to bring him closer to climax.

He would spend himself if she continued in such a way. "Elena," he said, pulling her up with more force than intended.

She smiled as she kissed him, her fingers seeking his cock, but he jerked away, shaking his head. "Nay, do not touch me or I will spill before I have you."

"We do not want that now, do we?" she said, helping him out of his clothes, before taking him by the hand and leading him toward her bed.

How long had he dreamt of this moment? Her body was beautiful. Not the body of a girl, but of a woman. Her full breasts were not as high as women half her age, but they were pleasing, as were the width of her hips and the fine silver lines on her hips where her body had stretched when she was pregnant with her sons.

He imagined her pregnant with his sons, and smiled. It was a dream, a fantasy. After all, she had been married to a Norman lord, and would never marry a poor soldier, the sixth son of a baron who could offer her nothing in way of lands or wealth.

The thought was more than a little sobering, but it disappeared a moment later when she lay on her bed, and opened her arms up to him. "Come, Galeran. Make love to me."

She did not have to say it again.

He sat on the edge of the bed and looked down at her, starting at her dainty feet, and moving slowly upward. Her finely shaped legs were long and lean, her stomach slightly rounded, and her large breasts more than a handful. He stared, wanting to memorize every line of her body.

When finally his gaze met hers, he was surprised to see a vulnerability he had never before seen. "You are beautiful, Lady Elena."

She smiled and pulled him down beside her.

He could no longer prolong what he had been waiting for since the first time he had seen her. The thing he had been wanting to do since he was a boy, and she a young lady. Covering her with his body he guided his cock between her legs but she stopped him. "Not so fast, Galeran. A woman needs to be touched and her body warmed before welcoming a man inside her."

A blush raced up his neck to his cheeks. He had always been with whores or experienced women, and not once had they asked him to touch them. It had always been about his pleasure. "How do you want me to touch you?" His voice broke.

She smiled softly, and kissed him gently. "Touch me anywhere, but especially my breasts, my nipples, my mound."

Trembling, he bent his head and kissed the swell of her breast, and then the skin between. She moaned low in her throat and encouraged him to continue.

Laving a nipple, he took his time and suckled one, before attending to the other. Her thighs opened wider, and his cock nudged against her heated cleft.

Her fingers brushed along his ribs, over his back, up his shoulders, and then down over his buttocks. It seemed she touched him everywhere, save for his cock, but it did not matter. He was so excited, and he loved her touch.

Growing a bit more daring, he touched her belly, before his fingers brushed over the soft curls that covered her sex. He swallowed hard when she lifted her hips.

She was so hot down there, and surprisingly wet. Slipping a finger into her heat, he smiled when she moaned softly. "I'm ready," she whispered against his ear, nipping at it, her tongue sucking on the lobe.

He thrust into her, moaning at the exquisite heat surrounding him. Her hands moved from his shoulders, slowly down his back, over his buttocks, where she dug her fingernails into his skin, urging him. Her inner muscles hugged his length, and she arched against him, meeting each thrust.

He watched her face, saw the passion in those blue-gray eyes. The intense need, and knew as her breathing increased along with her pace that she reached for completion.

Her nails bit into his back again as she cried out, her sheath tightening around him as she rode out the orgasm.

He kept his climax at bay as he watched her find her own release. Sweat beaded on his brow, and his body ached for completion, but he wanted it to last. Wanted her to remember him. He had waited too long for this moment to end in a matter of minutes. And he would not let her off so easy. He slowed his pace, wanting her to feel each thrust, each stroke to her very core.

Bending down, he took her nipple into his mouth, sucking and pulling on it lightly with his teeth. Her fingers wove through his hair, keeping him anchored there as her hips moved, urging him to do the same. But he did not move at all, loving the feel of her shifting beneath him, in order to take him further inside her.

He sensed her frustration as she arched against him and smiled against her breast, before his lips claimed hers and he thrust inside her, his strokes fluid, strong. "Yes, Galeran, that's it."

It wasn't long before she came again, her honeyed sheath hugging him tight. His balls drew close to his body and he groaned as he came, pulling out just in time.

He wanted to be a father one day, but not until he had attained lands and wealth.

Elena's fingers lightly played along his spine and he closed his eyes, content for the first time in his life to lay abed with a woman after intercourse. He could fall asleep right now. Mayhap he would return after checking with his guards for the night, and hold her until dawn.

A knock sounded at the door, interrupting the short-lived peacefulness. "What is it?" Elena called out.

"Forgive the interruption, but is Galeran in there, Lady Elena?" came a guard's voice.

"Aye, I am here," Galeran said, rolling off Elena. He pulled on his braies and tied them before opening the door.

"Lady Aleysia is gone."

Galeran's heart sank to his toes. "What do you mean?"

The young guard looked nervous. "The Scot came and took her. A servant said she heard them as they raced through the bailey."

He cursed loudly. "How is that possible? Her room was well guarded."

The soldier dropped his gaze. "They were killed, as were the guards at the gatehouse."

Elena, who had wrapped the blanket around her, stood behind Galeran. "I hope that they did not hurt her."

"Go, get the men together," Galeran said. "I need at least two dozen men ready to ride out within a quarter of an hour."

"Yes, sir."

As the soldier rushed off, Galeran turned to Elena. "Mayhap I should leave more men here to look after you?"

Elena squeezed his hand. "I will be fine, Galeran, as will the fief. There are plenty of soldiers to defend her. Aleysia is the one who needs you most. Go, bring her home."

If there was one thing Renaud could not stand, it was all the regality of his king's court. It seemed that every lord of the realm had journeyed north with William. Despite the fact the north had been in chaos, one would not know it. Men in fine clothing and women with expensive gowns and jewels dripping from fingers, neck, and earlobes, chatted amongst themselves, oblivious of the world outside the high walls of York Castle.

He hated it. Hated the crowds, all the pompous individuals who thought themselves better than those who served them. Personally, he preferred life in the countryside.

A young boy with long blond hair walked by, and Renaud smiled inwardly, remembering well when he had first met Aleysia, when she was dressed much like the lad.

How beautiful she was without all the ornaments of court life. A pure, sensual innocence he hoped she never lost. And once again his insides turned, making him wonder if he would lose her to another this very day. He prayed William would consider all of Renaud's years of faithful service before he took all he held so dear.

He prayed fate would smile upon him today.

Inpatient to have the meeting finished, and be back on the road to Braemere, Renaud took a steadying breath as he approached William, prepared to hear his fate.

This past week he had realized that he needed Aleysia in his life. He did not know if this was love, for he had never experienced such an emotion, but what he felt for Aleysia was stronger than anything he'd felt for any other woman, and he could not imagine his life without her.

Their last night together when they had made love, he had sensed a change in her. He believed that she honestly did not want Duncan. Though she had proven to be untrustworthy, he believed that was behind them now. Gone was the distrust, for he realized why she had done what she had. And then later, when she had touched each of his scars, kissing each one, his heart swelled with emotion.

No woman had dared touch his battle wounds, especially the one on his cheek. They had always been repulsed by the scar. But Aleysia had touched it—even kissed it lovingly, and she had been curious, sincerely wanting to know more about him. He had seen the softness in her eyes and something more. Could it be love? Aye, she felt something for him. Perhaps it was not love, but then again, maybe it was.

And he would not lose her to another. Not when they had come so far in such a short time. Nay, he would fight for her.

For now he must keep his wits, and have confidence that Galeran would maintain order at Braemere, and that William would show him mercy.

He hated to be so far from Aleysia, especially when MacMillan would be returning. Another reason to get this meeting done and over with.

He flinched, remembering the sight as he approached York Castle. The heads of traitorous Saxon's impaled on long pikes that lined the ramparts, a warning to all that William would not tolerate a rebellion. Renaud could not imagine Adelstan's head among the lot of those poor souls.

"De Wulf, it has been a long time," King William said, his tone kind.

William looked well, his eyes still fierce, but a kind smile on his face.

Renaud bowed. "Your Grace."

"'Tis good to see you."

"And you as well, Your Grace. You look in good health."

"As do you. But I understand that Adelstan of Braemere has escaped?"

He certainly had cut to the quick. "Indeed, Your Grace."

"You allowed him to escape." It was not a question.

Hearing the rumblings all around him, Renaud knew more than ever that he stood to lose everything. William did not like to be made a fool of, and he enjoyed making his point by example.

"Why would you do something so foolish, de Wulf? 'Tis not like you."

"Your Grace, I made a promise to Cawdor's twin."

William's brow furrowed. "What was this promise, and why would you make such a pledge to a Saxon before asking me? Cawdor should have been brought to York. You openly defied my request, and now who knows where this traitor might be? Mayhap he is plotting against me as we speak. What if this Saxon starts yet another uprising?"

"I promised Aleysia of Braemere that I would not kill her brother, and I could not, with good conscience, bring him to his death, Your Grace. The two lost their father and mother when de Pirou raided their fief years ago."

William's eyes narrowed. "And de Pirou took Braemere at my command."

"Indeed, Your Grace, but de Pirou made certain promises to the twins. Instead of following through with those promises, he treated them as servants and even tried to violate Adelstan."

William frowned, his fingernails tapping against the wood of the chair. "Such is the way of war, de Wulf. You know that. Not all promises can be kept. Remember, this man you allowed to escape killed de Pirou, a knight of the realm, one of your brothers in arms."

Renaud would never consider de Pirou a brother in arms, but he would not tell William that. "Indeed, Your Grace. Adelstan killed de Pirou, but he is a valiant young man, who felt compelled to fight with other Saxons, to take back the land his family—"

"You made a promise to his sister? Who is this woman? Why did you not bring her with you to York?"

"Your Grace, I would ask for the hand of Aleysia Cawdor, princess of Braemere."

William's brows drew together. "You did not bring her with you? Why, did you think she would be in danger?"

Renaud nodded. "Aye, I did, Your Grace."

Understanding flickered in the king's eye. "Ah, and so the story unravels. That is why you allowed her brother to escape. You have found favor in this woman—this Saxon."

The last was not a question. Renaud nodded. "I have, Sire."

"What of this Saxon's brother, whom you allowed to flee?"

"I believe him to be in Scotland, where he has lived these past years."

"But for how long? He is no doubt raising an army as we speak. Just as he did these past months. He is most dangerous, de Wulf. You knew this, and still you let him go?" William shook his head. "This is most upsetting news. I am most disappointed in you, Renaud."

"I ask for leniency, Your Grace. Adelstan is a faithful knight who may one day pledge fealty to you. He would be a loyal vassal to you, Your Grace, if given the opportunity."

"And you would give him this opportunity?"

"Indeed, Your Grace. I would consider it a privilege."

William shook his head. "I never believed in all my life that I would be having this conversation with you, Renaud. You were one of my strongest men."

Renaud's mouth went dry. "I still am, Your Grace. You have my sword, you know that."

"I trusted you with a mission. A mission you did not complete, and all for the will of a woman." William stood and paced. "I am sorry, but I cannot give you what you desire."

A stillness settled over the others in the room. Renaud's heart pounded loudly in his ears, fearful of his next words.

William ran a hand over his beard. "For allowing the Saxon Adelstan to escape, you will surrender Braemere."

A collective gasp sounded all around him.

Renaud could barely breathe, but he nodded. "As you wish, Your Grace."

"And I would like this Saxon princess brought to York."

Renaud forced himself to remain calm. "Your Grace, I would ask for Aleysia's hand."

"You are fortunate to retain your lands in Sussex, de Wulf." William's jaw tightened. "Bring the woman to me. I will decide her fate."

Renaud could not respond for a moment, so tight was his throat. "Aye, Your Grace."

"And if this Saxon Adelstan returns to Braemere with an army, you will also lose your lands in Sussex. Is this understood?"

Anger rushed through Renaud, but he forced it aside. He could not risk voicing his displeasure at losing both Braemere and Aleysia, because he could ultimately lose his lands and titles in Sussex and then he would have nothing.

"That will be all, de Wulf."

"Thank you, Your Grace," Renaud replied, turning on his heel and leaving the hall, feeling like he had lost everything he had worked so hard for, but most of all, he had lost the greatest treasure of all.

Aleysia.

TWENTY

Aleysia shivered against the cold rain that pelted against her. They had been traveling for most of the night, and now with the dawning of a new day, she wondered what awaited her when she arrived at Duncan's village. The large Scot had not said a word to her since leaving Braemere.

She had finally given in and leaned back against him, knowing she must appear relieved instead of repulsed. All along she had sensed his anger, and wondered if Renaud had told him the truth about their relationship, or mayhap he had guessed.

Even Duncan's men had been quiet, giving her sidelong glances as they rode by.

They had stopped only once, and that had been when she could no longer hold her bladder. She quickly relieved herself, but Duncan had stayed nearby.

"Be alert!" Duncan shouted, nearly startling Aleysia out of her skin. To the right a large, eerie-looking copse of trees was enshrouded with fog. The hair on her arms stood on end as she squinted, wondering what lurked in the forests. Even when they passed by, she was not able to brush aside the feeling that someone, or something, watched.

A little while later they came upon an old cathedral that sat on the border of England and Scotland. The stone building, full of stained-glass windows, looked out of place in the gloomy surroundings.

Duncan dismounted and held out a hand to help Aleysia down. She accepted, and his hands encircled her waist. "The priest is awaiting."

Her stomach turned. "Priest? What priest?"

The sides of his mouth lifted in an eerie smile that did not reach his eyes. "The priest who will marry us. I will not wait another day, Aleysia. I have waited too long already."

She swallowed hard, looking past Duncan to the cathedral, then to his men, who were busy making camp. "Do not fret, Aleysia. We will not be sleeping in a tent this night. I have secured a hut for us, so I can bed you properly."

Everything within her rebelled, and it must have shone on her face for Duncan laughed without mirth. "Do not act the virgin, Aleysia. I know what transpired between yourself and the Norman."

She could feel her face drain of color. How she yearned to tell Duncan she did not wish to marry him. That her heart belonged to another. But she could not. Duncan would only be more cruel.

"I am just surprised. Why here? Why not at Kilraney?"

"I am most anxious to bed my bride."

Aleysia, bit her lip to keep from responding.

"I imagine you are surprised, especially since you have been spending your nights in the bed of that Norman bastard." Before she knew what he was about, he slapped her hard, making her head jerk back. "You have acted the whore long enough."

She tasted blood on her lips and took a step away. Denying it would only infuriate him more. "I did what I must to save Adelstan."

"Well, you need not worry any longer about your brother or that arrogant Norman, who will taste the end of my blade very, very soon. You belong to me now, and you will never see Braemere again."

The door of the chapel opened and out stepped Audrey, Duncan's sister, a woman twice her age, who had always tolerated Aleysia, but no more.

"The Norman has been kind to us. He even let Adelstan go."

Aleysia felt him bristle beside her. "Did he now? You must have been a skillful lover for him to commit treason against his king." He ran a possessive hand over her hip, and finally her waist. "Smile now, Aleysia," he said, squeezing her hand painfully. "Let others believe you are happy to become my wife. Audrey will help you prepare for the wedding. I am off to see to my men." Without a backward glance, he left her.

"Are you hungry?" Audrey asked, taking Aleysia by the hand, her fingers ice cold.

"Aye, I am." Her face ached where he had slapped her, and she tasted blood.

"There is a hut on the other side of the chapel. It is where you will prepare for the wedding, and where you will spend the evening. In the morrow we will head for Kilraney. I expect you are ready to go home?"

Aleysia nodded. Apparently, Duncan had not told his sister everything.

The hut was very small, and housed little more than a bed, and a fire pit, where a pot of stew boiled now.

Aleysia glanced at the bed and shuddered. Tonight Duncan would be her husband, and she would be forced to have sex with him. She had no desire to make love to anyone but Renaud. But he was in York, and by the time he discovered she was missing, she would already be married, and there would be nothing he could do.

Her throat grew tight and she blinked back tears.

Audrey set a bowl of stew before Aleysia. "My brother says that you have embraced the Norman ways."

With cheeks blazing under the older woman's stare, Aleysia replied, "I have not embraced so much as I have accepted that King William is in England to stay."

"And you prefer England to Scotland?"

"My home is in England."

"I thought you considered Kilraney your home?"

"I realized how much I missed Braemere when I returned."

Her lips quirked. "I heard rumors when the men returned, but I chose not to believe them. I cannot understand why you would love a Norman, particularly the man who imprisoned your brother."

Surprised by the woman's bold remark, Aleysia replied, "You should not listen to rumors. They know not of what they speak." She hoped Audrey could not see through the lie. "I have done what I must in order to stay alive."

"You gave yourself to this Norman?"

"I do not wish to speak of it."

Audrey's lips curved slightly. "I have heard he is a handsome man. It is little wonder you had no desire to leave."

Aleysia tasted the stew, wincing because of the cut on her lip. "I wanted Adelstan's freedom, and that was the price."

"Aye, but you gave your maidenhead willingly enough. He must have pleased you well for you not to want to leave." Audrey laughed under her breath. "I do believe that is why Duncan abducted you. He could not bear the thought of you in another man's bed. You, a possession he has coveted greatly."

The discussion made Aleysia's stomach churn, and though she no longer had an appetite, she ate, wanting the conversation to end.

"Once we are finished here, I will take you to bathe in the river just beyond the forest."

Aleysia's heart skipped a beat. Mayhap she would be able to escape! "I look forward to washing away the dust."

She finished the stew in record time and looked up to find Audrey standing by the door, drying towels and soap in hand. "Come, let us get you washed while we still have sunlight. You will smell fresh as a rose for your husband."

Aleysia forced a smile and followed her out the door.

Duncan was nowhere in sight, but two of his men appeared out of nowhere and followed close behind them.

"Must they come?" Aleysia glanced over her shoulder at the burly man who made her skin crawl.

"Duncan would have their heads if they failed to keep you safe."

"Certainly, I am not going to flee when I am naked. I would freeze to death."

"'Tis true. Mayhap they can fall back a ways. Enough to give you some privacy."

"Thank you, Audrey." Aleysia hoped she sounded sincere.

As the forest closed in around them, she prayed for a miracle.

Renaud crested the final hill, and inhaled a deep, steadying breath as he took in the sight below.

He smiled. Braemere in all her glory.

It had been less than a month since he had first set eyes on the impressive fief, and he would never forget her beauty.

Much as the beauty within.

Every part of him ached for Aleysia, and had since he'd left Braemere a week ago. To see her face, to hear her voice.

Though he had lost this beautiful fief, he prayed he had not lost the woman he loved. Aye, and love her he did. He would do everything he could to regain William's favor.

He nudged his mount into a gallop, anxious to see the woman whose green eyes had haunted him so much these past days.

As he approached the gatehouse he heard Galeran's voice, shouting orders.

Unease rippled along his spine. Something was amiss.

The portcullis opened and Galeran rode out, two dozen men behind him, all dressed in armor.

Galeran, clearly surprised to see him, approached. "My lord, I fear I have bad news. MacMillan has taken Aleysia."

Anger and fear surged within him. "When?"

"Two hours ago. He killed six guards. I am sorry, my lord. I do not know how they managed to sneak inside the keep without being spotted."

Renaud turned to his squire. "Bring me a fresh mount."

The boy nodded, and raced for the bailey.

"How many men were with him?"

"Alexander said there are fresh tracks in the forest."

"Then we will take at least twice that and leave the others here."

They rode hard for hours, at a full gallop, following the path the Scots had left.

Renaud let his anger fuel him, and as they ate up the miles and approached the borderlands, he knew they were at a disadvantage. The terrain grew more treacherous with every mile, the weather worse. He could easily be falling into a trap. Two men were sent ahead, hoping they would not encounter danger.

Now those scouts came galloping toward him, a third man with them.

"Adelstan?" he said under his breath, recognizing the young man's blond hair and broad shoulders.

"Aye, it is." Galeran followed Renaud as they approached the trio. "What the devil is he doing here?"

"De Wulf," Adelstan said with a nod. "MacMillan passed this way just an hour ago. I followed them to a small valley where a cathedral sits. From what I could hear, I believe he intends to marry Aleysia this evening. We have little time to waste."

Renaud's blood ran cold. "The bastard certainly wasted no time."

"Aye, he wants to make sure that Aleysia is his."

"By God he will not!" Renaud replied.

"How many men are there?"

"I counted thirty."

"We will follow you then," Renaud said, motioning for his men. "Did you see your sister?"

"Aye, she is well. But scared. We just need to make it in time."

Adelstan pulled his mount up alongside Renaud. "I pray that we will not be too late."

"If we are, then Aleysia will be a widow by tonight. She belongs to me and no other."

The river was as cold as ice, but Aleysia clamped her teeth together and took another step out into the slow-moving water.

She wore just an under tunic, insisting on it due to her modesty. Audrey had shook her head while muttering under her breath. Aleysia wanted to make sure she had something covering her when she made her escape.

Duncan's sister stood on the riverbank, watching her closely. The two men who had followed them stood just out of sight, close enough that she could hear them conversing. The sun was slipping beyond the hills, which would work in her favor.

She must hurry though and take advantage of time. Taking another step, she waded out until she was in waist deep.

"Careful," Audrey yelled, as she tossed her the soap.

Aleysia made quick work of washing her body, then spent a little longer soaping her hair, looking toward the horizon where the sun was making its descent.

If luck was on her side, she could hide in the forests tonight, and then, God willing, make for Braemere in the morning. One thing that worked to her advantage was that she knew about soldiers and how to make due with very little. She also knew how to find shelter and how to hide and stay hidden from an enemy.

Problem was, the night was growing bitterly cold, and she would be on the run with soaked hair and wearing nothing but an under tunic, and a wet one at that. God willing she would find a hollowed-out tree, or some type of shelter that would keep her safe from the elements.

And the Scots who would be looking for her.

"Hurry, Aleysia."

She looked over her shoulder at the older woman, while her fingers curled around a good-size rock on the river's floor. It would have to do.

She hated to hurt Audrey, but she had no choice.

"I am finished." Aleysia stepped from the water, hiding the rock behind her back.

Audrey opened the drying cloth and came toward her. She put the cloth about Aleysia's shoulders and pulled her hair out from beneath it. She turned to grab Aleysia's shoes and that's when Aleysia brought the rock up and hit the woman square on the back of the head.

Audrey slumped to the ground soundlessly. Aleysia winced, hoping she had not hit her so hard as to kill her.

Aleysia hurriedly removed the other woman's shoes and put them on. Wrapping the drying cloth about her shoulders, she raced toward the south, far away from the camp, and crossed over a small bridge she had seen earlier.

She ran for miles, not looking back, ignoring the sounds of night all about her. She had always had Adelstan with her to calm her fears, but now in this unfamiliar terrain, she had never felt so alone.

Worse still, she would be hunted shortly.

Tripping over a fallen log, Aleysia stifled a cry, wincing as a short branch cut her calf. Blood seeped down between her toes. Ripping a piece from her soaked under tunic, she wrapped it about her injured leg and stood. The wound was deep, making walking exceedingly hard.

Tears burned the back of her eyes, but she blinked them away, praying for the strength to continue.

An owl hooted overhead, and she stopped short, hearing something else.

She closed her eyes, concentrating, and realized with a start it was horses' hooves.

Several in fact.

Fear paralyzed her.

No doubt Duncan had discovered Audrey on the riverbank. Looking for cover, she rolled up into a ball, her back to the trunk of a giant oak.

Her chest constricted, her heart rate accelerating the closer they came.

It did not help that both the tunic and linen sheet were white, and would no doubt stick out in the dark woods like a beacon. She gasped when out of the darkness came a large black horse . . . and riding it was Duncan.

Dear God, no!

He saw her.

She scrambled to her feet and ran, darting through the brush, hoping that the low-hanging branches would stop him.

But it didn't. The next thing she knew Duncan was off his horse, and he grabbed her none too gently by the neck, and threw her up against a tree trunk, so hard the breath left her lungs.

His men had stopped, not ten feet from them. There was nowhere to run. No way to escape them.

Two of Duncan's men dismounted, while the others stayed astride, watching her with wicked smiles.

"You think to escape me? You nearly kill my sister, and then disappear into the night. Do you return to him? To the Norman? What a little whore! Think ye I know nothing? Your father would turn over in his grave if he knew his daughter fucked his enemy." He shook his head while he untied his cloak.

Though it was dark, she could see the murderous gleam in his eyes. Cruel eyes.

If only Renaud were here with her now.

Duncan's dark gaze shifted from hers, to the neckline of her gown. She had thought for a moment he would give her his cloak, but now she realized with horror, that he had something else in mind.

Something that made her blood run cold.

He ran a finger along her jaw, down her throat, to the erratic pulse at the base of her neck, to where his hand covered her breast. "I have waited far too long for this moment."

His men snickered behind him. It would not help to cry out. There would be no one to hear her. Plus, he wanted her to cry. To hurt her.

"What are you doing, Duncan?" she asked, her tone surprisingly calm.

His lips curved into a sinister smile. "What I should have done years ago. What I have been waiting to do from the first moment I saw you."

Bile rose in her throat as with his free hand he untied his braies. A second later his erection pressed against her belly.

One of the men behind Duncan shifted on his feet. One looked away, while the men still astride their horses watched.

No one would help her.

She tried to wrench away, using every last bit of strength, but he held her firm.

Bringing her knee up, she caught him in the ballocks, but still he did not let go. However, he did take a moment to slap her, so hard she again tasted blood.

His rough fingers pulled on a nipple, tweaking it hard, sending pain coursing throughout her.

"Why do you do this here, in front of others? My father would kill you if he were alive. He trusted you."

He flinched as though struck. "Your father is dead, and soon you will join him."

She felt the blood drain from her face.

He ignored her, and she closed her eyes, unable to watch the men witness her rape.

Duncan kicked her feet apart, and his sex probed her women's flesh.

Her heart beat so loudly she could hear nothing above it.

One minute Duncan's lips were against her forehead, the next a primitive cry sounded throughout the forest.

Renaud hit Duncan so hard, Duncan's front teeth flew from his mouth.

Before the older man could stand, Renaud struck him again, this time on the jaw. Duncan's head snapped back hard.

From the corner of his eye he saw Adelstan covering Aleysia with his cloak, holding her tightly to him, while his men made quick work of the Scots, including the two who had taken off on horseback.

Renaud trembled with hatred, the image of Duncan as he'd nearly raped Aleysia while his men watched replaying in his mind.

He had seen the fear in her eyes before she closed them.

Thank God he had not been too late.

Duncan tried to fight back, but only managed a right punch to Renaud's stomach. The only thing Renaud could feel was the blood coursing through his body while he hit the Scot over and over . . . until the man's face was a bloody mess, and his breathing labored.

Let the man die like the animal he was.

Here in the forest.

"Kill him!" one of Renaud's men shouted.

Duncan fought to get on his feet, and when finally he stood Adelstan approached him. Silver flashed—the blade long. The Scot went to swing, but Adelstan was faster, his blade sinking into the man's barrel chest.

Shock showed on the highlander's face, a moment before he sank to the ground in a heap.

Aleysia went into Renaud's arms, holding him tight, like she wanted to step inside him. He embraced her in return, kissing the top of her head. "Thank God you are well."

She looked up at him, her lashes spiked with tears. How delicate she appeared. Her face bruised from the abuse she had endured. So frail.

"Adelstan is right. The others will return. We had best make haste for Braemere, but we will get you into some warm clothes first." Renaud glanced at Duncan one last time. The man's eyes were frozen open, staring skyward.

"How did you come to be here?" Aleysia asked her brother, who was already mounting his horse.

"I had been staying in a village near the border when I heard Duncan and his men pass. I followed you to the chapel, and when I realized what Duncan was about, I rode for Braemere. Thank God I did not have to travel far before I discovered Renaud and his men."

"Will you travel to Braemere with us?" she asked, needing him.

Adelstan looked past her to Renaud. "I do not know if it is safe."

"You will be safe, Adelstan," Renaud said. "I will see to it."

"First Aleysia must change out of the wet clothes." His men looked away while Renaud helped her out of the clinging, wet under tunic, and wrapped her in his fur-lined cloak.

Within seconds she was astride Renaud's mount. He settled behind her, and she snuggled up against his hard chest, finally relaxing. Her teeth chattered and he ran his hands up and down her arms, hoping to warm her.

"We're going home."

She glanced over her shoulder and smiled. "Yes, let's go home."

TWENTY-ONE

Aleysia had fallen fast asleep in Renaud's arms, and when she woke the next morning, she could scarcely remember the journey at all.

Renaud was not in the chamber, but he had called for a bath; the steam rose off the water, enticing her to step in.

She was disappointed that she had not talked to Adelstan last night. In their urgency to reach Braemere there had not been time for idle chatter. They had ridden as hard as their mounts could carry them, and thankfully, Duncan's men had not pursued them. Only one had gotten away. The others lay near Duncan's body in the forest.

She shivered, remembering how close the Scot had come to raping her. The one man her father had trusted to care for both her and Adelstan. Their father would be horrified to learn his friend had betrayed them all so badly.

At least Duncan was no longer a threat to her or her brother.

But that did not mean Duncan's people would not want vengeance.

Whatever the case, she would put it from her mind for now. She instead was anxious to see Renaud and her brother.

She dressed in a light blue kirtle with a delicate silver girdle Elena had given to her. Securing the cloak about her shoulders, she tied it, and stepped out in the drafty hallway.

The bailey was alive with activity and she smiled at a young boy who held a basket of freshly cut flowers. He handed her one, and she bent down and kissed the top of his dark head, thinking he could very well look like her son, if she and Renaud had a child. The boy's cheeks turned bright red as she stared. She had not had her menses yet and she wondered if even now Renaud's baby grew in her womb.

For some reason the thought of carrying his child no longer horrified her, but pleased her. She would love to give him many sons, and a daughter or two. Aye, she would enjoy having many children with the man she loved. Because she did indeed love Renaud de Wulf with all her being. She felt like shouting it from the rooftops.

She entered the great hall, which was full of knights and pages who were frantically setting the room.

"Good morning, my lady."

Adelstan!

Her heart leapt with joy. He grinned and came toward her in long strides. She rushed to greet him and flung her arms around his neck. He lifted her and swung her in a circle, his laughter vibrating against her chest. "I hoped you would still be here."

Over his shoulder she saw the flash of white teeth as Renaud smiled. He turned back to face the hearth and the fire roaring within, giving them a moment alone.

Adelstan set her back on her feet. "I told you I would stay overnight at Braemere."

She cupped his face between her palms. "I am so pleased to see you, brother."

"Aye, and you as well."

"Will you be staying?"

His grin broadened. "For now. I do not know how long I will stay. At least until MacMillan's threat is no more or William calls for my head." Adelstan sobered a little. "He is a good man, Aleysia. He forfeited much to make this happen."

She frowned. "What do you mean?"

"Renaud did not tell me, but I want you to know what happened with William so you prepare yourself for what might happen. I have heard whispers that he was stripped of Braemere."

Aleysia's stomach clenched. "Elena said that could happen."

"William says he must surrender the fief to another Norman baron who will be here in the near future."

Her mind reeled with the news. Renaud had sacrificed so much, and it had all been for her. She felt nauseous.

"What will we do?"

"Only time will tell, but you must be strong." He smiled, trying to soothe her. "You look beautiful in your gown," he said in an effort to comfort her from the sobering news. "Methinks this new attire suits you."

"It is hard to get used to," she said, tugging at the skirt. "I confess I miss the freedom breeches and a tunic allow."

"I think de Wulf appreciates seeing your feminine side," Adelstan said, motioning toward Renaud. "Perhaps later we can go to the cemetery?"

She nodded. "I would like that very much."

He kissed her cheek. "I will give the two of you time alone."

She nodded, and gave him another hug before she left him again and walked toward Renaud.

She drank in the sight of him. The broad shoulders, the lean waist, the tight buttocks, and long strong thighs. What a truly amazing specimen he was. Perfect in every way, and he had come to her rescue. This protector of hers.

Her blood quickened the closer she came to him, anxious for tonight when they could be alone together.

Uncaring of who watched, she walked right up to him and hugged him from behind, her arms wrapping around his waist, greedily feeling the muscles of his abdomen ripple beneath her fingers. Her cheek lay against his back, and she listened to the pounding of his heart. She inhaled deeply of his scent, realizing how much she had missed him while he'd been in York. "Thank you, Renaud. Thank you so much for all that you have given up for me."

His palms covered the backs of her hands, his thumbs smoothing over her wrists. "I would do it all over again, Aleysia." He turned and smiled down at her, pulling her into his embrace.

Desire pulsed in every nerve ending. An ache that went beyond just the physical. How perfect this man was, she thought, joy bubbling within her, taking in his striking features. The long eyelashes, sharp cheekbones that were even more pronounced. He looked like he had lost a stone in the past week. No doubt he had had little time for rest, and was exhausted from the trip to York and then her rescue. "What will you do now?"

"William asked me to bring you to York, but with MacMillan's threat I have sent him word and asked for time. We must await word."

Her heart hammered. "I am afraid, Renaud. I do not want to go to York."

He pulled her to him, crushing her against his chest. "Nor do I."

"What if William marries me to another? I have heard of such things happening."

He lifted her chin with gentle fingers, rubbing his thumb along her lip. "I will never let you go."

She remembered the words he had said on that day not so long ago. "Not now, not ever," she finished for him, and he smiled.

"Aye, and I mean it. Aleysia, you are my woman."

She knew he would never tell her what he'd given up for her. It was not in him to intentionally hurt another. Just as he had kept to himself the truth about Duncan not asking for Adelstan's release. He had done it to save her the pain.

"I asked King William if I could take you as my wife."

Her pulse skittered. "And?"

"He did not agree, but I believe he will think upon it." Renaud bent and kissed her. "I betrayed him when I released Adelstan." He brushed a thumb along her jaw. "I believe even I would turn traitor to have you as my wife, Aleysia. You belong to me and no other."

She could see the sincerity in his eyes. Knowing how devoted he was to his king, she felt humbled.

"Will you return to our chamber with me?" he asked, a devilish grin on his face.

Excitement raced along her spine. "Aye, I would."

Renaud removed his clothing and lay down on the bed, waiting for Aleysia. She slowly removed the kirtle, untied the ribbon holding her chemise together, and let it slide down her body to puddle at her feet. His heart thumped erratically. How beautiful she was. Knowing she would truly be his one day soon, in name and body, pleased him more than she would ever know.

Once he thought happiness was made by riches, castles, and land, but now he knew the true importance of loving, and how fulfilling that could be.

He felt that with Aleysia, and he would do whatever he must to make her his bride.

Renaud's gaze shifted over her slowly, noting how her nipples hardened into tiny buds. "Come here."

Her lips curved and as he stared, she climbed onto the bed, settling between his thighs.

She leaned over him, kissing him fiercely, only to break away to kiss a path along his jaw, his neck, his chest, his abdomen that tightened as her velvety tongue laved his navel. "You have a beautiful body, Renaud."

Her soft words surprised him, but pleased him greatly. "I am glad I please you."

She looked up at him and the hot look in her eyes had the blood in his veins boiling.

Her pink tongue reached out and touched the crown of his shaft, swirling around the edge, stroking the tiny slit of his cock head.

She opened her mouth and took him into her mouth, using care with her teeth. He moaned with pleasure as her hot and silky tongue worked magic.

Her fingers grazed his thighs, splaying there. She grew bolder, cupping his sac, her fingers stroking, exploring the sensitive flesh.

She took him farther into her mouth, and he groaned at the multiple sensations.

He reached down, his fingers weaving through her hair. He ached to touch her, but she stilled his hands, apparently intent on pleasing him.

His balls lifted as she continued, his blood coursing through him like liquid fire. "Aleysia, I cannot . . ."

She didn't stop, and knew he was close. Knew that he could not contain himself. He shifted his hips. She glanced up at him then, her tongue licking, rolling, teasing. "What do you want, Renaud?"

He looked to her glorious breasts, the tips erect, and then at his cock, remembering the fantasy he'd had the first time he saw her naked. For an instant he could see confusion in her eyes, then she leaned down, resting his cock between her breasts. She pushed them together and he moved his hips slowly. He closed his eyes, telling himself there would be time later for slow pleasure, but for now his body begged for release, and he came instantly, smiling when he heard her gasp of surprise.

He opened his eyes and she was beside him, resting her head on his shoulder.

Grabbing a corner of the bed linen, he cleaned his seed from her body. Finished, he kissed a path down her jaw, to the swell of her breasts, laving one, then the other. With a contented sigh, her head fell back on the pillows, her hands above her, fingers curling around the headboard.

He kissed her navel, his tongue circling it, dipping into it. The muscles of her abdomen contracted as he made a path to her slick folds. Already she was drenched, and he took in her woman's scent, the sweet musk, with a deep inhalation. He stroked her slit with his tongue, and he smiled, hearing her low-throated moan.

Her thighs fell open and he cupped her bottom, bringing her closer to his mouth, stroking her again.

He lifted her hidden pearl with his tongue, sucked it lightly, then hard again, leaving her squirming beneath him.

"Renaud," she breathed, with a sigh. "It feels wonderful."

He held her fast so she couldn't move, and plunged his tongue inside her sheath, which pulsed around him.

He watched her for a moment, the look of pleasure on her face, the smile, the hot desire in her eyes.

Then he stroked her again. Taking her to that pinnacle where she cried out, reaching for him. "Renaud," she said, her breathing uneven. "I want you inside me."

He could no longer hold back and thrust within her heated core. She moaned low in her throat, her thighs opening wider, her ankles locking behind his back.

For as long as he lived, he would never get enough of this woman.

Her fingers moved over his body, down his back, and his buttocks, curling there, holding him tighter, urging him deeper. He grit hit teeth as he kept his climax at bay, wanting to see to her pleasure first.

Hearing her breath hitch, he knew she was close, even before she cried out his name and lifted her hips. Looking into her forest-green eyes, he felt a peace he had never before known. He would never let her go.

And he told her in his native tongue exactly what she meant to him, and the joy she brought to him. Hopefully, one day he would be able to tell her in a language she could understand exactly how much he cared for her.

Her insides clamped tightly around him, and he thrust once more, following her over the edge.

Later that afternoon, Aleysia and Adelstan made their way to the home they had shared with their parents, which now served as sleeping quarters for some of Renaud's men-at-arms, including Adelstan, who reclaimed his old chamber as his own. She was elated that Renaud already trusted her twin, but was not so naive as not to know that Galeran's constant presence wasn't by accident—and though the two young men had become fast friends, they both understood Galeran would report anything and everything to Renaud.

Adelstan opened the gate to the cemetery, and hand in hand they stood before the large headstone. A sad smile came over Adelstan's face, and he squeezed her hand. "Mother, Father, we know you never wanted the Normans here in your beloved Braemere, but we have come to respect this man, and I believe you respect him as well. We may not be staying on at Braemere, but we will never forget her, nor will we ever forget you. Thank you for all that you taught us of loyalty and duty. We shall strive to make you proud."

The words pleased Aleysia, especially since she knew Adelstan was sincere. He liked Renaud. She wanted her brother to be happy for her. "I love him," she said the words aloud, surprising herself, and her brother as well, for he lifted a tawny brow, followed by a smile.

"See, she loves him and he loves her."

"Does he?"

Adelstan smiled softly. "Aye, one only needs to see you two together to realize it is so. So rest in peace, dear parents, and know that your children are well cared for."

Adelstan handed her a rose and together they each lay one before the headstone.

As they left the cemetery and walked toward the bailey, Aleysia caught Adelstan watching her. She stopped in midstride. "What?"

"Nothing," he said, shaking his head. "Who knew that a Norman could make you so happy? Especially, the merciless Baron de Wulf."

She laughed under her breath. How afraid they had been of Renaud. Instead of the fire-breathing dragon she had expected, she had found an honorable man. Now she no longer feared him, but she feared losing him. "Aye, and perhaps one day you shall find love where you least expect it."

He smiled as though to say he doubted it, then wrapped an arm about her shoulder. "I am relieved to see you happy."

As they approached the bailey, a loud roar of applause and laughter sounded. Adelstan looked at Aleysia with a frown. "What are they up to?"

They soon found out. Set up along the far wall were two targets. Two knights stood side by side, each with an arrow notched in his bow. One of the soldiers was Philip, who she had not seen since that night in the great hall when she had flirted with him.

"Release!" Galeran yelled, and the men released their arrows.

Philip smiled widely, and nodded to the men who yelled their approval. The loser shook his head and fell back, while the next in line took his place.

Renaud turned to Aleysia, a wide smile on his face. One that made her heart miss a beat. "Ah, here she is."

Everyone turned and looked her way. "What is he about?" she asked Adelstan.

"No doubt he has been bragging about your skill with bow and arrow."

Renaud stepped toward her and extended his hand. "Come, I told my men that you were a sure shot. I have the scar to prove it."

"And you are right." Adelstan's voice brimmed with pride. "Show them, sister."

Never in her life had she backed down from any challenge. All around them, men voiced their encouragement, all save the man she was going up against. Philip smiled widely seeing her, and she returned the smile, taking pleasure in the fact that Renaud bristled beside her. Yes, he was jealous of the young man who would never be the man Renaud was.

"Philip."

"Lady Aleysia, it is good to have you home."

"Enough of the pleasantries," Renaud said gruffly, handing her a long bow and arrow.

Flashing a smile, she took them from him, and concentrated on the target, extending her bow, ready for the command. Just off to her right she saw Elena, who shouted encouragement.

Aleysia extended her bow. "I am out of practice."

"Release!"

She released and a second later applause exploded all around her, for her arrow had hit directly in the center, a perfect shot. Elena gave her a conspiratorial nod, and then she looked at Renaud.

Clapping louder than anyone, he grinned, his pride obvious to everyone watching, which pleased her greatly.

Renaud stepped forward and took the bow from Philip, who relinquished it immediately. Aleysia watched him from the corner of her eye.

Galeran stepped forward. "Ready, release!"

The arrows landed side by side. Adelstan stepped forward, released his bow, and the arrow hit directly between Aleysia's and Renaud's.

The group laughed, and Adelstan smiled. "Let that be a warning, de Wulf. I shall always have my sister's back."

Aleysia kissed her brother's cheek, then turned to Elena, who grabbed her by the hand. "Come, my dear. We will leave you men to your games. I have need to speak to my friend."

"Not so fast," Renaud said, bending his head and kissing Aleysia.

Applause sounded all around them, and she smiled against his lips. Her cheeks heated, but she was immensely pleased. She did not care what others thought. She loved Renaud.

"I shall see you soon," he said, giving her a pat on her bottom.

"Careful, de Wulf," Adelstan said, his smile belying the steely tone of his words.

"I will make an honest woman of her, Adelstan." He turned deadly serious. "I swear it."

Adelstan kept his gaze and nodded. "You had better."

As they headed off, Elena took Aleysia by the hand. "Your brother is almost too pretty for a man."

Aleysia laughed, having heard that very statement a time or two. "Aye."

"What of Galeran?" Aleysia asked, motioning toward the knight who seemed more subdued than normal.

"He has not looked at me since your abduction. I think he partially blames me."

"That is ridiculous. How could either of you be responsible?"

"He is a stubborn soldier. He believes that he should have known. He lost six guards that night. All killed and on his first mission."

"I understand that he mourns his men, but how could he have stopped them when six men were caught unaware?"

Elena picked a thread off her skirts. "We were together the night you were taken."

Aleysia frowned. "Together?"

"We were making love, Aleysia."

Aleysia smiled. "You did?"

"For all the good it did me. He feels that had he been on duty, you would have never been taken, the men would have lived, and he would not have let Renaud down."

Aleysia nodded, understanding the young knight's plight. "What if Renaud spoke to him?"

"It is not his business. Plus, he may be angry with Galeran if he knew."

She shrugged as though she didn't care, but Aleysia could see the hurt in Elena's eyes. "'Tis my fault. After all, I seduced him into my bed. I should not have done it. I should have realized that he is still quite young."

"Yet you desire him still?"

"I do. Just as you desire my brother, but I am too old for such games."

Aleysia's cheeks burned bright under Elena's knowing gaze. "I am afraid, Elena. What if I am not given a choice and William marries me to Braemere's new owner?"

"I honestly do not know. It is our lot in life to do what our master says—be that master king, father, or husband."

Aleysia nodded, a sense of unease filling her. She had escaped one man in marriage, only to be possibly forced to take another.

"Why don't you go to Galeran? Ask him to speak with you?"

"I have tried, but he ignores me at every turn. In truth, I think he hates me."

"What if you send him word to meet you somewhere? How about the buttery, somewhere he will not expect to find you."

"You mean trick him?"

Aleysia shrugged. "If need be."

Elena nodded. "How fast you have learned, my dear."

TWENTY-TWO

Elena glanced at the buttery door. Every time she heard approaching footsteps, she stood up and held her breath, only to sit back down on a barrel when no one came.

Mayhap Galeran had realized it was she who had sent the message.

Just when she was ready to accept defeat, she peeked out the window and saw him coming her way. Her pulse quickened in anticipation.

A moment later the door opened and Galeran entered, shutting the door behind him.

Seeing her, he frowned. "What are you doing here?"

Her confidence plummeted. "I sent you the note. I wanted to speak with you."

He opened the door to leave, but she moved faster and closed it, blocking the way. "Nay, hear me out."

Galeran shook his head. "There is nothing to say."

"You have not spoken to me for days. Not since we made love."

"'Twas a mistake, Elena."

He may as well have slapped her. "A mistake?"

He nodded. "Aye."

"Well, I do not consider it a mistake. Not at all, and I thought more of you. You did not act as though it was a mistake then."

His brows drew together. "What do you mean?"

"Your groans and moans told me you enjoyed every second. Now you are behaving like a child."

He looked affronted. "I am no child."

"Aye, you are a man, but you have ignored me as though Aleysia's abduction was my fault, and such is the behavior of a child."

He blushed. "I should have been on duty. I was not, and because of that, six men have lost their lives."

"You did not kill them. MacMillan and his men did. Do you think my brother blames himself for each soldier he has lost in battle?" She shook her head. "He would make himself insane if he did. And what if you had been sleeping instead of making love to me? Would you still be so hard on yourself?"

His jaw tightened. She reached out to him, but he pulled away, and she felt the rejection all the way to her soul. "I was wrong about you."

He looked at her then, and she could see the warring emotions.

"I thought you were a man of honor, not a man who sulks. You are acting no better than a woman."

His throat convulsed as he swallowed hard. "First you compare me to a child and now a woman?"

She lifted her chin. "Aye, I do."

His nostrils flared as he stared at her, and to her shock he pulled her into his arms and kissed her, at first his lips gentle, but growing more aggressive by the second.

"I have wanted you from the moment you stepped foot at Braemere," he said against her lips. "And by God, I will have you again."

Elena's blood coursed through her veins, her anger diminishing.

His cock was hard against his braies, rising toward his navel, struggling to be free of the confines.

Her nipples tightened and she grew wet with need.

He set a barrel before the door, before pulling her into his arms and kissing her hard, his hands jerking her gown up about her hips. He turned her around, to where she bent over the table.

His cock probed her molten core, his hands on her breasts, his fingers teasing her already-sensitive nipples into hardened peaks. She arched her back, her ass high in the air, urging him to take her.

Galeran slid in slowly, sighing as her heat enveloped him, squeezing him tightly. She gasped as he filled her to the womb. He stayed like that for a moment, and then thrust, his movements slow and fluid.

Elena rocked against him, amazed at the size of his cock, and how full she was in that position. His fingers stroked her nipples, pulling them, pinching them, flooding her channel with honeyed warmth.

"You're so wet," he whispered, leaning over her, his lips brushing against her ear, while his fingers brushed over her clit.

"Aye," she said, her breaths coming fast as her body worked toward climax. "My body craves you, and only you."

He eased out of her, almost all the way, and she cried out, her hips following him, wanting him back inside her.

Galeran trembled with the need to come. He held back, just keeping the head of his cock within her dewy folds. She shifted, rotating her hips in a way that had him gritting his teeth as he sank into her.

She cried out again, her sheath squeezing his cock tighter, pulling from him the greatest orgasm of his life.

Galeran held her for a long time, content to hold the woman he had not been able to get from his thoughts. Unfortunately, the silence ended too soon. A loud knock brought him back to the present.

He helped to straighten her skirts, and pulled up his braies before stepping outside, leaving Elena inside.

"The scouts have returned and MacMillan's army comes this way," a soldier said, rushing toward the armory. "They are within an hour's ride. Maldor says at least two hundred strong, and they are being led by Duncan's brother, who is wanting Renaud's head. They must have rallied troops along the way."

Adrenaline rushed through his veins and he stepped back into the buttery and pulled Elena into his arms. "Come, let's get you to safety."

The sounds of swords clashing resonated throughout the chamber.

When would the madness end? All Aleysia wanted was simplicity in her life. She had her brother. She had Renaud. Now all she wanted was to live in peace and, God willing, at Braemere, but she was prepared to move anywhere, as long as she had Renaud and her brother safely with her.

And now, Adelstan, Renaud, Galeran, and the rest of the men were fighting, and all because of her.

If something happened to any of them she would be devastated. She pressed a hand to her stomach, wondering if a child grew in her womb. The chances were great that she carried Renaud's babe, considering all the times they had made love.

She caught Elena's sidelong glance and turned.

"Are you with child?" she asked, unable to hide the smile that came to her lips.

"I do not know."

"Have you had your menses?"

Aleysia shook her head. "Nay, I am late."

"And your breasts? Are they sore?"

They indeed had been sore of late, and when Renaud had touched them last, they seemed more sensitive. "A bit."

Elena clapped her hands together in joy. "I believe you are with child. Does that not please you?"

Aleysia bit her bottom lip. "I do not know. What if I am to marry another? What if I leave Braemere and never return? What of my son or daughter then?"

"You should tell Renaud."

"But I do not know for certain."

"Our bodies do not lie, Aleysia. Also, if King William knew you carried Renaud's babe, mayhap he would not be so quick to marry you to another."

Hope flared within Aleysia. "Do you think so?"

"Aye, I do."

"I shall tell Renaud the first chance I get."

Elena squeezed her hand. "He will be thrilled. My brother has always wanted a child of his own."

"And I have always wanted a child. I just did not think it would be so soon."

A loud scream sent them once again into companionable silence. She could not bring herself to look out the window for fear of what she might see. To hear it was bad enough.

"Come, let me brush out your hair," Elena said, motioning for Aleysia to take a seat before the fire.

She did as asked, sitting before the hearth, while Elena pulled up a stool behind her and began to brush. Aleysia's eyes began to close with each stroke. She smiled to herself, remembering the times her mother had done the same.

Time passed and they waited—until silence fell over Braemere. An eerie silence. Elena grew sullen as well, pacing the floor of the chamber, no doubt just as anxious to hear any news.

She heard footsteps on the stairs outside the door and she stood. "Aleysia, open the door!"

It was Adelstan. "Thank God," she cried, racing to the door just as he pushed it open. He no longer wore chain mail, but his hair was matted to his head, and blood splattered his face, neck, and hands. She ran into his arms and he held her tight. "Are you all right? Are you hurt?"

He shook his head. "I am fine, but you must come."

She put him at arm's length. "What is it?"

Fear consumed her seeing his worried expression. "Renaud has been wounded."

"Sweet Jesus," Elena said behind her, grabbing hold of Aleysia for support. "Where is he?"

"The men have taken him to the great hall, along with the rest of the wounded. I am afraid it is not good. He asks for you."

Sick with fear, Aleysia followed Adelstan down the steps, and into the hall where men lay on cots, all wounded—perhaps some were even dead, for they moved not at all. In the far corner she saw Galeran and knew that's where Renaud was. The younger man glanced at Aleysia and she saw concern in his eyes.

She released Adelstan's hand and raced to Renaud. Her heart gave a hard jolt. His face was a deathly white, almost gray. His eyes were closed, and his breathing shallow. His thigh had a huge gash in it, and blood flowed freely, soaking the blanket beneath him. "Renaud?" she said softly.

"He sleeps deeply." Galeran took Elena's hand within his own, kissed it. "He's said not a word since asking for you, Aleysia."

"Where's the healer?" she asked.

Adelstan looked equally nervous. "On her way."

Her hand moved to Renaud's forehead. He was so warm. Too warm. Sweat beaded his brow, and drenched the front of his tunic.

He opened his eyes and his gray gaze settled on her. Slowly, the sides of his mouth curved a little before his eyes closed again.

She had never been so afraid. She could not lose him. Surely, God would not be so cruel.

Aleysia bent down and kissed him tenderly. "You will be right as rain soon enough. Even now the healer comes."

"I am so tired." Even his voice sounded weary.

Her heart lurched. "Do not sleep, Renaud. We need you awake."

Renaud blinked time and again, as though his lids were too heavy, and finally they closed.

"Who did this?" Aleysia asked, full of murderous rage toward the man who had wounded her beloved.

Galeran cast her a worried look. "MacMillan's brother . . . and after the bastard had offered his hand in truce, promising to leave Braemere and never return. Instead of shaking Renaud's hand, he cut him through. Thankfully, Adelstan was quick enough to knock the Scot aside, or Renaud would not be with us now."

"And what of MacMillan's brother?"

"Galeran finished him off, so he will no longer be a burden to us ever again," Adelstan said. "His men surrendered and asked to take his body back to Kilraney, to rest beside Duncan."

"Thank God he is dead!" Elena blurted.

The healer came in and spread out her things. She fingered the wound. Renaud's face paled and he grit his teeth. "'Tis deep," the old woman said unnecessarily.

"You there," she said, nodding toward Adelstan and Galeran. "Hold his legs and arms." She handed a stick to Aleysia. "Have him bite on this."

Henry rushed into the hall. "Let me take care of him."

The healer shook her head. "Nay, he is my patient now. As you squabble, he bleeds that much more. If it continues, he will surely die for lack of blood."

Henry nodded, and helped hold Renaud's legs down.

Renaud had just bitten down on the stick when the healer poured wine on the wound.

A loud curse reverberated throughout the hall, Renaud's body arching against the men who held him down. A lump formed in Aleysia's throat, and tears slipped down her cheeks. How helpless she felt.

"The wound bleeds too much. We must cauterize it," the healer said, sopping up the blood that continued to flow from the deep gash.

Adelstan looked at Aleysia. "Mayhap you should wait outside?"

"Nay, I will stay." She winced as the healer took hold of the red-hot iron and placed it on the wound. A sizzling sound followed.

Renaud grit his teeth, his body shaking from the pain. The smell of his burnt flesh permeated her nostrils and she covered her mouth to keep from crying out. Elena hid her face against Aleysia's shoulder and squeezed her hand tight.

The wound was so large the healer had to take several swipes of the iron to it. She blended a mixture of raw egg whites and smeared it over the burnt skin, along with a thick salve. "It is important to keep the wound as clean as possible. We do not want it becoming infected. He will be in much pain, but the draught will help. It will be best if he can sleep. Better for the wound, too, if he does not move."

Sending the healer off to help others, Aleysia lifted Renaud's head and forced the draught down. He drank greedily and she smoothed back his dark hair. "When can I move him to our chamber?"

"Let him sleep first, Aleysia," Adelstan said, concern in his voice. "We will move him as soon as possible."

Elena stood and held out her hand. "Come, my dear, we will ready the chamber for him."

TWENTY-THREE

Renaud heard singing.

His eyelids were so heavy. Sleep lulled him, yet he felt restless, the music calling to him.

Light spilled into the room. The singing was louder now, and he turned his head a little to the right.

His heart missed a beat.

Sitting in the tub, her long hair falling over the edge was Aleysia, singing softly.

She lifted a shapely leg and washed it, her fingers sliding over the calf. He smiled.

How beautiful she was.

He moved a little and winced, instantly remembering the wound. He vaguely recalled the angry Scot who said he was Duncan's brother, on the battlefield. Renaud had been shocked by the size of the Scot. When his clansmen had fled, he had approached Renaud, calling a truce. And right after Renaud had turned his back, he had felt a searing pain.

He should have known better.

A second later, the man had lashed out with his sword. Had it not been for Adelstan, who had pushed Renaud out of the way, he would be dead, the wound fatal instead of a dull ache in his thigh that would no doubt pain him for the rest of his days. He vaguely remembered Henry saying the wound should have been mortal, so close it was to an artery.

But he had lived. Thanks be to God!

As though sensing his presence, Aleysia glanced his way, and she sat up abruptly, her glorious breasts bouncing. Heat filled him, settling low into his groin.

Grinning ear to ear, she stood, the bath water running down her body, over her full breasts and nipples, down her stomach and the tight curls that covered her womanhood.

His cock jerked in response.

She stepped out, grabbed a drying cloth, and wrapped it around her body. "You are awake!" she said, running to him, her gaze wandering over his face like she hadn't seen him for years. "You have slept so deeply for so many days. How do you feel?"

"Better now," he said, amazed that every time he saw her she seemed to grow more beautiful. Her long, thick lashes framed her gorgeous eyes, her full lips curved in a lovely smile that showed her small, white teeth.

She kissed him gently, as though he were fragile. "Did I wake you with my singing? I am sorry."

She did not sound sorry in the least.

He reached out, his palm caressing her jaw, before his fingers sank into her hair, weaving through the wet tresses. "I have missed you."

"And I you." Her brows furrowed. "You scared me. I thought you might die. You even took to fever."

"But you nursed me back to health?"

She nodded. "The healer as well. She has taught me much. I think you will be pleased with all I have learned."

"As long as you do not take to giving me sleeping draughts . . . or poison."

She laughed under her breath and kissed him. "Nay, not unless you betray me."

"I will never betray you."

"I will hold you to that, my lord."

"How long have I been abed?"

"A fortnight."

"That long?" He tried to sit up, but she pushed him back down. "Nay, Renaud. In bed is where you will stay until you are well and healed." Her expression was stern, yet her lips curved as he watched her. "The healer demands you follow her instruction, as does Henry. Two against one, I am afraid."

"I am well enough."

"Your skin is still the color of paste."

"You do not fancy me, then?"

Her brows lifted. "On the contrary—I fancy you very much, my lord."

His heart lurched, because he clearly saw the desire in her eyes as she watched him now. Fortune had truly smiled upon him to give him such a prize as this woman.

"Climb into bed with me," he urged, his gaze shifting to the soft swell of her breasts.

She frowned. "I do not think that is wise. The healer and Henry would not approve."

"The healer and Henry need not know."

With a halfhearted sigh she let the drying cloth fall to her feet.

His cock reared against his belly.

She pulled down the blanket and climbed into bed, cuddling beside him.

He held her tight, savoring the sensation of her soft body flush against his own. Her fingers lightly traced circles on his chest.

"Do you know how fine you are to me?" he asked, and she glanced up at him.

Her gaze searched his. "Am I?"

He nodded, his thumb brushing along the edge of a high cheekbone. "Aye."

"And do you know how fine you are to me?" she asked, her grin widening.

"Why don't you show me?" he asked.

She bit her bottom lip, and he saw the indecision in her eyes. "You are not well enough. The healer says—"

His hand found hers, and he guided it to his hard cock. She smiled as her fingers slipped around him. His blood pumped thickly in his veins, sending a fire throughout him as she stroked. He cupped her breast, rolling a nipple between finger and thumb. She released a low moan and arched against him. His other hand trailed down her stomach, over the soft curls of her womanhood to find her wet and ready for him.

So hot.

He groaned as he slipped a finger within her and she parted her thighs further.

He slipped another finger in her, brushing his thumb over her hidden pearl. In response, her grip on his cock tightened, her pace quickening as she pushed toward release.

He could not wait.

He lifted her so she straddled his thighs, and guided his cock inside her snug sheath. She stared down at him, love shining in her eyes. She kissed him, the taste so sweet he groaned with satisfaction.

For a moment she did not move, and he savored the feel of her heated sheath hugging him. So tight, like she had been made just for him. She kissed him passionately. "I love you, Renaud," she said against his lips, and for a moment he wondered if she'd really said the words, or he'd imagined them.

He sat up and took a nipple into his mouth, sucking it.

She squirmed against him, her hands moving up along his sides, then brushing over his nipples, circling them, then pulling them lightly.

She groaned again, and reached behind and played with his sac. Her teasing caused him to thrust deep into her, triggering her climax. She cried out his name as she came.

He followed behind, with an orgasm that had him fighting for breath.

She fell on him, her heart pounding hard against his chest. "We should not have done that," she said. "'Twas too soon."

How beautiful she was with her cheeks flushed from their love-making, her light green eyes shining brightly with love.

"How can you expect otherwise when you wake me from a slumber to find a nymph in the tub, singing softly, lulling me."

She smiled at him, her eyes still bright with their shared passion.

He kissed her, and whispered against her lips, "I love you, Aleysia."

Her gaze searched his, and her grin widened. "I love you, too, Renaud. More than life itself."

TWENTY-FOUR

Aleysia's heart pounded nearly out of her chest. They sat in the great hall, a first since Renaud had recuperated from his wound.

In his hand he held a letter from William.

Elena took her hand as Renaud read the letter.

He closed his eyes and the letter fell from his fingers.

No one moved, even though Aleysia felt compelled to pick up the letter and read it herself. As it was, she could barely breathe, so scared was she.

Renaud opened his eyes a moment later, and turned to Aleysia. He lifted her in his arms and held her tight.

"My woman. My bride."

Exhilaration washed over her in waves, and she cried in happiness. "It is true?"

He set her on her feet. "Aye, William has granted me a full pardon. He has given me Braemere. Even more, he has granted me your hand."

Relief, the likes Aleysia had never known, nearly brought her to her knees.

"Will you be my bride, Aleysia?"

She nodded. "Aye, I will."

He kissed her softly, gently. "I am the luckiest man alive to not only have you, but a sister who would write the king and plead my case."

Aleysia glanced at Elena, who wiped tears from her cheeks. "You did that for us?"

Elena nodded. "I could not stand to see you lose each other or this fief that you both love so much."

"So you sent a courier to William, telling him that I deserved Braemere, but more important, that I deserved Aleysia. You see, King William has always been fond of my sister, as has his wife, Matilda."

Elena smiled past tears. "And I am so happy that you have gotten what you so richly deserve, brother."

He kissed each cheek and hugged her tight. "I shall never forget it either. Forever I will be in your debt."

"I will remember that, brother," Elena said, a wide smile on her face.

"Come, let us celebrate this evening. Let us eat, drink, and dance."

"My lord?" Aleysia blurted, unable to hold the news from him any longer.

"Aye, my love."

Aleysia smiled at the endearment. "I have more news."

His brow furrowed as he lifted her chin with gentle fingers. "What news is that?"

"I am with child."

His gaze searched hers, and a smile came slowly to his lips. He lifted her in his arms, kissing her fiercely.

"I cannot breathe, Renaud," she whispered against his ear.

Startled, he set her back on solid ground. "Forgive me. Are you all right? I did not hurt the babe, did I?" he asked, his hand going to her stomach.

Pleased at his reaction, she shook her head. "Nay, you did not hurt us."

He bit his bottom lip and hugged her again. "I am so happy."

"As am I," Aleysia replied.

He turned to the others. "I am to be a father!"

"Congratulations, sister!" Adelstan said, hugging her tightly to him. "I am to be an uncle!"

"Come, let us celebrate our good fortune!" Renaud said, kissing her once more.

"I hope that entertainment does not include gypsies."

He tried to frown, but failed miserably. "Why is that?"

"Because I do not want anyone dancing for you."

He pulled her to him. "I want no other dancing for me, but you. My lady. My bride."

Elena sat in her chamber, writing her sons a letter. She told them of their uncle's upcoming marriage, and how happy he seemed. She said she hoped the same happiness for both of them. Indeed, they would be lucky if they met women like Aleysia.

Knowing she had played a small part in her brother's happiness made all of her effort worthwhile. It also served to remind her that she, too, sought that kind of love.

She had told Renaud this afternoon that she would be leaving by month's end, and he had tried to change her mind. Little did he know the true reason of her departure. Earlier, she had seen Galeran in the great hall, a young serving woman at his side. The girl had been on her tiptoes and whispered something in his ear. He had grinned, then patted her behind. Elena's heart had sank to her toes. What was she doing, pining for a man more than ten years her junior? Most would find it ludicrous.

Though she enjoyed being at Braemere, she wanted her brother and his new wife to have some much-needed time together once they married. Plus, she needed to put distance between herself and Galeran. He was not ready for a commitment, and she only served as a distraction by being here. Nay, she need not stand in his way of true happiness.

She heard footsteps outside her door, and figured it was a servant bringing her dinner, since she had sent word she would not be joining the others in the great hall.

The door opened abruptly, and Galeran stepped in.

Shocked to see him, Elena stood. "Galeran?"

"Renaud said you are leaving Braemere soon."

"Aye."

"I do not understand."

He looked like a wounded puppy.

"I will leave shortly after the wedding. I never planned to stay for long, and I want Aleysia to feel like the lady of the castle. I need not be underfoot."

"Did she say she did not want you here?"

"Of course she did not. Nor would she. My friend is far too kind." He ran a trembling hand through his hair. "I think it unwise for you to leave so soon, especially when we have just secured Braemere."

"I understand King William has squelched this rebellion."

"But danger continues from all corners. The Danes could attack from the east, and the Scots are always a threat, as MacMillan showed."

Touched by his concern, she smiled. "We live in dangerous times, Galeran. That cannot be helped. I ran a risk coming here when I did, but I had no problems. My men will protect me with their lives. I trust them."

He shook his head. "You are so stubborn!"

She hid a smile. "Why are you so upset, Galeran?"

He swallowed hard. "Because I do not want you to go. I cannot bear the thought of you leaving my life as fast as you've come back into it. I am not prepared to say good-bye."

Moved by the declaration more than he would ever know, she sat back down. "I am too old for you, Galeran. That became abundantly clear to me in the past week. There is not a future for us."

"How can you say that?" He was before her in three strides, surprising her further when he fell to his knees and took her hands into his. "I know that I have nothing to give you, save for what is here," he

261

said with hand over heart. "But I will spend a lifetime attaining riches, to give you the life you want. The life you deserve."

Her heart pounded an unsteady rhythm. "I do not ask for riches, Galeran. I am already wealthy and have homes in France and Spain."

He looked down, his thick lashes casting shadows on sharp cheekbones. She ran her fingers through his golden hair. "Galeran, one day you will fall in love with a woman your own age, and by that time you might have the things you have always desired."

"I love you, Elena. I've always loved you. I will never love another the way I love you. 'Tis impossible." Tears brimmed in his eyes and he blinked them back. "Do not leave me."

Her heart missed a beat, and she wondered if she had misunderstood. But she had heard him, and as she held his gaze, she was stunned to know he spoke the truth. "But I am so much older than you. I will soon have gray hair and more wrinkles than you could count."

"And I will love you just the same."

She brushed away his tears with her thumbs. "You say that now, but what if people say cruel things to you? What if they ask if I am your mother? Will that not embarrass you?"

"You are more beautiful than ever, and grow more so with each year."

"Soon I will be gray-haired and wrinkled," she repeated.

"And I will love you just the same as I do at this moment. Think you that your age makes any difference to me?" He shook his head. "It does not matter. I love your heart, your spirit, your body. *All* of you."

"Earlier I saw you with a young servant girl. She looked ready to leap into your arms, and you patted her quite intimately on her behind. That very girl might be better suited to you, Galeran. Someone who has not lived so long—someone youthful—who can still blush at pretty words."

"I knew you watched, Elena. I knew it." He squeezed her hand. "That girl, nor any other, could ever hold a candle to your beauty. Nay, your age matters not. It never has, and it never will."

How she wanted to believe him, but it was so difficult.

"Stay with me, Elena. Stay with me for as long as we have. Be my lady."

"I will not stand by while you pat servants' behinds, Galeran," she said, trying to keep from smiling, yet failing miserably.

Relief shone in his face and he stood, kissing her while cupping her face with his palms. "I will work hard to give you a good life, Elena. I swear to you. Be my wife, Elena."

She put him at arm's length and searched his face. "You would marry me?"

His lips curved. "Aye, my love."

"I wonder what my brother would say?"

"I think he would approve." Hope shone in his eyes. "Mayhap I should ask him, then."

"Maybe you should."

Renaud had never known such happiness. Aleysia lay beside him, a soft smile on her lips as she slept. They had come to the chamber to rest, for he still ached from the wound MacMillan had inflicted. Aleysia joined him, saying she was tired as well, no doubt due to pregnancy.

They had lain in each others arms, both smiling, talking of their good fortune. He still could not believe how quickly his life had changed. He could not have imagined being so happy when he had first arrived at Braemere. To think if he had arrived even an hour later, then he would not have known Aleysia. Now, because of that fateful day, all his dreams were coming to fruition. He had the home he'd always dreamed of, the woman he desired above all others, and a child on the way.

His heart was full to bursting. How shocked his father would be to know his son had found such happiness with a woman, particularly a Saxon who had tried to kill him the first day they had met.

He brushed back her hair from her face, smiling as she sighed contentedly. Her eyes opened, the light green orbs staring straight at him. She smiled as she stretched. "I was just dreaming of you."

His heart skipped a beat, and he kissed her softly. "'Twas it a good dream then?"

She wrapped her arms around his neck and smiled against his lips. "Aye, 'twas wonderful. You were there, as were our children. Loads of them, in fact." Her fingers brushed over his chest, down over his abdomen, and her smile broadened.

His cock twitched. "What are you about, witch?"

"Hmmm, I wonder?" she said, her fingers slipping over the cord of his braies.

"We will not hurt the babe?"

"Of course not. The babe will be fine."

He cupped her breast, surprised that he had not discovered her secret earlier, for she seemed bigger there, fuller.

He eased her out of her gown, and he sat up, looking at her gorgeous body. Her stomach, though still slender, had a bit of roundness to it, which he found pleasing. "I cannot wait to see you big with child."

"Ah!" she said, swatting at him. "You mean fat."

"Nay, I mean your belly round with our child. Already you glow, but in the months to come, I shall enjoy watching the changes in your body."

He leaned over and kissed her belly,

He still could hardly believe he was going to be a father.

"I hope it is a girl. As beautiful as her mother."

Aleysia reached out to him, her fingers running through his dark hair. "And I hope for a son. As handsome as his father."

"No matter what sex our child is, it will be well loved, and God willing, will know peace."

"Aye, I pray it is so."

He kissed her belly again, his tongue slipping into her navel, causing her to gasp. Before she could protest, he slipped lower, between her thighs and kissed the inside of each, before his tongue flicked over her pearl.

Her legs trembled, but undeterred, Renaud brought his hands beneath her bottom, bringing her closer to him.

She sighed and her fingernails dug into his shoulders as he licked her slit over and over again until her core tightened and pulsed against his tongue.

"Renaud," she said on a moan. "I want you inside me."

He ignored her, licking her again, slipping his small finger into her back passage. She tensed against the unfamiliar intrusion, and he murmured against her nether lips, "Let me pleasure you a new way, my love. I promise I won't hurt you." He went carefully, going up to a knuckle before going farther.

She relaxed a little, enabling him to grow more daring with her. He slowly pumped his finger inside her, and twisted it every few strokes. He was rewarded with Aleysia's whimpers of pleasure.

Aleysia forgot to breathe as the multiple sensations washed over her. The feel of his finger inside that forbidden place while he tongued and sucked her made her knees even weaker. But it felt wonderful and she did not push him away or tell him no.

When another climax hit her, she held onto his shoulders and moaned as she rode it out.

When she opened her eyes he had stepped out of his braies and lay her gently on the bed. Kissing her, he entered her slowly, watching her eyes close and her head fall back. He kissed her throat, her chest, the valley between her breasts, before taking a nipple into his mouth.

She sighed her pleasure, her fingers brushing along his back, over his shoulders, where her nails dug in as her release came.

"Renaud," she cried out, her sheath tightening around him, contracting with a force that startled her.

His climax was longer in coming, and she took joy in watching him, the tightening of the cords of his neck, the way his eyes became so heavy-lidded, the beauty of his body as he moved over her and inside her. The sight of his huge rod sliding in and out of her. And he was to be her husband. They would be together for the rest of their lives.

She had never known such happiness.

He thrust twice more and came, his seed spurting heavily into her. The feel of his release triggered her own, and they came together with satisfied groans.

Panting, he rolled them on their sides, face-to-face, and then he kissed her, pushing the hair back from her face. "How fine you are with your cheeks so pink."

"I am deliciously sated," she said with a coy smile. "I could sleep for an entire week."

He laughed, pleased by the replete smile on her lips. "Aye, and you must sleep, my love. Our child needs you to rest."

"Already I enjoy this pregnancy," she said, closing her eyes. "You spoil me."

"Aye, and I always will. You can stay in bed all day and I would not care. I just want you happy and healthy."

She opened her eyes. "Renaud."

Seeing the unspoken question in her eyes, he went up on his shoulder. "Yes, my love."

"What will become of Adelstan, do you think? I worry that one day someone will turn him into William. I have heard such has happened before. A man turning in another for a reward. What if that is what happens with Adelstan? William might have pardoned you for allowing him to escape, but what happens if he discovers that Adelstan resides at Braemere? Will you not be in danger for harboring a traitor to the crown?"

"Worry, not. I will do whatever I must to protect Adelstan, for very soon he will be my brother."

Aleysia smiled. "Aye, he will."

"And I will talk to William when the time is right."

"Thank you, Renaud."

"Now, I have things I must see to. You get some sleep. I shall return after."

"Come back soon, my love," she said, her eyes already closing.

TWENTY-FIVE

Every bench in Braemere's chapel was full. Not a seat to be had. Soldiers even lined the walls to watch the nuptials and the doors were left open so all could hear, even the villagers who packed the bailey.

A fortnight had passed since Renaud had asked Aleysia to be his wife, and now that the day was here, she could hardly believe it.

Aleysia's throat tightened as she took her place beside Renaud. How handsome he was dressed in a black tunic and black braies. Such a contrast to his silver eyes.

How strange fate was, that she would marry the very man she had feared not so long ago.

Outside the sky grumbled, promising rain on the horizon.

However, the small chapel was warm and filled with the people she loved the most.

She looked over her shoulder to Adelstan, who stood at her side, a wide smile on his face.

The two men she loved most in the world, together.

The preacher, a tall man with a long gray beard nodded at them both. "Shall we begin?"

Aleysia and Renaud nodded.

"We are come here at this time in the name of the Father, Son, and Holy Ghost, to join, unite, and combine these two persons by the holy sacrament of matrimony, granted to the holy dignity and order of priesthood."

And so it went. They pledged their love amongst God and their friends, swearing to love until death parted them.

When the priest announced them husband and wife, Renaud lifted her in his arms and carried her to the festivities in the great hall. She belonged to him now. Forever. What a wonderful feeling.

Throughout the celebration he kept her at his side, danced a time or two, or watched with sparkling gray eyes as she danced with Galeran or another solider. Though he spoke with a friend, his gaze did not waver from her, and she felt a flicker of satisfaction knowing he was jealous.

She glanced over at the hearth to find Adelstan talking to a few knights. How easily he had blended in with the Normans, earning their respect and admiration. How she hoped he would one day find happiness, too.

Elena came up beside her. "Come, are you ready?"

Aleysia nodded.

"Renaud, I am taking your bride and helping her prepare for her wedding night."

Renaud looked surprised, and intrigued. "Indeed, I shall be counting the minutes."

"I will come get you when she is ready," Elena said, and taking Aleysia by the hand, they left the hall.

Aleysia looked at the reflection in the mirror and could scarcely believe what she saw.

In the space of an hour, with Elena's help, Aleysia had been transformed from bride to vixen. Her hair had been brushed out and curled about her hips. The golden top barely covered her breasts, which had grown larger in pregnancy. The skirt, made of a deep red silk floated about her hips, and fell only to midthigh, enhanced by a golden chain that hung snugly about her waist. On her wrists and ankles were golden bracelets, both of which had bells that rang out with every movement.

"You are a vision, Aleysia. In truth, Renaud will not be able to keep his hands from you."

"I hope he is pleased."

Her eyes had been rimmed with kohl, emphasizing the light green color. They seemed to glow from within. Her lips and cheeks had been rouged, and Elena had suggested rouging her nipples as well; Aleysia had, shocking herself by her boldness.

"I wish I could see his face when he enters the chamber and sees you," Elena said with a laugh, heading for the door. "I will get Renaud. I told Galeran to signal the musicians when we left the bailey. If all goes right, you will be able to hear them from your window."

The chamber was dark, the only light from two candles on the bedside table and fire.

Aleysia waited nervously, pulling the cloak tight about her as Elena went to fetch Renaud. What would he think when he saw her? How nervous she was! A thousand times she had reconsidered and thought it would be best to wash her face and rid herself of the outfit, but they had come too far and Elena had worked so hard finding the gypsy outfit for her.

Nay, she would play this out.

Outside she heard footsteps approach and turned her back to the door. The door opened and closed. "Aleysia, what are you doing?"

"Lie down," she said, her voice shaky. She willed herself to relax, and waited as she heard him sit on the bed.

"I am lying down now."

"Close your eyes."

"All right." A hint of laughter touched his voice.

She had no idea if he actually had closed his eyes, but taking a deep breath, she dropped the cloak and turned toward him. His eyes were closed, and a soft smile played upon his lips.

"You may open them now."

Still smiling, he opened his eyes and the smile slowly slid from his face as his gaze shifted over her.

She did not know if he was pleased or disappointed. As though on cue, the music drifted in from the window. Now was not the time to lose her nerve. The hypnotic sound of the lute and drum blended together, and Aleysia moved her hips.

Renaud sat up on his elbow.

She lifted her arms up and over her head and snapped her fingers, while rotating her hips in a circle.

She heard him release a breath and smiled.

272

She moved closer, twirling about in a circle, her skirt flying up.

Renaud could not catch his breath. He could hardly believe the transformation in his wife. How beautiful she was, perfect in every way. He was relieved she had not tried such a stunt in public, for he would have had to kill every man who looked at her. She was so desirable. As it was, he could not wait to take her to bed.

Now as she rotated her hips his cock grew achingly hard—the blood burned within his veins. Her breasts were barely contained by the golden silk that hugged them, her nipples rock-hard against the material, and he could see the tiniest hint of rose as one peeped above the fabric. If he wasn't mistaken, she had rouged her nipples as well.

Her eyes, outlined in black kohl, focused on him, then moved down his body. She stared brazenly, her hands moving down her body as she rocked her hips, her fingers splaying over her own breasts, cupping them.

His mouth went dry.

Her fingers drifted lower, along her waist, her belly, toward the apex of her thighs, and then just shy of touching herself, she flung her arms wide and whirled about in a circle, the motion sending her skirts up, showing her naked bottom and her shaved femininity.

His cock jerked. She came closer, her hips moving faster, her breasts bouncing with each movement.

He had never been so hard in his life.

Her gaze shifted to his cock, which strained against his braies.

She lifted a tawny brow, and he could not help himself. He reached out and grabbed her, pulling her down on top of him.

He kissed her hard, and rolled over so she was beneath him, and he pushed his braies down.

She seemed as anxious, for she guided him, sighing as she took each inch inside her.

She moved her hips and he grabbed hold of them, steadying her, knowing he would spend himself if she moved.

"Did you like my dance?"

He brushed the flimsy material of her top aside. Seeing the rouge on her nipple, he grinned devilishly. "Aye, I did," he said, before taking a nipple into his mouth.

She gasped and cradled his head while he paid homage to one breast, then the other.

She came instantly, her hot sheath contracting around him like a glove. "I am glad you were pleased. I never want you to look at another gypsy again."

"I have no need to. Don't you know that you never have to dress up and be something you are not? I love you, Aleysia de Wulf, my woman, my wife."

He rolled over so she was on top and lifted her up and down, her breasts bouncing with the tempo he set. "Ride me, wife."

"So you do not want me to dress like this again?"

"Nay, I did not say that," he said a touch too quickly.

She laughed again and kissed him. "I am glad that you are pleased, husband."

"I love that word coming from your lips, wife."

"As do I."

Her head fell back on her shoulders as another climax claimed her.

Renaud lifted her off of his lance and had her kneel on the bed. He entered her from behind slowly, deeply, moaning as he touched her very womb.

His strokes were fast and sure, the slapping of skin against skin, the entire bed rocking against the wall. So much for taking her gently. He couldn't help it, especially when she called out his name, her inner muscles squeezing him tight.

He came with a satised moan, and pulled her down, into his arms. Kissing her, he smiled against her lips. "I love you, wife."

She ran her fingers tenderly along his jaw. "And I love you, husband."

Epilogue

Aleysia stood beside Elena on the platform that had been set in the center of the bailey. At the foot of the steps stood Renaud, looking handsome in white tunic and dark braies. Beneath him, dressed in a white linen tunic and trunks, silk stockings and shoes ornamented with golden lions, Adelstan bowed.

In front of God and everyone, he took the pledge of knight, swearing allegiance to King William and the Norman cause.

Trumpeters played as several knights helped Adelstan with his armor. His sword, which had been blessed the night before by the priest, was brought to him, and he kissed the hilt.

Renaud executed the colee, an open-handed whack that nearly knocked Adelstan off his feet.

The soldiers shouted their approval.

"Go, fair son! Be a true knight, and courageous in the face of your enemies."

Adelstan nodded. "I shall."

A loud roar sounded and Adelstan turned and flashed Aleysia a smile.

"'Tis done," Elena said, hugging Aleysia tight. "How proud you must be."

Aleysia nodded, doing her best to hold back tears. She had prayed for this day, and now that Adelstan had sworn fealty to William, she knew she could finally live in peace.

She lay a hand on her swollen stomach. In three months her babe would be born. Never in her life had she thought to find such happiness.

In a few weeks' time Elena and Galeran would marry. They spoke of moving back to France in time for the birth of their child, but Renaud grumbled each time it was mentioned, so they never spoke about it in front of him.

Aleysia would miss them both desperately. Elena had become her dearest friend and companion.

But at least for now she had her brother, and he did not seem to be going anywhere.

Another loud cheer rang out as Adelstan turned and bowed.

As was customary when a man became knighted, Adelstan displayed his skill with lance and sword.

Galeran came to Elena and pulled her into his arms.

Renaud bent down and gave Aleysia a kiss. "Are you happy, my love?" he asked, his eyes shining with love.

"Aye. I feel like I could burst."

He placed a hand on her stomach. "Our son is not yet grown."

"He will prove an able soldier, my lord," Galeran said, watching Adelstan with a smile on his face. "He's as fierce as they come."

"Aye, he will make an excellent sergeant-at-arms."

Galeran looked stricken and Elena turned to her brother with a frown.

Renaud laughed under his breath. "I need a new sergeant-at-arms, for you will no longer be serving with me at Braemere."

"My lord, if I have done something that—"

"Nay, Galeran, you have done nothing wrong. On the contrary, you have done everything right, and that is why I am bestowing my lands and titles in Sussex to you and my sister."

Galeran swallowed hard and shook his head as though to clear it. "I cannot accept it. 'Tis too much."

"Braemere is my home, and I have no desire to leave her. Except perhaps to visit my sister and her husband on occasion."

Elena looked up at him, a wide smile on her face.

Galeran kissed her, then bowed. "Thank you, my lord. I am honored."

Adelstan galloped toward the quintain, a dummy fashioned in chain mail that had been fastened to a post. Her brother attacked it, hitting it straight in the heart.

The crowd roared their approval, and Adelstan dismounted and took a bow. Now they would feast and celebrate this wonderful day.

"He will make a fine sergeant, my lord," Galeran said, smiling widely.

"Aye, he will," Renaud replied.

Aleysia lay her head on his shoulder. "I am glad it was you who came to Braemere that day."

He smiled devilishly. "You did not seem happy to see me."

"Nay, I was not, but I am happy now."

"Are you?"

"Aye. I have never known such happiness."

He leaned down and kissed her. "Nor have I, my love. Nor have I."